BOOK 3

CLANS OF MUIL

THE
ANGUISH OF THE
Scottish Lairds

KEIRA
MONTCLAIR

PROLOGUE

L OGAN STOOD IN the clearing waiting for his informant to arrive. He glanced over at his wife, situated in a tree with her bow ready to fire. "Logan, I don't like this. You are no longer a spy and besides, everyone knows you were a spy so why would they trust you?"

"I offer an equal sharing of information, Gwynie, and you know that. I lie. They tell me something I need to know. Sometimes, I can send them in the wrong direction, but it's best to keep your eye on your enemy."

Gwynie let out a loud sigh. "As you wish, husband, but be careful."

"I heard that eye roll, Eli's grandmother."

Gwynie giggled, something he didn't hear often anymore. Her life was often painful still, but he still adored the woman he married so long ago that he didn't recall how long it had been. She'd beat him fairly on the archery field, something he couldn't ignore, so he married her.

"He's coming, Gwynie."

The man stepped into the clearing and said, "Tell me what I need to know."

"I don't know what you want to know. You tell me."

"Tell me about the forces at Clan Grantham. How many did the old chieftain bring with him?"

"More than you have. Who is attacking the isle? And why don't they leave the bairns alone?" Nearly everything Logan told the man was a lie, so he carried no guilt for meeting the fool. He hoped to stay ahead of the evildoers on Mull.

"They want the faery and the gifted bairn."

"You touch my grandbairns or nieces and nephews again and I will hunt you down, you weak-kneed bastard."

"They're just bairns. What the hell good are they?"

Logan lost all control. Perhaps he was an old man, but only evil men picked on bairns. He rushed the informant, tripped him, then landed on him, his fist high in the air. "I'll tell you this and you remember it well. You hurt any bairns from my clan, and you'll regret it. I will hunt you down myself."

The man snickered. "Why are you so upset? You got them all back, did you not?"

"We did, no thanks to you." Logan climbed off him but stayed close. This was difficult for him. His experience told him that any time an enemy wished to speak with you, it was wise to take the time. Weak-brained men liked to brag about all they knew, and Logan preyed upon them knowing that. He always walked away with more information than he ever gave. But this fool's ignorance was nearly more than he could bear, especially knowing he took part in the kidnapping of the bairns. He stared up at the canopy of the tree branches over his head, the leaves just starting to turn color. The glorious oranges and yellows brightened his outlook, the hint of red just beginning. He had to remain calm and learn what he could about the fools who would not leave them alone.

The man pushed Logan away. "I don't have much time. They still want the green maiden. Is she the golden-haired one?"

Logan thought for a quick moment. If Lia were truly a faery, then she could get herself away from anything. It was the lad who worried him. Maitland and Maeve's son. He walked in a circle, then replied, "Aye. The golden-haired one, not the white-haired one, is the faery. The white-haired ones are related to me, so you'll pay if you touch them. Why do you want a lad?"

"Because it's said he has special powers too."

That comment confused him. No one knew of any powers Grant had.

"I need to know more about the attack on Mull. Who and when?"

"I have no problem telling you that. There are two who plan to take over different parts of the isle. One will start with Clan Rankin."

"Why?"

"They say he's the easiest one."

"When?"

"Soon. That's all I know. Your turn. How many?"

"He has three score, but that can change any

time. You know the Grant forces are over a thousand, do you not?" Still lies, but it would get him the information he wanted. Grants and Ramsays with Menzies and Camerons were well over two thousand now.

"Aye, but getting men with swords and horses on the isle will not happen quickly. You know that. And horses won't cross from Oban. Mayhap to Ulva you can get a few, but not from Oban to Mull without a big ship or two."

Logan tugged on his mussy locks, knowing it was time to jump in a loch somewhere, but he'd been too busy. The thought of anyone touching Maitland and Maeve's wee laddie was more than he could handle. "Leave the lad alone. Take the faery and leave the others. You'll bring some powerful forces down on you if you are fool enough to persist."

"I'll pass on your warnings." The man stared at him, a twisted grin on his face.

"What the hell is your name?"

"You don't need my name. We don't use them at all. Our chief refuses to use names."

Logan stared at the man, taking in everything he saw. Dressed in black from head to toe, he wore no clan identification and spoke more like an Englishman than a Highlander. Perhaps he was from the Lowlands. "A Borderlands man up this far. That does not happen often."

The man appeared flustered by his guess.

"Och, I guessed right." Then it was Logan's turn to grin. He had to leave the man unsettled and a bit afraid of him. "What powers have you heard the lad possesses?"

"Don't know. Said they think he'll be another Alex Grant, but he had no special powers that I was ever aware of."

"It'll be a long time before the lad can fight like the Grant. Time and many raggies. Who's planning on changing them?"

"Not my concern. I just get the information, grab my coin, and run."

"Names. Give me a name."

"Don't have any for you. I already told you that we are not allowed to use names."

He could see this line of questioning was not productive, so he switched to the other issue at hand. "How soon for the attack on Clan Rankin?"

"Soon." The man took a step back and said, "Later, old man." He moved a short distance away, then turned around and chuckled. "I can't believe you are fool enough to think I'd believe you were a spy."

An arrow landed in the tree less than a hand away.

He ran like a wee bairn.

"Did you shite your raggie on that one, fool?" Logan called out after him. Then he chuckled. "Nice one, Gwynie."

CHAPTER ONE

Eva

Early autumn, 1316, the Isle of Mull

EVA MACVEY'S HORSE bolted, nearly tossing her out of the saddle, but she managed to hang on. "Snow Queen, stop!"

The horse ignored her, tearing across the path and into the forest, exactly as Eva feared the frightened beast would do. "Snow Queen!"

Eva glanced over her shoulder in time to see a horse and rider she didn't recognize following her. Was the strange horse the reason her sweet mare had gone off the path?

She pulled the reins, urging the horse to slow, but she sped on, branches scratching her arms as she flew through the trees. "Stop, Queenie. Please!"

They were only a short distance from her home with two guards not far away—her brother insisted since she was sister to the chieftain of Clan MacVey—but she'd never been accosted on her horse before.

"Easy, Snow Queen. Whoa, girl." Eva spoke in a

low tone, attempting to calm her mount, yet she also feared the horse behind her might catch up. When she turned around, the strange rider had disappeared, but three other horses followed. Two were her guards, but the closest one was nearly upon her.

In one smooth move, the closest rider leaned over and lifted her off her horse, then settled her on his lap at first before adjusting her to sit in front of him. The loss of her rider slowed Snow Queen, the terror leaving the animal.

Sloan Rankin, chieftain of their neighboring clan, asked, "Are you hurt, Eva?"

Nearly falling off, she grabbed the saddle at the same time that Sloan wrapped his arm around her waist, steadying her. "I've got you."

Something flipped inside her belly at his touch. She whirled and shoved at his chest, nearly knocking both of them off the horse. He tugged the reins and stayed on, helping her to keep upright on the beast, too, and his mount slowed.

As soon as she could, she took another swing at him. "Leave me be!"

"Eva, it's me." Sloan finally stopped the horse. "I'll not hurt you."

Embarrassed by her reaction, she mumbled, "I'm sorry, Sloan."

Ahead, Snow Queen was heading back toward them. Eva turned sideways so she could face Sloan. "I didn't mean to fight you. My thanks for coming after me."

Her brother's two guards came abreast, but Sloan waved them back to the path. "Eva," he said, waiting to make sure the guards were far enough away not to hear his words. "What the hell did the earl do to you? You've never been afraid of me."

He was right. She'd known Sloan all her life and knew he would protect her from anything and anyone. He'd just proven it. "I'm not afraid of you." She swiped a falling tear from her cheek, hoping he wouldn't notice.

Her brother had arranged for an English earl, Sir Basil de Stain, to meet her two moons ago. He'd come on two occasions, hoping for a match. Eva had felt more like a prize set on a table. He'd studied her, rarely speaking to her except for polite discussion, instead focusing on her brother, the chieftain. They'd conversed at length, to the point where her mother had said, "Are you interested in marrying my son or my daughter, my lord?"

The earl had shot daggers at her mother, but that never stopped Rut MacVey, who'd responded by crossing her arms and taking a step closer. "You're ignoring my daughter."

He'd replied, "She's a lass. I have more important discussions available to me."

Rut ground her heel on his instep until the boor winced. "Oh, pardon me." Then she'd smiled and whisked her daughter away.

"I heard it didn't go well, Eva. Your brother wasn't fond of the earl, but did he hurt you?"

She shook her head. He hadn't hurt her, just offended her. He'd asked to see her breasts when they were given a few moments in private at his request. Eva had been shocked, unable to speak, so he'd reached for her and attempted to yank off the top of her gown, but she'd pulled away and kicked him.

That had ended the impending betrothal.

And stirred a new hatred for men, though she reminded herself that Sloan was not like the earl.

Or was he? Were all grown men so crude? This question forced her to rethink her desire to ever marry. Even if her dear father were here to choose her betrothed for her, she would feel doubtful about marrying anyone after the way the earl treated her.

"Eva? I'm not convinced he didn't hurt you."

Eva smiled at Sloan. "Nay, he didn't hurt me. He wished for more than I cared to give him, but my refusal upset him, so the betrothal ended before it even began."

The look of fury on Sloan's face went straight to her heart, but then his expression changed as quickly as a bolt of lightning in the night sky.

"You don't deserve such treatment. If anyone ever abuses you again, please let me know and I will deal with it." The fury had been replaced with a tenderness that warmed her insides.

There had been times over the years when she'd thought she and Sloan would suit, but after all she'd been through with the earl, she'd decided living alone would suit her better.

Now all she had to do was convince her mother and her brother.

CHAPTER TWO

Sloan

———◆◆◆———

SLOAN LED EVA'S horse to the gates of Dounarwyse Castle. He dropped to the ground, then turned and set his hands at her waist and lifted her down. He placed her an appropriate distance away from him.

If he had his preference, he would have kissed her sweet, rosy lips, but Eva would not have been receptive to any such thing from him. He'd always had a soft spot for her, but he knew the feelings were not reciprocated.

That was why he'd proposed to Gormal. He'd thought Eva was going to be betrothed to an English earl, Sir Basil de Stain, or whatever the hell his name was. Sloan's father had been pressuring him to marry and get an heir or two, but he'd procrastinated, hoping Eva would change her mind. It had never happened.

He liked Gormal. She was a sweet lass, but apparently she hadn't been interested in marrying him at all. She'd fallen to her death from a cliff after telling her sister she couldn't bear to marry him.

He never knew what the lass had hated about him, but he had to admit that her death had a major effect on him still being unmarried.

He surely couldn't survive another lass taking her own life over his inadequacies. In fact, at one point, he wished to ask Eva why she wasn't interested in him, but after Gormal, he decided never to ask that question.

Clearly, there was something very wrong with Sloan for a lass to choose death over life with him. Others had told him she had problems thinking clearly, but it did nothing to change one fact he knew for sure—he was a total failure at romantic relationships.

He'd nearly given up on the idea of Eva as his wife, but after what de Stain had done to her, would she possibly reconsider his offer? Perhaps he should visit Lennox and ask him.

He vowed to give it more consideration.

"My thanks to you, Sloan, but I must go inside now."

He nodded and went on his way. He had many things to tend to on his land. His brother's wanderings, the issue of the activity on the bay, the seed count, the harvest of the summer's plantings, and his father, forever complaining about one thing or another. Sloan headed home, two of his guards flanking him.

As he approached Rankin land, he noticed Miles waving to him from afar.

"Just in time, Chief. Please follow me to the water's edge."

Sloan followed Miles, his second-in-command,

down to the coastline past his castle. "I don't understand what you're saying, Miles. What have you seen, exactly?"

"I am not sure," Miles said, then stopped at the edge of Dun Ara Castle where they could see Coll, Kilchoan on Ardnamurchan, and Rum on a clear day. He took in the activity at Kilchoan, where ships often docked. "There's more going on than I'm used to seeing."

Sloan's brother, Rinaldo, joined them. "What are you looking for?"

Sloan shrugged. "Naught in particular. Miles thinks he's seen more activity around Kilchoan than usual. What do you think, Rinaldo?" Since it was his brother's job to watch the vessels on the sea, he should have reported any change in activity to him, not Miles. What was his brother doing?

"I haven't seen anything unusual. I'm not as bright as Miles, but I can see ships easy enough. I would report it to you, Chief, if I saw anything odd." Rinaldo gave the wide smile he was known for. Easygoing and always helpful, his brother did the best he could with what he had, but a problem at birth had slowed his faculties, or so their mother thought.

"What the hell are you looking for, Sloan?" his father, Dermot, asked. He strode down the hill carefully, his steps slow and deliberate on the rocky path. His father had aged much since losing his wife nearly a year ago.

Sloan nearly groaned because he hated it when his father got involved with any of his affairs with his men. No matter what Sloan was doing, he was wrong. His father loved to point out his failings, and the more ears there were around to take it all in, the happier his sire was. Dermot had been miserable ever since his wife, Ailis, had passed on.

Sloan had paid the price ever since. Even more so since that fateful day nearly a year ago, the day he'd lost Gormal. Another of Sloan's supposed failings that his father loved to mention.

"Miles says the activity in the seas has picked up. We just started our discussion."

"Ask Rinaldo. He's always here to watch for you. It's his job, and he does it well."

"There's nothing out there, Da. You are looking well this morn. You must be feeling better," Rinaldo said, moving over next to their sire to clasp his shoulder.

"I am, Rinaldo. I'm glad one of my sons is concerned about me," he grumbled, glaring at Sloan.

"Da, you just got here." Sloan held out his hands to let him know that he was being unreasonable. Again.

"You wouldn't care, Sloan. Don't deny it." His father spit off to the side.

Sloan decided it was best to ignore the old man with all his aches and pains. Everything had turned worse since Mama had passed. He'd had no idea that he should have thanked his mother daily for listening to her husband. How he wished she were still here to listen to the man.

"Miles, any special type of ship?"

"Galleys sailing, mostly. Oarsmen, but not the

usual amount. I see the most in Kilchoan Bay. But I don't understand why."

Sloan made a mental note to speak with Lennox about the matter. He'd been on Ardnamurchan recently, and he recalled some prediction the wee lass Lia had made then. Should they take the word of the lass?

That much he hadn't decided on yet. When had the chieftains of several clans ever listened to the warnings of a lass of only six summers? Surely, they were daft considering it. He had more important things to think about.

"Did Eva accept yet?" his father asked.

Sloan held in the growl he wished to let loose on his father. The old man just wouldn't let things rest, instead believing in constant pestering, like a toddler. "I don't know. Nothing is official. I'm waiting to speak with Lennox. You know these things take time, Da."

"Shouldn't take time. The lass should consider her good fortune to be asked by a chieftain and say aye. Arrange the wedding next week. No reason to wait for her approval."

Rinaldo took a step closer, his face bright. "Eva hasn't answered yet, Sloan? I think you will make a fine couple. I would love to have her as a sister." Rinaldo nodded to let Sloan know he approved vehemently, another one of those things his brother loved to do.

"First of all, I haven't asked her or Lennox yet. I'll let you know when I decide anything. I need to venture into our stores and decide what seed to order. I'll be going to the mainland for more soon."

"I told you that you didn't order enough seed. The beans are slim this year."

Sloan stopped in his tracks, grumbled to himself, then turned around to his father, ready to argue the point with him because he kept careful records and did frequent calculations to make sure all was well, but that was another thing his father believed he failed at. "Is your belly full, Da?"

"Aye, it's full. But you should have ordered more."

A voice called to them from the top of the hill. "A word with you, Chief, if you have the time."

Sloan was more than happy to meet with the speaker, whomever it was. It meant he could get away from his sire. "Rinaldo, help Da up the hill. Miles, come with me."

"I don't need anyone's help," his father yelled, then dropped his voice and said, "Rinaldo, give me your arm so I can hang on to you."

"I heard that, Da." Sloan headed toward the castle, facing the opposite direction so his father couldn't see his smile.

"Heard what? I didn't say naught. You need to get your hearing checked, Sloan."

Miles said, "You are a patient man, Chief."

Sloan peered up ahead, then said, "Ramsay, what brings you here? Come," he said, nearly at the top. "I'll find a nice ale for you. I even have a new batch of our best amber liquid if you'd like a taste."

Logan Ramsay smiled widely, something Sloan hadn't seen often. "I'll accept on the amber brew. My favorite. Let's see how your barrel brew matches to others I've had. Who brews the finest on the isle?"

"It would have to be ours or MacVey's. Thane hasn't started to brew any yet, though his second, Artan, has been asking many questions about it."

"I'll have to test both a few times before I decide," he said, waggling his brow.

"I'm sure you'll find ours the best."

The group of three headed toward the castle, Sloan leading the way. "When we reach the solar, give me your news quickly, Ramsay. My sire will be here as soon as he can, but some news is better not for his ears these days."

"Turning daft, is he?" Logan asked.

Sloan said, "Not daft, but he's become a true curmudgeon. He's not going to like anything you say."

Miles nearly snorted but held it in the best he could. "That's a true understatement. Naught suits the old chieftain these days. He's missing his Ailis."

Sloan could only hope he'd find someone he'd miss as much as his father missed his mother. He'd had one attempt to marry, and it had gone terribly wrong. So wrong that he feared to even attempt a betrothal again, which made him wonder if he'd dared to approach Lennox about Eva. She'd seemed fine with him. Perhaps she would accept him after dealing with the cruel earl. He'd have to consider his timing. If so, he'd return to MacVey land and have a chat with Lennox about Eva.

Logan said nothing, probably thinking of his own wife, who he'd nearly lost recently. Doiron had saved her life, but not her leg. It had been difficult for them both to see the woman in that shape. But she was still with him.

"How does Gwyneth fare?" Sloan asked.

"Better now that she's around her family. Eli is here, and our daughter Brigid is on her way. She and a few others have created a contraption to help Gwynie walk. Our niece Jennet is quite crafty, and her husband, Ethan, is just like her. I pray it works."

They made it inside the solar and Sloan unlocked a cabinet, pulling out two goblets and his best brew, setting the three vessels on his desk. "None for you, Miles?"

"Nay, I'll pass on the brew, Chief."

Miles always did. As his second, he preferred to keep a level head during the day. He would only imbibe during the few big celebrations in the keep, something they didn't do often enough. He should change that, especially now that it had been over a year since Sloan's mother had passed on.

Sloan poured a draft and handed the goblet to Logan, who swirled it, sniffed it, and smiled before tasting it, rolling the amber liquid over his tongue to savor its taste. "A fine batch, Rankin. I thank you for it."

"I'll send some home with you."

"I'd be pleased to accept." Logan nodded, eased into a nearby chair, and took another sip.

"What news have you?"

Logan swallowed his brew and said, "You're first."

Sloan set his drink down, sat in his chair, and moved closer to the old warrior. "What?"

"The idiot who thinks he is going to overtake the entire Isle of Mull has decided to make his move, and he's chosen your clan to be first. Someone has advised him that your clan will be an easy takeover. All he has to do is kill you and your brother and the rest will fold and pledge allegiance to him. What say you?"

"The bastard is full of shite if he thinks he can battle us that easily. Who the hell is this leech?"

"I don't know who he is. He doesn't reveal his name or where he is established. I discovered him … I'd prefer not to give my sources away. I thought I'd give you warning."

"Did he say when?"

"Nay, he's waiting for the Grant group to leave is my best guess. Connor Grant is planning to leave in a couple of days, and he'll probably take most of his guards with him, though Dyna will ask for some to stay. Then I guess he'll make his move. He's gathered three score men. How many have you?"

"Only a score and a half." Sloan sighed, afraid he'd failed in this endeavor, though there was little history of battles on the isle of late, so he'd not worried until all the bairn stealing had started.

"Miles has been training our men harder in the lists after all the foolish kidnapping. We've gained a few new ones. Have you any other suggestions?"

Miles said, "I'm open to any advice. Ingelram is working with them now." Ingelram was one of their most loyal guards and also one of the strongest swordsmen.

"Derric Corbett is willing to trade sword-skill training for some fine brew. They didn't bring any barrels with him, and with Connor and the others, what little they brought has gone fast. What say you to some extra training? He's a mighty fine swordsman, and any guard trained by Grant men says he's one of the best."

Sloan decided to push the old warrior's loyalty and leaned back in his chair. "Who is the best? Ramsay guards or Grant? And who has the best archers?"

Logan's eyes narrowed and a slight smile curved his face. "Always a man of wisdom, are you not, Rankin?"

"I try my best." He waited, hands folded in his lap, for Ramsay's answer.

"All right. I'll be honest. Dyna is a fine archer, but the finest are Ramsay archers. My son Gavin has trained Eli to be one of the best. I think she'll end up overtaking Gwynie's reputation as the finest in all the land. Dyna is a fine second. But swordsmen? Since my age has done its job on my shoulders, I am no longer the finest. I'd give it to Connor and Alasdair, but Broc is coming up close. The man works hard. Trust me that Derric has been trained hard by his wife's father. Connor pushes him hard, and it shows. Your men would be fortunate to learn from him."

"And Maitland? Where does he fit in since he's the chieftain?"

"He and Dyna share it. You don't wish to meet Maitland on the field either. Now that he has a lad to defend, he's been working harder than anyone I know. Alasdair has been training him."

"Alasdair and Broc are returning with Connor?"

"Broc will be staying. Not sure about Alasdair yet. He may bring his wife and two bairns here."

Miles shook his head.

"What?" Logan asked.

"I don't know how you keep them all straight, Ramsay."

Logan said, "You remember who's on your side in battle. I hope you don't need to learn the truth of my words."

Sloan said, "We'll gladly take Derric's offer. Should I go to Clan Grantham with you?"

"Nay, I'll send him your way."

Logan stood and stepped out of the solar at the same time that the door to the keep opened, Dermot entering.

"I want to hear the news from you, Ramsay. One old chieftain to another."

"I've never been a chieftain. I was my brother's second."

"They say you were a spy for King Alexander and for King Robert. 'Struth?'"

Logan gave a slow nod to the man.

"Da," Sloan said. "Let the man take his leave."

Logan moved over to the door, but Dermot

grabbed his arm. "What's the news? More attacks? More bairns to be stolen? My grandson Rowan still won't step outside the curtain wall." Rowan had been one of four bairns kidnapped over the summer.

Logan glanced over at Sloan, then back at Dermot. "Keep him inside the walls. And everyone else. There's a madman who wishes to take over Mull, but he comes by boat. No one knows where he's from, so be aware."

Dermot looked at Sloan and said, "I told you!"

Sloan sighed and stepped outside, Logan along with him. "Many thanks to you. I have a flask in the stables I'll give you. Send Derric when he's ready. Our men will work with him whenever he arrives."

He settled with the old warrior and sent him on his way, just as Ingelram approached.

"Did Rinaldo come this way?"

Sloan shook his head. "Why?"

"He disappeared on me again. He was going to work in the lists."

"I'll worry about my brother. Go back to the lists." Sloan knew that Rinaldo was too weak in the head to handle much physical exertion, so he let him do as he wished.

Sometimes they had no idea what he did with his day.

CHAPTER THREE

Eva

EVA LEANED OVER the parapets to watch the activity taking place down near the water. Voices carried so well over the sound that she could hear everything as clearly as though the speakers stood next to her.

"It's too cold, Lennox," Meg declared. "I'm not going in."

Her brother removed his tunic and his plaid, now dressed only in his trews. "You're going in with me." Lennox took two steps toward his wife and Meg squealed, running off in the opposite direction.

"Run, Meg!" her sister shouted after her. Tamsin had married Thane MacQuarie and they visited often.

That made spying on the four Eva's favorite pastime. How she loved watching her serious brother turn into someone completely different, and only because he'd become smitten with Meg and married her quickly. Their antics entertained her more than anything else these days, and the love between Tamsin and Thane gave her hope that someday she'd find her own partner to love. One who would love her for who she was and not what they wished she could be.

Down the bank, she heard a loud scream and an ever louder splash from Lennox lifting Meg and jumping into the sound with his wife. She came up sputtering and pushed his head back underwater, but Lennox tugged her under with him.

The two laughed so much that it made Eva smile.

Tamsin headed toward the two, but Thane rushed along behind her. "Careful, love. There are tree roots sticking up. Don't trip."

"Thane, I'm not going to fall into the water. I am much better at swimming than I used to be."

Eva listened with a twinge of jealousy. Meg had told her that she thought Tamsin might be carrying, but her sister hadn't said anything yet.

Eva let out a sigh as a golden bird approached, closer than any bird had ever done before. Eva sat up straight, leaning back, and the bird landed on the edge of the parapets, moving across it as if it were king of the isle.

"Greetings to you, mighty bird. Where did you get such bright feathers? I've seen many yellow birds, but you are the first golden one I've ever seen."

The bird squawked and pranced a bit, then stopped to stare at her, an eerie feeling creeping up her neck.

"What do you want?" The first word that

popped into her mind was marriage. Eva laughed. "I don't think I can marry a bird, though you are quite regal."

The bird flew off toward the northwest corner, then returned. Eva had never seen a bird try to communicate with anyone. Was this bird making an attempt to tell her something?

Once it landed again, it lifted its left leg, revealing a scratch down the extremity. "Your leg has a scratch. That must have been painful."

The bird let out a loud squawk, then took off because footsteps from the staircase carried to them.

Her mother opened the door and asked, "What about a scratched leg? Yours?"

"Nay. A bird. A silly bird that sat on the parapets and stared at me." She glanced around the area, but the flying creature had disappeared.

"Your father had a deep scratch on his leg." Her mother stood in the doorway with a stool in her hand. "May I join you?"

"Of course. Would you like my assistance, Mama?"

"Nay, I do it myself all the time. What color was the bird?"

Eva replied, "The oddest color of gold I've ever seen. But never mind about the bird. Please join me."

"What brings you here? Are you spying on your brother?" Her mother tugged her stool across the stones before settling it so she could sit down next to Eva.

"Nay, not spying. They are fun to watch." She

sighed, not able to catch it before her mother heard her.

"Eva, just because the earl was unkind to you does not mean that all men will treat you that way." Her mother patted her hand. "You will find him. I am confident you will find him in less than six moons."

"I wish I could believe you, Mother."

More than anything, she wished to marry, but only to the man her sire had chosen for her. Her dear father had passed on two years ago and left an ache in Eva's heart forever, but he'd chosen someone for her.

Unfortunately, he'd passed on before he could reveal who he'd chosen to be Eva's husband. It had haunted her ever since. How would she ever find out?

There was only one way. Her father must have approached the man and arranged the marriage. Eva had to be patient. She would not tolerate another betrothal to someone like the earl.

Surely one day, her perfect partner would arrive on her doorstep to ask for her hand in marriage. Then she'd live happily ever after.

∞

Eva crossed her arms and glared at her brother two days later. "Because I'm not ready yet." What better reason was there to deny a betrothal offer? She wouldn't discuss the earl because they all knew about what had happened.

"That is a most foolish reason," Lennox MacVey replied to his sister.

"Do not dare to stand there and tell me who I'll be marrying, brother dearest," Eva MacVey said, rising from her chair near the hearth, her arms now by her side. How could he try to do to her what he told their mother she had no right to do with him?

"Eva, you are two and twenty. Past time for a lass to be married," Lennox said, the twitch of a grin trying to break out across his face, but he contained it, something he was a champion at. And it pissed her off even more. "I know the earl insulted you, but he's gone. This is a sound offer for you, and you should accept it before you're are labeled a spinster."

"You just married Meg, and you are seven and twenty. Do not tell me about being old." Eva had been on his side for years, both arguing with their parents about forced betrothals. He'd refused his mother, but a couple of months ago she suggested she would choose Lennox's wife. "You have forgotten your reply to Mama when she suggested she'd choose for you?"

"That is irrelevant in this conversation. We are not choosing for you. *He* chose *you*. You and Sloan Rankin will make a fine couple. He has proposed, you've known him all your life. What is wrong with a betrothal to Sloan? You'll be mistress of your castle and living not far from here."

Eva tipped her head back and made a very unladylike growl, her hands grabbing at her dark hair, yanking the pins out because her waves had already become unruly. "Mama! Tell him to stop."

Rut MacVey sat in the chair closest to the

hearth. "Now dear, you've known Sloan forever. He's a fine man. I believe you should consider his offer. What's wrong with him?"

"Naught is wrong with him except that I'm not ready yet." She'd just finished getting rid of a man she hated, the earl. Besides that, her dear father had died not long ago, and he had promised to choose a wonderful man for her. He'd promised to find her a fierce, strong warrior, a Scottish warrior who was the best in all the land. She knew he would be the most handsome and the kindest man too.

Papa had promised. Since she was but a wee one bouncing on his lap, he'd told her about the man who'd have the good fortune of marrying her. Strong, fierce, handsome. Those were his exact words.

Not Sloan Rankin.

Her mother rolled her eyes and sighed. "Here we go again. Lennox, she's not acting any differently than you did when I tried to convince you to allow me to choose your betrothed. Listen to me again, Eva. I know your father promised you all kinds of things—handsome warrior, the fiercest in all the land. I've heard you talk of it since you were a wee bairn, but your sire is gone and cannot choose for you. He's been gone for two years now. We will forget about everything that happened with the earl, but you must move on. Lennox and I have given you enough time to choose someone, but you have not.

"But the earl tried to propose to me. That counts too."

"He didn't suit you. And while I was glad he refused to offer for you in the end, you were not overly willing to get to know the man." Her mother had that look on her face that told Eva she'd never win this argument.

"I refused him," she said, nearly stomping her foot. The man had come from England on two occasions, but she hadn't taken a liking to him. The hard part was that she couldn't identify exactly what was wrong with the man, just that she didn't find him appealing. But when he'd asked to see her breasts since he was about to purchase her, Eva had refused, sending him into a fury. But Eva's fury had been stronger than his, and she'd told him to get out. Since the man had been English, Lennox had agreed with her and sent him on his way.

He'd told Lennox that women were property, no more, and he'd had a right to inspect his property.

Eva had nearly put a fist in his face.

"Think what you wish, but you refused him, so he'd have gone on his way. You were right in making that decision, but it doesn't change the fact that you are beyond twenty with no prospect in sight. No one will want you soon. It's time, and Sloan is a fine man."

"Sloan is a bit gruff, don't you think, Mama? The man hardly ever speaks. He just growls at people." Her mind flew from one characteristic to another—there had to be one that would get her mother on her side. She had known Sloan Rankin her entire life, back to the days when he would find a frog near the water and toss it to her as if it were a prize.

The slimy, disgusting things one found in the sea.

Or the time they had all been swimming in the sound, and Sloan had found a fish that he wished to give to her as a pet.

She'd yelled at him when he tried to hand it to her. Ugly, scaly thing. Fish were not pets; they were meant to be eaten for supper. Dogs were pets, and she'd always wanted one but never had one. She'd crossed her arms and glared at the lad as if he were from England.

Lennox glanced over at his mother, his jaw twitching. "I see Eva is still going to be unreasonable. If I have to, I'll force this. Why not take a few months so he can court you, see if you suit, Eva? I'm sure you'll grow fond of the man. He has offered, and I'm not about to turn away the only solid offer you've had. If you wait much longer, you'll be an old spinster."

Eva wished to slap both her mother and her brother. He'd just refused to settle for an arranged betrothal of his own and instead fell in love with a perfect match for him, his wife Meg. He'd married her so quickly it had shocked everyone.

The door opened and their other brother Taskill stepped into the mostly empty great hall. "Oh, I think I should go back out. I can feel the tension from here." Taskill's brown hair curled about his face, the wind clearly rearranging his usually fine-looking style. "Should I go back out? It's about to storm, and I'm guessing that would be more enjoyable than whatever this conversation is." He grinned as his glance went from one stony face to the next, but no one spoke. "Och, storm it is." He spun on his heel to take his leave.

But this brother would agree with her. "Nay, Taskill. Stay." Eva reached his side and took his arm, turning him back to face Lennox. "Tell him I will choose my own husband."

Taskill smiled and said, "I will choose my own husband." Eva smacked his arm, so he chuckled and said, "Eva will choose her own husband. And I will choose my own wife."

"My thanks. As you can both see," she said, facing her brother and mother. "He agrees with me."

Taskill said, "I'm next in age. I should marry before you. I just haven't found the right person yet."

"There you go, Mother. Find him a wife. Arrange his marriage. He has four winters on me. Leave me alone." She picked up her skirts and moved over to the door. "I'm finished with this discussion."

Meg approached from the kitchens, a confused look on her face. Eva said, "Never mind, Meg. Lennox will explain how I refused to accept a betrothal from a man I have no interest in. I'm sure you would agree with me."

Meg looked from Eva to Lennox to Rut but said nothing. "I haven't been part of the family long enough to offer an opinion, Eva. Sorry!"

Lennox wrapped his arm around Meg's

shoulders and kissed her forehead. "Forever the negotiator, are you not, love?"

Meg smiled and nodded, but still said nothing as Eva moved over to the doorway.

"And what do I tell Sloan, Eva?" Lennox called after her.

"Tell him I'll find my own husband. You need not say anything else." Then she banged the door shut to let them know how serious she was. She had to get away from them. Oh, she knew their intentions were good because she understood their thinking.

It was exactly like her own.

And she knew that her time was running out, but her father had promised her. Somehow, she still believed this handsome man was about to arrive at their castle, calling her name. Telling her that her father had chosen him years ago, and they'd agreed that he would come for her now.

Her brother called her foolish, as did her mother, but to her, it was still real. To let that go was to admit that she'd never see her dear father again.

That he was gone forever and never to return.

She believed he'd taken care of her, chosen a man who would offer for her soon. And she trusted her father to choose the perfect man for her. If he'd only told her his name before he passed on two years ago. "Da, please come back," she whispered to no one.

She'd thought all about what marriage would look like for her. She'd watched Tamsin and Thane fall in love, then Lennox and Meg. Clan

Grantham, the place where she spent more and more of her time because she was training in archery, had two of her favorite couples. Dyna and Derric were so much fun to watch together, but even more? She was entranced by Eli and Alaric.

One day she'd seen them stroll out of the keep together, but Eli had moved ahead of him and teased him like Eva had never seen before.

Dyna noticed her distraction and said, "Don't watch them. They're still newly wed and they couple like rabbits."

Eva had averted her face back to the archery target, lined up her arrow, and was about to let it fire when she heard a moan unlike any she'd ever heard before. Her arrow flew wide, but she stopped while Dyna strolled around the field, retrieving arrows and giggling.

Eva took two steps and saw Alaric and Eli locked together against a tree as if they'd become one person, their gazes unmoving while they panted. Glad she couldn't see everything because of a few nicely placed branches, she definitely could hear everything.

Everything. Including Eli's scream of Alaric's name when she crossed over that precipice she'd heard so much about from others.

She had the sudden urge to do the same thing, if she could find a man willing to teach her a bit about intimacy.

But how was she to find a husband when they were all afraid of her? Hard to find one to marry when she found most of them wouldn't even speak with her. Well, except for her brothers, though Lennox was trying to get to the hated side of her list. Now that she'd been to Clan Grantham, she'd met so many men that she'd created her own special list in her mind, and they went on one side or the other. Hated on one side, loved on the other. There was no in-between.

She'd been interested in various men over the past few years, but if she ever attempted to have a conversation with one at the festivals or other events, they'd greet her, then smile and walk away, making her feel as if she were the most unloved lass on the earth.

At one point, she'd asked her only friend, Alycia, what was wrong with her, and Alycia had tried to make her believe it was only because she was the chieftain's sister. But she knew the truth.

Eva was not pretty enough. She'd even reached the point of considering herself ugly. Her hair fell into unruly waves that took forever to straighten, and it was as dark as night, a far cry from the golden colors in Dyna's hair or many of the bairns at Duart Castle. Her hips were not curvy enough and her breasts were not as large as most lasses. She had tiny feet, and her nose looked as if God forgot to give her one when He made her, tossing her the last one he had before she was born without one.

She'd only find a husband if her father found one for her. She was convinced of it. After years of being ignored, no one was going to offer for her now. She'd overheard talk of other lasses, like Theebet MacKinnis with her generous curves.

The lass had so many suitors that her sire had sent them all away.

Eva hadn't had any other than an English earl. None. Zero. Over twenty summers and noble blood with no offers. She had to be ugly. Well, she supposed she could count Sloan Rankin as her second. How she wished that offer made her heart soar, but since she'd known Sloan for so many years, there would be nothing new to their relationship. Why marry him?

Clan Grantham's arrival and Lennox's recent marriage had given her a reprieve. Her mother had left her alone because she'd focused on Lennox. In the meantime, Eva vowed to be more like Eli and Dyna, strolling around in tight leggings instead of fancy gowns, and wearing a bow and quiver with her hair tied back. Dyna even wore hers tied at the top of her head at times, wild braids on either side. She'd learned that Dyna's mother was Norse, but Eva admired the look more than any other she'd seen. Perhaps she needed to go for a visit to Duart Castle again.

Eva strolled across the courtyard, internally bemoaning the fact that she didn't have a close enough friend besides Alycia to tell her the truths of the world. Alycia worked as a maid in the keep, sometimes working as a cook's assistant or a serving lass, so it was hard to pull her away from her work to discuss the issues Eva needed help with. Her mother had advised her on multiple occasions to stop fraternizing with the help.

Her mother gave her the foolish advice that naught good would come of it. Clearly, her mother didn't understand what it was like to be a young lass with no one to talk to. How she'd wished she'd had a sister, forever envious of the relationship Lennox had with Taskill. The two men discussed everything, though not with her because she was a lass.

On one occasion, she'd asked Taskill what a one-eyed spitter was because the serving lasses had been laughing about it, but Taskill had just stared at Lennox, who let out a barking laugh unlike she'd ever heard from him before.

And she'd told them the truth—someday she'd find out on her own.

Lennox had yelled after her, "The hell you will, Eva! Do not repeat such vulgarities!"

Sard, tarse, one-eyed spitters, shite, and fusty skunks to all of them.

How she wished she had a close friend, one like a sister. Meg had Tamsin, and they were as close as anyone. Eli and Dyna were cousins and related by marriage, another relationship Eva envied. If not for Tamsin, perhaps she could get close to Meg, but whenever Lennox was around, Meg couldn't leave him alone.

And her dear brother, who'd never looked at a lass before he met Meg, was totally besotted. He couldn't take his eyes from her and preferred to be touching her.

Touching made Eva think of fusty skunks. Ick.

A sister could have helped her to understand the confusions of growing up, of men and their oddities. Of intimate relationships and all the secrets kept within and away from her ears.

Her thoughts interrupted by her only friend, Alycia, crossing to the stables, she called out to her. "Alycia!"

Alycia stopped to turn toward her. "Oh, greetings to you, Eva. How do you fare this morn?"

"I'm fine. Are you going somewhere?"

"Aye, I'm going to help the Granthams for the rest of the day. Elvard is going with me. He loves to play with Sandor. You look flushed. What happened?"

Not willing to admit where her thoughts had been, still on the intimate relations of Alaric and Eli, she shook it off and said, "I'm mad at my brother and my mother."

"Why?"

"Because they want to marry me off, someone of their choosing." Even though Alycia was part of the housekeeping staff at Dounarwyse Castle, she could pick up extra coin by working for the Granthams when they needed her. Rut didn't mind. And Alycia was Eva's only true friend, always willing to tell her the truth of the world, something her brothers and mother would never do.

"Who? Someone you don't like?" Alycia asked. "You are getting up in age for a lass, Eva. I've told you that before. I had Elvard when I was six and ten."

"Sloan Rankin wants a betrothal."

Alycia let out a whistle, her face lighting up.

"What?"

"Lucky you. You agreed, did you not?"

"Nay," she said, wondering why her friend had thought it such a good idea. Probably because she hadn't been able to find a husband since she'd had her bairn. She'd never admitted to anyone who the father of the bairn was, just that he'd moved on. "I don't wish to marry Sloan. I've known him forever. He growls too much."

"So why does that matter?" Alycia asked as she saddled a horse, flipping her long plait over her shoulder.

"Because I want to marry someone I'm in love with. Someone with mystery, someone who travels the world and will take me with him." Someone who would follow her everywhere the way Alaric followed Eli.

"Have you kissed Sloan yet?"

"Nay. I don't like the thought of that."

"Well, then he's not for you. But until you've kissed the man, any man, I don't know if you'll know if he's the one for you. He could be. You should try."

"Nay."

"You are daft, lass. He's a handsome man. Chieftain of his clan, loads of coin, lives on the water. What more do you want?"

"Love. I want love and I'll not settle for anything less. If he's so handsome, why don't you go after him?" And she wished for the assurance that her father had chosen the man for her. Something she'd never know now that he'd passed on. The thought made her teary-eyed.

Alycia snorted. "I don't think I'm Sloan's type."

"And what is his type?" Confused by Alycia's

quick denial, she had to wonder what was wrong with Sloan. She'd liked him as a friend, just nothing more than that.

"A lass with her maidenhead still intact. That's his type. He's a chieftain and needs to make sure any bairn born by his wife is his. Besides, he would not be interested in me if I were a virgin. I'm not noble blood like you."

"Well, I don't care. You can have him if you like."

Alycia rolled her eyes. "As I said, he'd not be interested. I'll see you later. I have to get Elvard and move along."

"What's the event at Duart Castle?" Eva had heard about something, but she couldn't recall.

"Just a small family gathering. Dyna's sire is leaving soon, so this is their last celebration of the new bairn before Connor and Sela leave. Not too many will be there."

She had a sudden idea—Broc. Mayhap she'd go along and see if she could get to know Broc better.

It was the only way she'd get her brother to leave her alone. Find her own husband.

Broc MacNicol was unmarried.

"I'm coming with you."

CHAPTER FOUR

Eva

DYNA WATCHED EVA arrange her stance and her bow before she set herself to fire again at the target. She hadn't been training that long and had learned quickly, but she was definitely off this morn. "Your elbow, Eva. Lift it or your arrow will go up into the trees." This day, she couldn't hit any target.

Eva cursed, something Dyna hadn't heard before.

"You wish to stop, Eva? You don't seem yourself this morn."

Eva fired her arrow, which missed by half a horse. She dropped her bow on the ground and stared at Dyna. "I'm distracted. I apologize." The truth was she was a terrible archer, no matter how much she tried. "I don't think I'll ever get any better at this."

"What's wrong? Anything I can help with?"

She grumbled under her breath, then decided to tell Dyna the truth. Perhaps she had some insight as to how to make her brother change his mind about betrothing her. "Lennox wants to marry me off to someone."

Dyna appeared surprised. "Did he choose someone yet?"

"Sloan offered for me, but I don't wish to marry him."

"Sloan? He's a fine man in my eyes. You surely could do worse. Come sit with me for a moment." She pointed to two tree stumps.

Eva flopped onto the stump. "And now Mama agrees with him."

"You are not interested in Sloan at all?"

She shook her head, afraid to speak or the tears would flood her cheeks. "Were you forced to marry Derric? Was Eli forced to marry Alaric? Is that how everyone does it?"

Dyna's eyes widened. "Nay. No Grant or Ramsay lass has been forced. My great-grandmother, Elizabeth, made my grandfather Alex promise not to force any of his siblings to marry. Told him it was wrong. One sister married a Ramsay, so she refused arranged betrothals for the entire Ramsay clan. And his sister Jennie did the same for Clan Cameron."

"Truly? You are so fortunate."

"What about your mother? Doesn't she agree with you?"

"Nay, she wishes for me to marry Sloan because he's a chieftain and he lives nearby. She doesn't care how I feel about him."

"Do you know him well?"

"Aye. He's too stubborn. He always has an opinion on things. He's bossy and gruff. He thinks he can do numbers better than anyone. And he doesn't believe in anything unless it's directly in front of him."

"Ah, I think I recall a bit of that conversation. He said there's no such thing as faeries or seers, didn't he?"

"Aye. How could you speak with him if he denies your abilities? Everyone knows Tora is a seer now. Even Magni says so."

"Some people are a wee bit more stubborn than others. It doesn't bother me that he doesn't recognize my abilities, so please don't let it bother you. Some men are hard to convince."

"Most men."

Dyna arched a brow at that comment. "I'm sensing that this is more than believing in seers. Something you wish to tell me about most men?"

Eva shook her head and stared at her boots. "Nay. I just don't have any luck with them. Any man I've ever been interested in refuses me."

"How do you know that they refuse you? Are they that direct?"

"Nay, I have Alycia ask for me."

"The same Alycia who is here now?"

"Aye. She asks and tells me they don't want me. Is it my appearance? Is my hair too wavy or is it my nose?"

Dyna's expression changed to one of surprise. "Nay, you are a beautiful lass. You have the most beautiful blue eyes I've ever seen. Do not allow anyone to tell you otherwise. There is the possibility that they refuse because you are the chieftain's sister. I had trouble because my father was the finest swordsman in all the land."

Eva tipped her head in question.

"Connor Grant was second in skills after my grandsire Alex Grant. No man would come near me because they feared they'd be tested by my sire, like Logan tested poor Cailean. They were all afraid of him, so I had to find my own husband."

"How did you meet Derric?"

Dyna laughed. "That's a story for another day. Ask Derric because he tells it better, but I met him when I flipped him onto his back and set my boot on his chest. He says he was smitten with me after that."

"Where were you?"

"Not on Grant land. We were searching for the English who were after my grandsire. Derric was working with King Robert. Perhaps you need to look outside your castle."

Eva didn't always believe her sire had chosen the perfect man for her. There were days when she dreamed of finding a nice man on her own, one like Alaric, to have a relationship like Eli and Alaric had, but she didn't see it happening. It was best for her, given her past, to not set her sights on any man. It was unlikely to happen for her. She'd never find out who her sire had thought was the ideal husband for her, and no one wanted the chieftain's sister, so she'd be a spinster living alone at Dounarwyse Castle, though now she hoped to have some nieces or nephews to love.

Someone let out a squeal, so Dyna stood, looking toward the gates. "Oh my goodness, I think the group from Clan Matheson is here. We can finish this discussion later, if you like. But trust me that it is not your appearance, Eva. It is more likely that most guards fear Lennox. He has that intimidating stare that makes some lads shrink away. You can keep practicing as you wish, but I need to greet them. They've come a long way, all the way from Black Isle." Then she shouted, "Look, Brigid brought wolfhounds! We've been waiting for them."

A man behind Brigid opened a crate and a pile of puppies flew out, two larger dogs with them. Eva had never seen anything so adorable, and she'd always wanted her own dog, but Lennox had said there weren't enough dogs on the isle. Eva followed Dyna out to the gates, watching as a beautiful older woman hugged Derric and Dyna.

Then Logan came flying out of the keep, bellowing, "Get out of my way, that's my daughter, and I need to hug her and then bring her to see Gwynie."

Dyna called out to Eva and said, "Logan's daughter Brigid and her husband Marcas have arrived. Join us for a brief repast, Eva, before you take your leave. Visit with the pups. Bring one home with you, if you like, though Marcas will insist you take two, I think."

Eva joined them and was introduced to Brigid and Marcas Matheson. Another happy couple, or so she guessed. She decided to follow them in so she could ask questions. If all the Ramsay women were able to choose their own husbands, she wanted to know how they went about it.

She followed the group, surprised to find a pup bumping her feet. "Oh my, are you not the cutest thing I've ever seen?" She bent down and picked up the wee pup, snuggling and brushing its soft brown fur.

Marcas said, "The smallest of the litter has found you. I think it's a sign that she belongs with you. Though I would only send her along if you take her older brother. They've been inseparable since her mother set the pups free." He bent down and picked up another dog three times the size of the first one. "Meet Goldie, the wee one in your arms, so named because she has this shock of gold fur amid the brown and gray strands. Her protector is Shadow because he's always following someone."

"I would love to take both home with me."

"You are welcome to the pair. You live nearby?"

"Aye, the next castle."

"Here, allow me to clean up the pups and ready some food to take with you while you go inside for a visit."

Eva handed Goldie to Marcas and turned back to the keep. She then followed Brigid inside, even when she stopped to look at her mother by the hearth. "Mama, you look so much better." Hurrying over to her mother's side, Brigid stopped short when her mother let the blanket drop to the floor, her stump of one leg now visible. "Do I, Brigid? It's not pretty, but it doesn't pain me the way it used to."

Brigid fell to her knees in front of her mother, her hands feeling through the soft leggings. "I'm sure it was hard for you, Mama, but you are still here. I feared we lost you. Who helped you? I know it wasn't Aunt Brenna or Aunt Jennie."

"Doiron, the MacVey healer. We stayed with them until I healed, then came here. I wanted to do it in private."

"Whatever you needed is what we all needed. I couldn't bear the thought of losing you, Mama. I'm glad Da brought you here where no one else would bother you. I know how private you are about some things."

Overcome by the love flowing from Brigid to Gwyneth, it nearly brought tears to Eva's eyes.

Brigid continued, "I love you, and we brought along an odd contraption that Jennet and Ethan created for you."

"How does it work?" Logan asked, coming up behind Brigid.

Marcas walked through the doorway, carrying their bags. "It is quite crafty. There's a strap to go over her shoulder to hold the thing on. It looks almost like a leg without a foot. More solid than just a peg, but there is a way to tighten it. You probably won't wear it all the time, but it will get you to a garderobe or the kitchens when in need. Jennet even managed the few stairs to the keep with it on."

Brigid chuckled. "Jennet has tested it so many times it's a wonder it hasn't broken."

Eva took a seat at a nearby table, watching everything transpire. Gwyneth Ramsay was indeed an inspiration. Losing her leg had to have been quite an ordeal, yet she still kept up her archery skills.

Logan seemed harsh at times, but never with his wife.

The group finished their greetings, and Dyna insisted they sit for a brief repast. Alycia came down the staircase waving to her, so she waved back, but then her friend headed into the kitchens while Elvard played with Sandor.

The conversation covered everything that had happened.

Brigid asked, "Maeve is here with the new bairn? I cannot wait to meet him."

"Aye. She and Maitland are in the tower so we don't wake the babe. They fuss over him all the time. He's precious," Dyna said. "Have you heard his name?"

Brigid shook her head, her eyes widening. "Do tell."

"Alexander Drew Menzie Grantham."

Brigid gasped, then said, "I love it. Oh, I love it so much!"

Logan came over and took a seat across from Eva while the others babbled on and on. "Have you ever heard the story of how those two met, Eva? It's a great one."

"Nay. Please do tell." She couldn't wait to hear another love story, a tale about true love where the couple chooses each other instead of an arranged marriage.

"He kidnapped her."

Stunned by this revelation, she leaned forward. "Truly? Tell me more."

"They had a curse on Clan Matheson because everyone became suddenly sickened. Marcas had lost his wife and couldn't handle the thought of losing his bairns, so they went in search of healers. He snuck into Clan Ramsay one night, thinking he was abducting Brenna, but took Brigid by mistake. Jennet slept in the same chamber back then, so he took Jennet too. Foolish lass volunteered because the two were inseparable at the time."

"And he forced her to marry him?" She couldn't imagine that Brigid would accept that. "And you let them?"

"Nay," he said with a wide grin. "She fell in love with her captor. Not an unusual occurrence. And Jennet fell in love with his brother. We had to go to Black Isle for two weddings. They only leave for holidays, but both lasses became healers, so they were needed there."

A tall lad came in carrying a large crate and set it down on the table next to the group eating. "There, Mama. See if Grandmama likes it."

"My grandson Hawk. He's a giant, is he not?" Logan asked, the pride in his eyes evident. The man may have seemed overly harsh, but he loved with his whole heart.

Hawk was a giant. He had brown hair that he kept just below his ears and green eyes.

Marcas stood and pulled the contents out of the crate and held it up for all to see. Logan strode right over to it, studying it. "Hellfire, but Jennet and Ethan did a fine job on this, Gwynie. Try it out."

It took a while, but Gwyneth was finally able to

arrange it quite right and took a few steps with it. The expression on her face let them all know how pleased she was. "There is a small problem, but it could be a big problem."

"What?" Brigid asked.

"It hurts. It could rub a sore into the stub. Can we adjust it?"

Eva watched as four different people tried to adjust the straps to fix the problem, but from where she sat, that didn't look like the issue. She made her way to the basket next to the hearth and pulled out a small squirrel fur. Returning to the group, she asked, "May I?"

"What are you doing?" Gwynie asked.

"I think the problem is because your stump isn't level. If you attach this to one part where your leg connects, I think it will even out, make up for the uneven part of your stump."

Brigid said, "Here, I'll fix it, Mama. I think Eva is right." She fussed over it and Gwyneth tried it out, stopping to turn to Eva.

"My word, you fixed it, lass. Many thanks to you."

Marcas came over and clasped her shoulder. "Well done, Eva. What clan are you from?"

"MacVey. Excuse me, but I have to go. Thanks to you, Dyna, for the lessons."

"Allow me to go with you," Marcas said. "I'll get the dogs ready to travel and give you the food we've used with them. If you have any questions, we'll be here for a sennight, at least. After that, Maitland has raised many pups. He can help you."

Eva headed out with Marcas, surprised to see Goldie run straight for her, Shadow behind her. The two lunged for Eva as soon as she kneeled.

Finally, an animal that liked her that she could fuss over.

Anything to help her stop thinking about earls and betrothals.

CHAPTER FIVE

Maitland

M AITLAND STRODE INTO the great hall with wee Grant tied to his chest, facing out, while he held Maeve's hand. He'd never known such joy as he'd experienced since he'd married Maeve, the exhilaration of holding their son in his arms, something that had brought him to tears on more than one occasion. And the lad's smile was the most beautiful sight he'd ever seen.

After many discussions, they'd decided to call the lad Grant. Maeve couldn't call him Alex because it reminded her of her father. Sandor was already taken. Their last choice was either Graham or Grant, and they both preferred Grant.

Maitland had been married once before, had thought to have a child one day, but he and his wife had been kidnapped and held in a dungeon by the English, both beaten, but the true torture was when he'd been separated from her by a stone wall, not thick enough to prevent him from hearing her cries of pain as she delivered their bairn, both dying within an hour.

He carried many scars from those times, but he'd promised Maeve not to dwell on the past and to look to their future. He did his best to honor that promise, though he fell back into the darkness occasionally.

But this wee laddie of theirs brought him out with his smile, his wee fists, his kicking legs, and the way his gaze would lock on his father. As Maitland stepped into the hall, Grant began to kick with excitement because of the bairns near the hearth and the hall full of people laughing and enjoying the meal.

The first one to see him was Brigid who flew out of her seat. "Maitland! Maeve! I've been so excited to see you and that sweet bairn."

Suddenly surrounded by well-wishers, wee Grant bounced more and more. Brigid reached for the bairn, Maitland helping to remove him from the wrapped plaid he was tucked into. "Come to me, sweet bairn. We've all waited so long for you to arrive!"

Grant gurgled and kicked, his fist in his mouth whenever he could calm enough to do so. Brigid bussed both cheeks, and the lad smiled. "I love the name, Maeve. Maitland, have you seen your parents yet?"

"Nay, they are on the next ship, I hope. In a day or two, they should arrive."

Dyna said, "We need Avelina here to help us figure out what's going on with my daughters." She shook her head and rolled her eyes at Brigid.

"Gwyneth, you have a new device?" Maeve asked.

"Aye," she said, joining the group on her own. "And I think Jennet has done a fine job." Gwyneth nearly teared up but swiped the tears away. "My niece and nephew have given me some freedom."

Logan drawled, "And my back too." No matter what the man said, everyone knew Logan would still carry Gwynie wherever she wished to go.

While everyone fussed over Grant and Brigid and Gwyneth, Maitland nodded to Logan and tipped his head toward the solar. Connor entered just in time for Maitland to motion for him to join them. He turned around, not surprised to see the wee odd lass named Lia standing right next to the baby and Brigid. The lass was surely taken with their son.

Maitland motioned to Alycia. "Three ales, if you please."

Once she'd brought them their goblets, she left and closed the door behind her, smiling extra at Maitland.

Logan said, "You better ignore all those lasses' eyes, Menzie. Or Connor will have you at the end of his sword. He'll uphold his sister's honor."

Connor laughed at Logan. "Maitland does not have wandering eyes. I've never seen him so happy. And my sister too. It pleases me to see Maeve settled."

"You were fortunate to have the one bairn because Maeve is up in age. Probably the only one for you," Logan added.

"One bairn is enough for me, and I'll never want another. I adore my wife." Maitland stopped to stare up at the rafters. "I never thought I'd love another at all, but my love for Maeve grows stronger every day. I will protect them both with my life, Connor."

"I know that, Menzie. Did I hear someone outside say your sire is on his way?"

"Aye, my parents are on their way. My mother cannot wait to see Grant. You'd think it was her first grandbairn."

Connor shook his head. "That's not why she's coming."

Maitland frowned and looked from the old chieftain to Logan, who said, "Connor is right. She's coming to see her son with his son. No better happiness in the world."

Connor said, "I loved seeing Sylvi when she was born, but I was more taken by the joy on Dyna's face. Avelina and Drew are coming for that, not the bairn. He's a secondary reason. Especially after all you've been through, Maitland."

Maitland couldn't argue with their reasoning. His difficulties had indeed been reflected in his parents' mannerisms. "Either way, I'm pleased they'll soon be here. You will stay, Connor?"

"Aye. Dyna has begged us. Sela talked with her last eve, and Dyna convinced her to stay. She was feeling the need to return, but with Astra here and Dyna still unsettled, we agreed to stay another fortnight. Sela said she'd send word for Hagen to come with the next group if he wishes."

Logan said, "We're staying. Gwynie is thrilled with that contraption. We have enough family to keep us busy for a while. Something happening, Maitland?"

"Nay, but I heard you visited Clan Rankin. And thanks for the brew. Derric will be visiting for some training," he said with a grin. "Especially if he can get more of any fine beverage."

"Tell him to talk to Dermot. I think he knows where it's hidden," Logan said with a smirk. "The elders always keep track of the finest barrels. I wish I had brewed some."

"My sire will bring more wine, though we had a good supply here, which was wonderful." Maitland took a swig of his ale, then said, "Tell all, Logan. I'm waiting."

Logan sighed. "There is some fool who believes it would be easy to conquer the entire isle. I've told his friend how reckless an endeavor it is, especially now that there are so many Grant guards here, but he's young and stupid. Thinks I'm an old buffoon."

Connor snorted. "I don't think anyone has ever had a conversation with you and walked away with the idea that you're a fool, Ramsay. Old, mayhap, but never a fool."

"And?" Maitland persisted. "You tried to distract me, Logan. I want the whole story. Why did you go to Sloan?"

"Because the idiot said he's going after Rankin first. No idea when, but I told Sloan he needed to be ready. He said they've been training more ever since Rowan was stolen away, but he's not pleased yet. That's when I offered Derric's sword-skill help in exchange for some brew. He's glad to make that exchange."

"Hellfire." Maitland stood and moved over to

the window, pulling the two furs back to stare out over the landscape.

"Don't get too upset. I don't think their forces are that strong," Logan said.

Maitland spun back around. "You don't know who they are. What if they're Norse? Or Sutherlands or someone else with massive numbers? These isles are ripe for overtaking. If I had known this, I would not have brought my wife and son here, Logan. This isle is in a state of unrest, not where my family belongs."

Connor stood up and placed a hand on Maitland's shoulder. "You have many supporters here. And if it makes you feel any better, I'll send a score of guards to Rankin land. I'm sure we'll receive word when it happens, and we'll be there to help."

"And how many will we have left to protect our bairns here? I should have told my sire to bring a score of guards."

Connor said, "We can send for more, if you think they are necessary. We may not get the horses here, but we'll have a good number of men to protect the castle."

"That's what I want, Connor. I want a hundred guards to protect everyone in the castle. Mayhap that sounds foolish, but how many total do we have now? I counted around four score."

"I have a score with MacQuarie. I can call them back anytime."

"Nay, but please call for another score or two. We'll build another stable if we must."

"You still have plenty of room, but I can request more pallets and blankets."

"Aye, request more grain, more ale along with the pallets and blankets. More swords." Maitland tugged on his hair, feeling helpless. "More. We need more of everything."

He was glad his mother was coming. With her odd gifts paired with Dyna's seeing abilities, surely they'd be warned if anything were to happen. Maitland would not survive anything happening to Maeve and their bairn.

He'd surely die of a broken heart.

CHAPTER SIX

Avelina

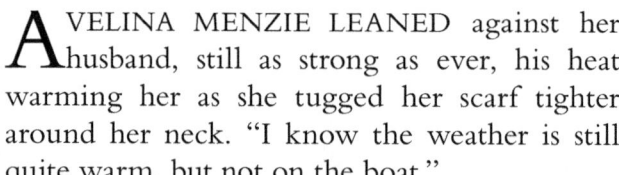

AVELINA MENZIE LEANED against her husband, still as strong as ever, his heat warming her as she tugged her scarf tighter around her neck. "I know the weather is still quite warm, but not on the boat."

Drew pulled her in closer, wrapping both arms around her in a hug, grinning. "I love having you this close. When do you hold still for this long except when you are cold?"

"So true." Her breath caught as she watched the landscape come closer as they crossed the firth, heading toward Craignure and the Isle of Mull. "I cannot wait to see Maitland with their new son. And I just adore Maeve. She will be the perfect mother."

"He deserves every bit of happiness coming their way. I've already heard that the isle is wonderful. Lots of fish and deer, good clans, and the castle they say is finely built."

"I'm so excited. I hope Connor and Sela are still there."

"You never know who you will see around Clan Grant."

"Or Clan Ramsay. I wonder where my brother has gotten off to." Logan was one of the two brothers who remained since Quade's passing many years ago. "I hope Gwyneth is still with him. I worry about him. Where do you suppose they went?"

"Probably to Edinburgh or even London to find a strong healer."

"Better than Brenna or Jennie?" She glanced back over her shoulder at her husband. There were no better healers, in her opinion.

"Mayhap he's found one of the doctors who've come from Europe. I've heard of them."

"Only the best for his Gwynie." She leaned back against the railing, the narrow seat as cold as the wind. "Oh!"

"What, Lina?"

"I'm not sure. Just a moment." She blinked several times because sometimes she feared her eyes had aged enough to deceive her. The clouds had begun to change, rolling quickly over the mountains on the isle, darkening, the wind now picking up.

The captain of the ship yelled below. "The wind is buffeting us in the wrong direction. Keep rowing. I have to pull the sail down. We must hurry. I don't like those clouds."

"Neither do I," she whispered to herself, but Drew heard her.

"What is it?"

"The clouds. They remind me of the day when

Alex came out of the mountains, the time of the sapphire sword. Those are ominous clouds, the kind I've only seen twice in my life. Oh, Drew."

"What are you saying?"

Avelina stood, tugging her husband with her to the other railing so she could see better. But what she saw was not good, and what she felt was worse. "There's an aura, a type of warning from the heavens. The gloomy yet menacing forces behind it, the kind I cannot control."

"But what does it mean, Avelina? Tell me it's not about Maitland or Maeve or their bairn. Please."

"I can't tell what it means. I can only tell you one thing."

"Do tell. Please."

"It's hovering over Duart Castle."

"And?" Drew asked, holding his breath.

"We better get there soon. Someone at Duart Castle is going to need our help."

"Your help. I can do nothing when it comes to your special talents, Lina."

"Nay, but I need you there to support me. Between Dyna and me, we'll find out what is happening. I'm certain of it."

"Can you stop it?"

"I don't know, but I will fight with all of my being."

A sudden gust sent the ship rocking, the rain suddenly coming down in sheeting waves of a pulsating force she didn't like.

"Captain!" Drew yelled. "Do something!"

"Get below deck!" the captain yelled to the half-score of passengers. "Take your things with you. This will not let up, and it's dangerous up here."

Drew tried to push Lina over to the stairs to head below deck, but she shoved his hands away. "Nay, Drew. This is about our son or our grandson. I'll not allow this to happen to him again! I'm staying here!"

She shoved away from him and threw her arms up over her head with a scream of fury, her head dropping back so she could stare at the clouds above. "Nay, nay, nay! Not now!"

The boat rocked back and forth, the captain grabbing her arm, but she pushed him away. Avelina chanted and prayed and begged for assistance. "Angels above us, I beg for your help now. I beseech you to bring us to the port safely and to send the ill-omened clouds of doom to another place."

Drew came over and stood behind her to support her, the rocking of the boat and the winds nearly knocking them both over. "I have you, sweet Lina. Help them," he whispered while the storm buffeted them back and forth. Her arms swayed and moved rhythmically, and as if lifted by an unknown force, the boat propelled toward the port, docking in less than a few moments, the pelting rain stopping as soon as they tied off.

Avelina fell into her husband's arms, exhausted from the battle she'd just endured with unknown forces. "I've got you, Lina. Come. We have a grandson to meet."

Avelina kissed her husband's cheek and said, "I can't wait to get to know Grant."

"Is that what they are calling him?"

"I think so. We'll see."

They gathered their things and headed up the incline to the small village. He found the local stable and paid for a horse to take them and their belongings to the castle. They were halfway there when they saw six horses approaching from Duart Point.

"Who is it, Drew? Is it Maitland?"

They approached the group of horses, pleased to see familiar faces. Drew said, "Aye, I see Maitland with a wee lad strapped to his chest, a bald head sticking out, just like our wee ones. On one side is Connor Grant and the other side is Dyna. I think Alasdair and Broc are behind them. And the last horse? Saints above, I think it's your brother Logan, with a wee lass riding in front. Golden-haired. One of Dyna's daughters, possibly?"

Lina studied the group, pleased to see it was indeed her brother and their youngest son. Maitland looked as happy as she'd ever seen him, his bairn carefully protected from the weather, riding against his chest. The Grants all looked strong and intimidating, but that wasn't what caught her attention.

"You see Maitland, aye?" Drew asked.

"I do."

"And your brother?"

"Aye."

"Then what is it? I know something else has your attention." Drew had learned to pick up on her strange auras.

Avelina patted his arm. "Aye. It's a good thing."

She'd keep telling herself that, no matter what else she thought. "The lass with my brother."

"Dyna's lass?"

"Nay."

"Then who?"

"Alexander has his own angel. Her name is Lia."

"What are you talking about?"

"The wee lass. Do you not see the rays from heaven surrounding her?"

"Nay, I see naught."

"I do. She's an angel. A guardian angel. She's here to protect our grandson."

From what, she didn't know. For now, she was grateful to see the tiny warrior, her powers shining around her. They had a grandson who was indeed special.

And a wee angel sent from the heavens to protect him.

CHAPTER SEVEN

Sloan

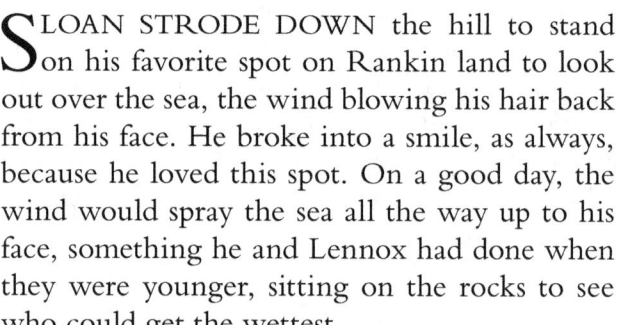

SLOAN STRODE DOWN the hill to stand on his favorite spot on Rankin land to look out over the sea, the wind blowing his hair back from his face. He broke into a smile, as always, because he loved this spot. On a good day, the wind would spray the sea all the way up to his face, something he and Lennox had done when they were younger, sitting on the rocks to see who could get the wettest.

From there, one could see everything that goes on across Bloody Bay.

And something was definitely going on. He'd seen more boats than ever going from Kilchoan to Coll and back. He had no idea what the ships were transporting, and he was curious, but he was more interested in why Rinaldo hadn't mentioned the increased activity. It was his brother's primary responsibility, and he was failing at it.

It was a simple task for a simple-minded person. His mother had always insisted that Rinaldo's birth had been difficult, and so she considered him lacking. His father had insisted that he not push Rinaldo too much.

Oh, there were times when they were young that Rinaldo had demonstrated some limitations in his thinking, but not as much as his parents thought. At least, not in Sloan's mind.

He dismissed these ideas, changing over to a different topic as he strode from one spot to the next. Lennox hadn't returned yet to give him his answer to his offer for his sister, and he was long overdue.

Sloan had suffered from more jealousy than he'd ever admitted as he watched his friend fall in love so fast that it had shocked everyone, Lennox included. He'd met Meg and swore he'd known she was the one for him from the moment she'd swung an axe over her head and aimed it straight for his chest.

How Sloan wished he'd been there to observe that, but he'd heard much about it from his nephew Rowan, one of the bairns kidnapped and saved by Meg, Lennox's new wife.

Lennox and Meg, Thane and Tamsin, Maitland and Maeve, Derric and Dyna, Alaric and Eli—more couples to watch than he'd ever paid attention to before. It was as if they were inundated with happy couples. Deliriously happy couples, Logan and Gwyneth Ramsay included. The entire situation fostered more of a yearning deep inside his belly of a happier life, of one where everything wasn't decided by his father and whether he measured up to the old chieftain's standards.

He wished for the same happiness. But he'd been rebuked too many times by the one lass he'd known for years.

Whom he'd loved for years—Eva MacVey.

Eva with her long dark waves that fell down her back, her rosy lips, and a smile that could stop any man in his tracks. Petite, she was a powerhouse when it came to her mind. He could recall numerous times when one lad or another would pick on her when she was young, and she'd stand up to them, bold as ever, her clever taunts putting each boy in their place.

One summer, a group of lads had headed to the loch on foot, and Eva had followed. A boy had told her to go away, and she'd marched right up and said, "I'm staying," with a wild scowl on her face. Then she'd stomped hard on his foot and asked, "Shall I stomp on the other boot too?"

He'd moved to shove her a short distance, but Sloan caught the bully's hand, squeezed it, and said, "The lass asked you a question."

The boy cried and ran away.

Eva's response had been to smile up at Sloan. That had been the first time he'd known that Eva was going to be more than a wee lass living in the next castle. Eva had sent the first stirring to his loins he'd ever had.

Lennox had snorted. "You have half the hour, Eva. Then you go home."

And she pranced ahead, following the group into the loch.

Sloan had always been drawn to the lass, but sadly, the feelings were not reciprocated. He'd waited patiently for her to grow up. She was two and twenty to his four and twenty, but she still had no interest in him.

Every time he approached her, she shunned him, just as she'd done not long ago at Dounarwyse Castle.

Tired of waiting, he'd approached Lennox and asked for her hand, expecting his old friend to accept with a smile and a congratulatory clasp of his shoulder, only that hadn't happened. Lennox had told him he would have to ask Eva.

Sloan sighed because he knew what her answer would be. What he was most curious about was her reasons for the refusal he knew would be coming. Was it his looks? His demeanor? Was he not tall enough? Not smart enough?

He'd never gotten the chance to kiss the lass, so he knew that wasn't her reason.

Miles called down to him. "You have a visitor. MacVey is here."

Sloan nodded, heading up the hill to accept the refusal, but he was anxious to hear the reason. Being good friends, he felt Lennox owed him that much.

"MacVey," he called out as Lennox approached, coming down the hill to meet him, he guessed because he didn't wish to be overheard. His friend would save him the embarrassment of being refused in front of all his guards.

"Rankin. Something draw your attention down here?"

"Nay, I just enjoy the tranquility of the sea and the birds. My favorite place. You have the sound,

I have the sea." He shrugged, not wanting to push the issue, so he waited to see why he was here.

"I came to give you my sister's answer to your offer. She accepts."

Sloan couldn't have been more shocked. Nothing anyone could have said would have surprised him more. "Eva accepted? She agreed to marry me?" He had to admit his heart soared a wee bit, though he'd not say so, but the answer pleased him. Mayhap with a lengthy betrothal, he could help Eva learn to care for him. See his better qualities. It would give him the time to learn more about her and how to make her happy.

The possibilities were endless. He couldn't stop the smile from breaking out across his face.

Lennox grimaced and said, "Not exactly." He scratched his beard, a move that his friend often did when he was about to lie.

"What do you mean by that? It's an aye or a nay. There's no in-between, Lennox."

"In this case, I am accepting for her. She will see the wisdom of my decision in time."

Sloan stepped back. He knew that was the way of it for many. The elders of the clan decided who would make a good match and ordered it. He didn't want that for his marriage.

No way on this hallowed ground would he want a lass to be forced to marry him.

"Did you speak to her at all or is this your decision?"

"I did speak with her."

"And?"

"And she refused. Some foolish reason or

another about our father choosing her husband, but she doesn't know what she's talking about. He's gone and I'm here, so I'm choosing for her. You're a good match for her. She'll adjust."

Sloan was nearly at the point when he was about to lose his temper completely. It didn't happen often, but when he reached that point, there was no stopping his fury. But he managed to hold it in for a bit longer. "You think to make such an important decision for your sister like that? And you think I want a wife who is forced to marry me? Hellfire, you better think on this again, friend. Or is it about to become enemy, MacVey?"

"What the hell, Rankin? I'm giving you what you want. My sister's hand in marriage. Why are you upset about it?"

"Because I want her willing. Do you not know your sister? Do you think I wish to see her in chains at the altar? You know that's what it would take to get the stubborn lass to marry me if she's not inclined. You are as daft as my sire if you think I wish for that."

"The hell I am."

"You are. You're only thinking with your cock. You are so taken with your new wife that you can't see what's in front of you. Eva doesn't want me."

"Then why the hell did you ask? I'm giving you what you want and you're going to refuse me now?"

"Aye. If Eva can't come to me willingly, I don't want the match." He did his best to lower his voice, but he couldn't stop it. And of course, out of nowhere came his brother.

Rinaldo approached. "What's all the yelling about, Sloan? Can I help with something?"

"Nay, we're done here. Take your leave, MacVey." Sloan's hand went to the hilt of his weapon, though he'd never draw it on his friend.

Lennox nodded. "I'm sorry you feel that way. As I said, we accept your offer. We'll come on another day to discuss the impending nuptials. She'll come to understand it's best for her." He headed up the hill with a nod.

Sloan waited until he was gone and turned to Rinaldo. "If you speak a word of this to anyone, I'll beat you until your tongue swells so much, you'll never be able to speak again."

Rinaldo paled but then smiled. "But from what I heard, Eva is going to marry you. Does that not make you happy?"

"Not when she's being forced!"

Sloan headed up the hill, yelling behind him. "Remember what I said, Rinaldo. Tell no one."

CHAPTER EIGHT

Eva

———————

EVA SAT ON the floor in the great hall, just outside her brother's solar, where her two brothers argued on about some seed discrepancy, a topic she found totally uninteresting.

"Come, Goldie. Sit with me." Absolutely enamored with her new plaything, Eva smiled when the wee hound ran straight for her, bounding onto her lap and landing in the middle of her skirt. Shadow followed, his nose pressing against the wee dog as if to tease it, then ran away in a wide circle.

Goldie responded, leaping off her lap and falling face-first because she'd misjudged the distance. Shadow rushed to the pup's side, encouraging her to get up again, which she did, frolicking behind Shadow.

The two were such a delight to watch that Eva had been sitting ever since Taskill had gone inside the solar.

His voice carried to her now. "I'm telling you that there is not enough grain for everyone. I counted it out carefully this time, and Jasper confirmed my count. Your calculations must be wrong, Lennox."

Lennox paced, the same way he always did while the newest member of the family, Meg, asked, "May I look at your calculations, husband?"

Lennox said, "Of course, sweeting."

Jasper asked, "You can do numbers, my lady?"

"Better than any of us," Taskill said. Eva knew he grinned from ear to ear when he made that statement. It tickled all of them that Meg was such a whiz with numbers, able to multiply and calculate in her head faster than any of them.

"I think there is a mistake here, Lennox," she said.

Eva lifted her head, leaning back, that statement calling to her. Oh, how she would love to be in there to witness the horror on her eldest brother's face at being caught in a mistake. She waited, ignoring the dogs for now, her mother coming down the stairway.

"Meg, you are correct. I did make a mistake. Let me look again, if you please."

All was quiet while Lennox probably studied the paper over and over again before making a final decision, if she were to guess.

Lennox said, "I did. Let's recalculate, and we'll go into the storeroom and hand out more bags of grain to those who need it. My apologies to all, Taskill. Please tell them it was an honest mistake, that my head was clouded by this beauty in front of me."

Taskill laughed and Meg giggled, but then the group left, all headed to the cellars.

Once they were alone in the hall, her mother called out to her, "Eva, how many times must I tell you that those dogs do not belong in the hall. Dogs belong outside."

"But she's just a baby, Mama."

"A baby with fur that is getting everywhere. I see that no matter what I say, you'll ignore me, so please would you at least confine the wee beasts to the area in the corner? I do not care to have dog hairs all over the bottom of my fine gowns. How I wish your sire were still here to set you straight, young lady."

"I wish Da were still here too." Eva sighed but got up and took the dogs over to the designated area, taking a blanket with her. "This is going to be Goldie's bed. She needs something soft to sleep on."

"Not your bed or I shall suffer apoplexy. She has something soft to sleep on. Shadow. They always huddle together. They're animals."

Rut approached, keeping her distance from the pups, choosing a chair close to the hearth. "Eva, have you thought more on Sloan Rankin's proposal? He would be a good match for you. You should reconsider and accept it."

"Nay, Mama. I'm waiting for the man Papa chose for me. I believe he will show up at my door someday. Then I'll marry someone I love. And that's not Sloan Rankin."

"Oh, hog spit. Your father thought he would choose for you someday, but he was taken ill. He cannot choose for you, so trust your brother and me. You are well past marrying age, Eva, and you've mentioned no one. Are you sneaking off with a local guard and rolling in the hay in the stables?"

"Nay, Mama. How could you suggest such a thing?" Appalled by the comment, she had to admit that perhaps it was time for her to consider a roll in the hay.

"Listen, my dear. I've allowed you enough time to mourn your sire. You were Da's wee lassie, his only one, and I know he spoiled you. But you've had enough time to recover. You will be an old spinster if you do not find someone to marry. Soon enough, no one will have you. Don't you want bairns? If you wait too long, you won't be able to have any."

"I am not spoiled, Mama. Just because Papa loved me dearly, it does not mean I'm spoiled. I hate it when you say that. You say it so much that others say it too." She knew it was true that her father gave in to her requests much quicker than her mother, causing her to approach her sire with nearly every request she had, but that didn't mean she was spoiled. How she hated it when Alycia would call her that.

"Who would dare say my daughter is spoiled?" Her mother stood up and crossed her arms over her chest, something that did not bode well for whomever was not in her favor at the moment.

"No one specific. I've just heard from others."

"What others?"

"It doesn't matter." She'd never tell her mother that her only friend Alycia had told her she was spoiled on multiple occasions. And she didn't stop when Eva told her she didn't appreciate it. There was something about Alycia thinking it was her own private joke. "Either way, you know Papa always said he knew who he wished for me to marry. That someday he would tell me. I believe his ghost watches over me and somehow, he will let me know who it is. I wish to wait."

"How in blazes can he tell you when he's not here? And if he had chosen someone for you, don't you think he would have discussed it with me?"

"Nay, Da and I had private conversations."

"Fine, keep your secrets."

"There may be another way. There are seers living at Duart Castle. Suppose I ask Dyna or her daughter if they could talk to Da. Surely, they could reach him, and he'd pass the name on to me."

"You will not go over there and bother the chieftain of Clan Grantham about talking to the dead."

"What about Lia? They say she's a faery. Mayhap she can tell me. I'm going to ask her the next time I see her."

Her mother shook her head in exasperation. "There's no talking any reason into you, lass. Fine. But I think you'll be waiting a long time to hear anything from a dead man." She dropped her arms and moved back to her chair, settling a fur over her lap. "Tell me why they would think you were spoiled. Has this mysterious person given you a reason for such a judgment?"

Eva knew the reasons, but she thought mayhap

to keep it to herself, but then Goldie came almost up to her face and barked at her. As if the animal was telling her what to do. "All right, Goldie. I'll tell. This person said that I have no responsibilities. That I don't have to work like the others in the clan. That the mistress runs the keep and the servants and the cook, but I do nothing."

"And what did you say?"

She didn't like one bit that her mother's tone had softened as if she saw some truth in Alycia's cruel words. "I told her that I have many things to do. I take care of my own chamber. Now I am the caretaker of two dogs. And that I am learning archery."

"You have learned to read and write, lass. Not many have."

"You're right, Mama. Many thanks to you."

"Why don't you read a book and tell me about it?"

She frowned. There weren't many books about and the ones that were here were quite boring. "I've asked Lennox to try to locate more books, but he tells me he doesn't know where to find any. I do love to read, Mama."

"I know, dear. You used to read to your father whenever he was taken ill. He loved to hear your voice. He always believed you were a bright girl, that there would be many suitors clamoring for your hand."

Eva scowled again, dropping the fabric animal she had that she used to play tug with Goldie. "No one has come but Sloan. What's wrong with me, Mama?" She hated to ask because she feared the answer, but the question had dominated her mind for the past year. What was wrong with her? Why had no one but Sloan offered for her? She refused to consider the earl as a suitor. He was not interested in her, just with the womb in her belly. Was she long in the face, too homely, or too talkative? Alycia was always teasing her about her small breasts, though Eva didn't think them that small. In her mind, they fit her just right.

"Naught is wrong with you. 'Struth is there are not many suitors of noble blood here on the isle. I've told Lennox we should take you to court, but he resists. Sloan is your best choice on the Isle of Mull, Eva. Think on it, please."

Her mother set the fur aside and headed off toward the kitchens. "I'll go check with Cook on the meals. Meg is doing a fine job learning her new tasks. She's a bright lass as well. You should talk with her more."

"Mama? Why didn't you teach me some of her tasks? I would like to be useful, but you've always told me it was your job. I could have helped you. Could I not help Meg?"

Her mother stopped and tapped her foot, thinking. "I suppose that is my fault. I didn't wish to burden you, but you are old enough. Let's ask Meg if she would like your assistance. Think on which chore you would like. I know you are not good with numbers, but you could work with Cook or handle the linens or the cellars. What about the wine?"

None of those chores sounded the least bit

appealing to her, so she said the only thing she could think of. "I'll give it careful consideration."

"You do that and let me know. And what about Clan Grantham? Is there not someone there you are interested in? There are plenty of Grant and Ramsay lads in this world. Surely one of them would appeal to you. They are all of noble blood."

She thought of Broc, wondering why she hadn't approached him the other day. She'd been too taken with her new pets. "I'll talk with Dyna when I go for my next archery lesson."

"I think that's a fine idea, Eva. I must move along to my duties." Her mother swirled her skirt as she turned, something Eva couldn't begin to mimic.

That conversation left her feeling as though she had no worth at all.

Meg came up from the cellars, the men heading out the front door while Meg approached the hearth. "It's so cold in the cellars. I have to warm my hands. Are you hale, Eva? You do not look well."

"I'm fine. It was just the conversation with my mother that frustrated me." She moved over to sit in a chair by the fire. Meg was close to her age and so she should understand her problems.

"Can I help?" Meg asked.

"I'm curious. How did you know that you were good with numbers? Did you work hard at making yourself good with them?"

Meg sat down and shook her head with a smile. "Nay. It came easily to me. Part of it was that I loved numbers."

"You do? But why? They're quite boring to me."

Meg laughed. "Because they're always true. They don't change, they are fun to play with, and they are exact. You don't need to think on anything with numbers. The truth is there for you, and they'll never lie to you. And there's something about their rhythm, the way they work together, the patterns are so intricate sometimes." She ticked her fingers as she talked, staring into the fire. "Sometimes, when Mama gave us something to draw with, I made pictures based on numbers. The results were quite pleasing to me, though Tamsin often said she didn't see it. I always like things to balance out evenly. Do you understand what I mean?"

"Aye. Both sides of your skirt must be the same length."

"Exactly!" Meg smiled.

"How did you know to love numbers? And how did you become good with the axe? I keep trying to perfect my archery skills, but I'm quite terrible at it." She'd tried so hard, but she nearly always missed the mark, her arrow flying wide.

"I didn't know I was good at either. It just came about. You know what a young lass told me out in the forest one day?"

"You mean Lia?"

Lia had been kidnapped along with three other bairns, Magni, Rowan, and Tora. Meg had been stolen to care for them. They'd gotten away and traveled through the forest, headed for the port, finally running into Lennox who brought them all home. Lia was now six but at times spoke as though she were forty summers.

"Aye. Lia told me that the heavens know what your purpose will be, but they may not tell you until you need it most."

Eva thought about that for a moment, then said, "Does that make sense to you?"

"It does. I didn't think I was skilled at throwing an axe until I had to save the four bairns from that evil man. He came at us and something inside me said to throw it, and I did. He dropped instantly."

"You mean you didn't know you were good at axe throwing before then?"

"Nay, I did not. It was a total surprise to me. I'd done it before, so it was the only weapon I had to bring along with me when I ran away. I never planned to use it."

"And the numbers? When did the heavens tell you that you had a special gift for them?"

Meg grinned. "The heavens never did. I learned numbers from my father but never used them other than to play with in my mind. It was your brother who told me I was good at adding and calculating. I've used numbers more than ever, and I love using them."

"So, the heavens didn't tell you anything about numbers."

Meg smiled and said, "Nay, but they sent your brother to me." She stopped because her eyes misted, something that surprised Eva. "He was heaven sent, not the numbers."

"And did you love him when you met him?"

"Oh, nay."

"You didn't?" Now this admission she found more interesting than anything else she'd heard this morn.

"Nay. I hated him. Ask your mother. I think she heard us arguing down near the boat launch. He tried to give me orders, and I didn't like it. He told me I was ignorant, and I didn't like that either."

"Then how did you end up loving him?"

Meg shrugged. "I had to spend time with him, see all his good qualities. And he took care of me right from the start. Something I'd never experienced before. It didn't happen right away. Be patient. Believe in what Lia tells you."

"What would Lia say about finding a husband, one that I could love?"

"She would say that the heavens will find him for you when the time is right. She'd say not to worry."

Somehow, Eva couldn't quite believe that, but she knew one thing for certain. Whoever she was meant to be with, it would not be Sloan Rankin.

CHAPTER NINE

Sloan

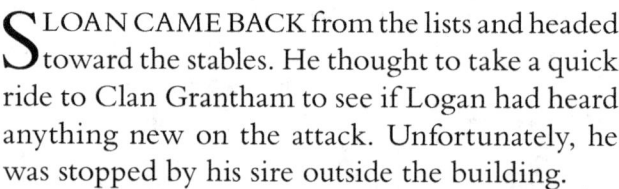

SLOAN CAME BACK from the lists and headed toward the stables. He thought to take a quick ride to Clan Grantham to see if Logan had heard anything new on the attack. Unfortunately, he was stopped by his sire outside the building.

"So you can't even find yourself a wife, I hear."

That comment halted him in his tracks. "What, Da?"

"I said I heard Eva refused you." He crossed his arms and stared at his eldest son, his eyes telling Sloan exactly how upset he was about this.

He let out a loud groan, wishing his brother was nearby so he could throttle him. "Who told you that?"

"Doesn't matter, does it? The truth matters. MacVey was going to force her to marry you, and you refused. What the hell is wrong with you? Women don't get to make decisions. If Lennox said he'd accept the betrothal, you should have agreed. Did I teach you naught?"

Sloan was too angry to sort out his thoughts, but he knew better than to yell at the old man.

He moved until he was a hand length away from his sire. "You taught me too much, Da. How to punish lads. How to favor one lad over the other. How to ignore the lasses of your clan. How to run the clan without listening to your clan members."

His father waved his hand in dismissal. "Stop your whining, boy. I did a good job raising you and your siblings. But you don't do what I ask you to do. Why not?"

"What have I ignored?"

"You should force the marriage. You need to marry, Sloan."

"I'm trying, Da. But honestly, it is none of your concern. I want to know who told you."

"I'm not saying."

"Rinaldo did. And where the hell is he today? He was supposed to brush down the horses, and I see it hasn't been done yet. Does that upset you, or do you prefer to stay mad at me and me alone?"

"He'll get to it. He wanted to go on a boat ride. Rinaldo will be back. He's a good boy. He always does what I ask him to do."

"I know. You remind me of my lackings often enough."

"Sloan, I don't mean to be so hard on you, but you have an important job. Rinaldo doesn't, and he has a hard time being second to you. He always has. You were fortunate to be the heir to my land. I think it's important to keep him involved."

"Da, I give him responsibilities, but he shirks them." Right now, Sloan could jump in the sea and swim over to Coll and his father would still be talking about the wonders of Rinaldo. "I have work to do. I'll see you at the evening meal."

Sloan headed down the hill toward the coastline, grumbling at his brother along the way, waving off his father. He thought he'd seen a boat out of the corner of his eye. Sure enough, it was Rinaldo coming back from some unknown destination.

"Rinaldo, where the hell have you been?" Hellfire, but he sure looked like a fool when his own brother refused to do whatever he asked of him.

"Greetings, brother. I have new information for you that I'm sure you'll find pleasing."

"Where have you been?"

"I went to have a brief repast with our neighbor, Angus MacKinnis. Interesting enough, he's been trying to find a husband for Theebet. I suggested your name, Sloan. She's a fine lass. Verra pretty. I told him you'd call for her soon."

Sloan stared at his brother wide-eyed, denying his need to choke the breath from him. He shook his head, certain that he'd heard incorrectly. "You did what, Rinaldo?"

"I suggested a betrothal between you and Theebet. She smiled when I asked her if she would be agreeable."

"Why would you do such a thing?"

"Because Eva refused you. And I couldn't bear to see you arguing with your best friend in the entire land, Lennox. This way you and Lennox won't fight again. You're welcome."

Rinaldo put the oars away and headed up the hill, a wide smile on his face.

"Rinaldo, halt!"

His brother turned around, that innocent expression that he always wore still there. "What can I do for you, Sloan? I'd be glad to help you in any way at all."

Hellfire, but the simpleton pushed his patience. He loved his brother, but he truly pushed him too far sometimes. "Why did you tell Da about Eva when I asked you not to?"

His brother frowned. "I didn't tell him. He overheard the whole discussion. I overheard him asking Miles about it."

Sloan slapped his forehead, closing his eyes. Blast the stars out of the sky, but his name was doomed to be on the end of every wagging tongue on the isle.

"Pardon me, but I must go brush down the horses as you have requested, Sloan."

And Rinaldo disappeared.

Sloan wished to rip every single hair out of his head, one at a time. In fact, perhaps he'd hire a bird to come along and peck at his scalp while he yanked on them. Or a flurry of crabs to crawl up and tear at his bare feet when he swam the next time. Or mayhap he'd fall onto a pile of nettles while he was taking his next pish.

His sire was daft and hated him, his brother was a simpleton who could not be controlled, and now the entire clan would know Eva refused him.

Miles and Ingelram came down the hill toward him, and he knew what he had to do, the purpose twofold. "Ingelram, I need you to go with me. We are heading to Clan MacKinnis to undo what my brother has done. Miles, you are in charge."

He'd relax by rowing across the calm sound, then he'd explain to MacKinnis that he wasn't in search of a bride, and his brother should not speak for him.

"Aye, Chief. Rinaldo went into the stables. Is that where you wish for him to go?"

"Aye, Miles. Make sure he brushes all the horses in the stalls at present. Keep him busy, if you please." Grumbling, he waved Ingelram over to the boat and the two pulled it out, finding another set of oars so both could row.

They made it halfway across their short trip to Kinlochaline before Sloan could speak. "So the tongues are all wagging thanks to Rinaldo, I'm guessing."

Ingelram cleared his throat before he spoke. "I've heard some rumblings, but we don't believe everything Rinaldo says, Chief. I know he's your brother, but many times he tells tall tales. It's my preference to wait to hear the truth from you."

"I appreciate that. Does anyone else agree with you?"

"Many do. Some prefer to listen to Rinaldo, but they wag their tongues more than I do."

"This trip is to chat with Angus MacKinnis. Rinaldo offered for his daughter, not for himself, but for me. My brother has decided to start arranging marriages, apparently. I'm going to undo his promises before there's too much damage. We'll put the boat in, and you can chat with Isaac in the stables while I try to smooth things over."

Nothing was said until they arrived at the neck of Loch Aline, but then Ingelram said, "I cannot believe he would do something so careless, Chief. I believe it to be one of his worst actions, to come over here on his own. Mayhap the chieftain never truly entertained his words. And I hope Theebet never found out about it. She's not your type, in my opinion."

Sloan couldn't help but be surprised by his words. As they glided down the tranquil waters of the loch, he said, "And what is my type, in your opinion?"

"Someone strong, someone not afraid to back down. Theebet strikes me as timid, Chief. Not your type."

Sloan couldn't argue with that, so he said nothing as they approached the dock near Kinlochaline Castle. Isaac was on the hill above the coastline, talking with Angus. Sloan waved as they approached.

Angus smiled and moved over to the dock, waving them in. "Not surprised to see you, Rankin. Come in for a brief repast."

Sloan accepted the help of one of MacKinnis's men, who managed the boat with Ingelram's assistance, and followed Angus up to the castle.

Once they were inside, Angus spoke to one of the serving lasses. "A goblet of ale and a meat pie for our guest, if you please." Then he led Sloan into his solar at the top of the staircase, leaving the door open for the lass to enter.

"I'm not surprised to see you here, Sloan, though I didn't expect you'd arrive until the morrow." He smiled, and Sloan knew he was thinking about his brother's meddling.

Sloan made small talk until the lass brought his ale and pie, then once she closed the door behind her, he decided there was no reason to delay. He took a swig of the ale and sighed, deciding to deal with the issue first thing. There was no reason to avoid the discussion about the irresponsible act his brother had committed. "My apologies that my brother came and acted on my behalf when I did not give him the rights to do so. I honestly don't know what came over him, but I'm not in a position to offer for your daughter's hand, Angus. I hope you will forgive us."

Angus leaned back in his chair and folded his hands across his abdomen, his eyes sparkling. "Your brother. He is changing. He certainly surprised me with that visit. I'd heard of Lennox's quick wedding and I'm happy for him, but I've heard little about you. Only that you offered for Eva MacVey and you were refused."

"You heard that too?" Sloan closed his eyes and rubbed them with his thumbs. Would his embarrassment never cease?

"Only from Rinaldo," he said, sitting up. "Did you offer for her?"

"I did. Lennox is in favor of the match. Eva is not, so we are not betrothed. That's all I care to say, but either way, I had no plans for offering for another so quickly. I think that would be an insult to Eva, saying that I was not truly bothered by her rejection. While others might like her to think that, I do not. I hope you have not informed Theebet."

"I did not. She overheard us speaking, but I told her once your brother left that it was a false offer."

"And she was not upset?" he asked but wasn't quite sure what he hoped the answer would be.

"Nay, Sloan. I would have accepted as I think you would make a fine match, but Theebet considers you a bit—*gruff* is the word I believe she used."

Gruff? Had he ever been called gruff before? Only when he dealt with his brother and his father and his men. Well, that meant nearly everyone. He'd have to ask his sisters. Either way, he wouldn't dwell on that. It needed to be shoved into the back of his mind where he could hopefully forget the words.

"It would be an honor to be betrothed to your daughter, but this is not the right time, Angus. And I thank you for understanding."

"Sloan, I wish you much happiness. After what happened to your first fiancée, I'm sure it must be hard to find another. I hope it will work out for you."

Sloan had been betrothed for a few months, but his betrothed threw herself off a cliff into the sea. Gormal was probably dead before she ever hit the water, but it had been tragic and horrific for everyone, no one else more than himself. He'd known Gormal for many years but had only agreed to the match after he'd learned of Eva's impending betrothal to an English earl. Gormal was the daughter of the armorer, and though he hadn't been in love with her, he had hoped for a good marriage. He respected and trusted her, so he'd hoped for the best with the match.

Even though his heart had belonged to Eva.

It hadn't come to fruition, so it was another one of those things he pushed into the caverns in his mind, locking it up and throwing away the key. He couldn't dwell on Gormal either. The event had affected him for so long that he'd sworn to let the pain of it go. He couldn't dwell on what had happened forever. He honestly had no idea why the lass would take her own life. He thought she'd been pleased with their betrothal and had been excited to be his wife.

How wrong he'd been. He'd done his best to ignore the wagging tongues, to not take the awful situation as being his fault. A few others had tried to place the blame on his shoulders, as he'd done for a short while, but Gormal's sire had insisted it was not Sloan's fault.

It had taken nearly six moons for him and his clan to come out of that darkness.

If only Eva would allow the two of them to explore a relationship between the two of them, but it was not to be.

He took a bite of the meat pie and said, "Please excuse my brother's ignorance, Angus. He doesn't understand the implications of his words. I apologize for him. If you wish for me to apologize to Theebet, I will." Not that he wished to, but the honor code of his clan said he would.

"Nay, she knew it was not a true offer. But I wish to bring something else up to you."

"I'm listening," he said before taking another bite of the meat pie.

"Your brother is wiser than you think he is, in my opinion. I think that, as he has matured, he's come into a better understanding of the world and its ways, if you know what I mean."

Sloan couldn't have been more surprised by his comment. "In terms of lasses and marriage? Those types of ways?"

"Nay." Angus leaned back again and sighed. "I don't know how else to say this other than to be blunt about it. Many consider your brother's mind to be simple." He glanced at his hands, then back up at Sloan. "I do not. I tried to tell your sire that once, but he got upset. However, I want you to know that I've seen your brother in some situations that are not the type that a simple-minded person would be in." Sighing again, he sat up and said, "I'll put it simply. Rinaldo is smarter than you think he is. Please consider that in all your dealings with him. And now, I have somewhere else I have to be, so I'll escort you back to your boat."

Sloan felt as if he'd been dealt a blow to his gut, but after a moment or two, that feeling changed. It blossomed in a good way. "Many thanks to you, Angus. I'll take my leave."

Had he been right about his brother all along? Was the favor his father gave Rinaldo false?

Angus escorted him back, and they chatted easily. "Sure was glad to see Lennox marry. Meg's quite a lass. I chatted with her at the wedding, and she has a quick mind. Quite a beauty too. I wish them much joy in their lives. I've never seen Lennox happier."

Sloan said, "I agree. He's found his mate, and I'm sure the bairns will follow soon enough."

Now if he could only find his own wife. He'd be able to survive living with his father and his brother much easier if he had someone like Eva in his life.

But he forced himself to a topic he couldn't ignore.

Was Rinaldo putting on a show for everyone?

A year ago, he'd have dismissed the thought without considering it, but now he had to reconsider.

Was Angus right?

Was his brother a phony?

CHAPTER TEN

Maitland

MAITLAND SAT IN the great hall with his son, enjoying the early-morning quiet. The wee laddie was usually the first one up, so Maeve fed him quickly, then handed him over to her husband, her eyes often still closed.

This was only fair, in Maitland's mind. The boy was such a voracious eater that he still woke his mother up in the middle of the night to eat. Maeve deserved her sleep, so he changed the boy's raggies and headed out into the great hall with Lia not far behind them, allowing Maeve a couple more hours of rest. He set the boy in the fabric lounger he'd fashioned in front of the hearth and got the fire going again. He'd made a small boat and packed it with furs and plaids to prop him up and keep him warm, and the lad loved it. It gave him the chance to kick his legs and watch everyone.

Cook was busy readying the morning meal in the kitchens, cooking porridge and fruit for everyone.

Other men left bairn care to the women, but not Maitland. He was young the first time he'd seen Alex Grant walking around with one of his grandbairns strapped to his chest. He especially recalled Dyna, who giggled and kicked all the way through training at the lists, though Alex did keep her a distance away from the swinging swords. Maitland had admired the way Alex raised his bairns and helped with his grandbairns, part of the reason he had agreed when Maeve suggested naming their son after her adoptive father.

Maitland let Lia keep Grant occupied while he grabbed a clean linen square and soaked it in his own bowl of porridge, then handed it to the boy to suck on. He and Lia always laughed at his face, covered with oats as he sucked and chewed on the succulent treat, his legs kicking away. Maitland had tried to give him honey one day, but Lia yelled at him.

"No honey!"

"What? Why not? I'm sure he'd love it," Maitland had asked, surprised by the vehemence in her words.

"He probably would, but I'm telling you it's not good for wee bairns. Not yet. Not until he can walk."

He had discussed this with Maeve, and the two had decided that with Lia's dedication, they would honor her wishes. Alexander would not know what he was missing, after all, so they kept the honey away.

His mother came down the stairs, floating like an angel.

"Good morn to you, Mama. How did you sleep?"

"Wonderfully, Maitland. The heather mattress is lovely. And the lad is up already?"

"I bring him out every morn with me. And Lia."

Avelina kissed his cheek, then bent down to plant a kiss on her grandson's forehead. "My but the laddie enjoys that porridge, does he not? He's wearing most of it on every part of his face but his lips." She laughed at the boy and the bairn laughed back, wrinkling his nose. "And a lovely morn to you, Lia."

His mother had asked him about Lia, why she always followed Grant about, but Maitland had advised her to ask the lass herself. His mother had some otherworldly talents, had been the keeper of the sapphire sword for years, and had passed it on to Alex Grant to give to his great-grandson, John. She had seer talents that Maitland had never understood, but somehow, he thought she might have a special connection with Lia.

He and Maeve had discussed the similarities between Lia and Callie, the wee lass they'd met in a snowstorm before they married. She'd been several years older than Lia, but Callie had many similar characteristics. They both spoke as though they were decades old, never let anything bother them, and went about everything as if it were their primary task in life.

After all he'd learned about Lia and Magni, especially the haunting tale from Logan about how Magni had found Lia, he didn't question.

The lad had simply whispered that he'd found her as a faery under a frond in the forest. They all wondered about Lia but let her do as she wished, even staying by Grant's side at all times. Some things were not meant for him to challenge, and this was one of them.

Maitland looked at his mother until he caught her eye, then nodded and tipped his head toward Lia, hoping she understood his meaning. No one else was around but the serving lasses, so this was a perfect time to question the girl.

"Lia, you are so wonderful with Grant," his mother said, catching on to his meaning quickly. "How have you learned to handle bairns so well?"

Lia smiled, stopping her play with the laddie to give Avelina her full attention, handing Grant a toy to occupy him while she spoke. "Different experiences. I do adore the wee ones. Don't you, Mistress Menzie?"

"Please call me Avelina."

"What about Lina?" the girl asked, her brow raised in question. "It is verra much like my name. Do you not agree? Or would that be too confusing for others?"

No one had called her Lina since she arrived. Her brother Micheil did all the time, but he wasn't here, and Logan hadn't used it yet that she had heard. "How did you know?"

"Oh, I picked it up somewhere." Lia smoothed her skirt as though she were the queen of the royal court.

"May I ask you a prying question, Lia?"

"Of course. As long as I may ask you the same."

Maitland shrugged his shoulders. He faced his mother and now stood behind Lia, watching his son.

His mother replied, "All right. I'll agree if you ask your question first."

"I'd be happy to," Lia replied. "If you had one wish, what would it be, my lady?"

"That's an easy one to answer. I would wish that no harm would come to my son, his wife, and their son until Alexander was of marrying age."

Lia tipped her head. "Hmmm. I must reflect on that as it could be considered three wishes. But while I do that, please ask *your* question, my lady Avelina."

Without hesitation, she asked, "Why do you stay by my grandson's side?"

"Because it's my duty."

"Who gave you this duty, lass?"

"The universe. I sleep at night, and that's how I learn of my duties. Where my time can be best spent. It's most difficult to explain. First it was Magni, then Tora, Rowan, and Magni. Then Thane. Now it is your grandson. I have other smaller tasks to accomplish, but I always have a focus. Does it please you that he is one of my duties?"

"I think so."

"Why would you doubt this? You have special talents, as well."

"Because I fear it means there could be danger coming to him. Is there? Is that why you are here, Lia? Is my grandson in danger?"

Maitland took a step forward, afraid to hear her answer. But he convinced himself that no matter what, he had many people who would help him. He wasn't alone in a dungeon. He was in a strong castle with a curtain wall that was nearly two horses thick, and he was surrounded by the best swordsmen in all the land. And archers. So many strong ones. Alasdair, Broc, Connor, Logan, Derric, Dyna, Gwyneth, Eli, and Alaric, plus countless guards. And the MacVeys, the Rankins, and the MacQuaries were but a short distance away.

Yet something still bothered him. Four bairns had already been kidnapped. Would it happen again? He couldn't help but wonder if that was why Lia was here.

That fear ate at his insides all day long. Every time he looked at Grant in Maeve's arms, he was nearly ripped in two by the fear of losing either one of them. He knew that pain well because he'd been through it and almost didn't survive it before.

He and Nesta had been traveling back to visit her parents on Drummond land when they'd been captured by the English and thrown into a dungeon. Unfortunately, they'd been thrown into two separate cells. He'd listened to his wife's cries of pain that night, thinking she was being beaten, but it had been a wee lass named Callie who had informed him that Nesta had delivered their bairn in the cell. She'd cried from the pain of bearing the child, not from any beatings. But their child had been born dead, something that couldn't be helped.

For many years, Maitland had carried the guilt of their deaths with him, thinking he should have been able to break free of his restraints so he could have saved them. But Callie, the guiding angel who had revealed herself to Maeve and Maitland, had said that there was naught he could have done. And she'd told him it was time to marry Maeve so their son could be born.

He'd never survive it if any such thing happened again. The pain of it still gripped him on occasion, much as he tried to fight it.

Lia did something that surprised him more than anything else she could have done. She pushed a stool over next to his mother, then turned back to him and took him by the hand, a movement that was a bit ridiculous, but he allowed it, the girl leading him over to the stool, pointing for him to sit. She glanced over at his son, but he was happily chewing on his snack, his legs still kicking.

Maitland sat as requested, his arms touching his mother's side. Lia leaned forward and cupped Maitland's cheeks with her tiny hands. In a quiet, soothing voice, she said, "I need you to listen carefully to me, Maitland Menzie. I am here to protect your son from any harm, and I wish to tell you that I have been granted special powers to see that it happens. I cannot explain it all to you, but I am charged to bring the heavens down to protect him if I must. And Nesta is standing behind me to inform you that we will not lose him and for you to stop worrying so. She says that Callie assures you the same. Trust me, even when the skies are darker than you have ever seen them before, the light will prevail."

She stood back and lifted her arms over her head, a green aura surrounding her. She smiled and tipped her head to bask in the light.

Immediately, Maitland's mind jumped to when he had fallen for Maeve. They'd met Callie in the snow. Lia reminded him of Callie, and Maeve had been with him when Callie appeared in front of them later, angel wings and all. She'd said the universe had sent her to them. Callie had been the one who told them they would have a son together, and that he would be quite special.

Had the universe sent them Lia?

A voice on the staircase interrupted them and Lia's aura fell away.

Lia turned back to Grant, finding another toy for him, acting as if nothing had happened. How grateful Maitland was to have his mother next to him, so he had another witness to Lia's words.

The person on the staircase was his father, who'd seen and heard enough. But even his father wasn't prepared for what he found when he reached the group.

Maitland sat on the stool and cried giant tears, ones that choked him.

Nesta was the name of his first wife. Was she that close to him now?

His mother leaned over and kissed his tears,

whispering, "Maitland, you must trust in the heavens and the universe. She's just like Callie was not so long ago. You're not going to lose him."

CHAPTER ELEVEN

Eva

———❦———

A FEW DAYS LATER, Eva came down the stairs with a plan. She moved over to the corner of the hall, picking up her new best friend. "Good morn to you, sweet Goldie." She gave her dog a snuggle, then set her down, petting Shadow and throwing a toy for him to grab. "Come, puppies, you must spend the day outside because I'm going on a visit later."

Her mother entered the hall with Meg, both coming from the kitchens. "There," her mother said. "And now we have the next two days' meals set. You handle it well, Meg."

Meg said, "Only because of your help, my lady."

"Rut."

"Rut." Meg patted Rut's forearm.

Eva wasn't surprised that Meg was taking over her duties so well. She was a bright lass who had worked her fingers to the bone long before she'd met Lennox. The lass still had horrible calluses on her hands the day of the wedding. It never bothered Meg, but it surely caught Rut's attention.

Eva's mother had recovered quickly and mumbled to Eva, "Not a concern. Lennox is finally getting married, and her hands will heal."

They had. It was hard to dislike Meg because she was sincere and hardworking. How she loved her brother, Eva didn't know, but then again, she'd been a witness to behaviors from Lennox that Eva had never seen before. He was so much in love with Meg that Eva often found it quite amusing.

Would she ever find someone to love her like that?

"Where are you going, Eva?" her mother asked.

"I'm going to Clan Grantham for a visit. I'm taking your advice, Mama. I'm going to ask to borrow a book, so I have something to read."

Rut stopped, the surprise on her face making her smile. "The Granthams have books?"

Eva grinned and leaned toward her mother. "Don't tell, but Dyna said all the Grant and Ramsay women have to learn how to read. And write! In case they are healers. They must keep notes of all they've done. Dyna told me they have many books they brought with them, and Connor has brought more. So, I'm going to promise to return one if they'll allow me."

Meg's eyes widened. "Ooh, would you borrow one for me too? Anything interesting. I used to read with Tamsin and our mother."

Lennox entered and said, "Books? Why did you not say so, Meg? I'll order some to be delivered on the next ship from Europe."

"You can do that?"

Lennox pulled Meg in for a kiss and said, "Come to my solar, and I'll show you the letter I received offering such shipments."

"I'm so excited," Meg said, clapping her hands. Lennox arched a brow and got an odd look on his face that Eva didn't quite understand.

Rut said, "Take it to your bedchamber, you two. You never know when a child might walk through the door." She gave Lennox's shoulder a shove, and he chuckled, leading Meg to his solar.

Eva whipped her head around at her mother. Surely, she didn't mean they were talking of intimate relations. Slime, but she'd have to ask Dyna another question. And when had she ever thought of the word *slime*?

Eli was rubbing off on her.

"Mama, I shall return before the evening meal. I may practice my archery if Dyna is available."

"Please make sure you take five guards with you. Taskill will choose them."

Eva rolled her eyes but grabbed her shawl and headed out, the dogs directly behind her. Taskill would watch the animals for her because he adored dogs almost as much as she did.

They arrived at Duart Castle two hours later, telling one of the guards, "I'll be a few hours probably." They were used to escorting her, so they spent their time in the lists watching the Grant men spar.

She was surprised that Broc appeared at her side. "May I?" he asked as he reached for her waist.

"My thanks to you, Broc."

He lifted her down with a wide grin, showing off his beautiful smile. Broc was fine-looking, but he didn't send her heart aflutter like her future husband would do someday.

"What brings you here, Eva? More archery? I think Dyna is still in the great hall."

"That, and I'm interested in borrowing a book. Do you have any available?"

"Och, many for you to choose from. And I believe Dyna brought a few of my grandmother's picture books she used to tell the bairns stories. I doubt she would let you borrow them because they are treasured by many, but Maitland and Dyna both love to read, so there are numerous books inside. Just leave a note if you borrow one. As I said, Dyna is inside. Maitland's parents are here so there are more meetings going on. Probably where they all are at present, but she'll be about."

"Where do they keep the books?"

"In the tower room in a bookcase. Maeve is probably there with wee Grant."

"My thanks, Broc. I'll look for Maeve or Dyna."

Eva strode inside, nearly grumbling to herself because she could tell Broc had no interest in her at all. Broc was a cousin to Dyna and Alasdair but was unmarried.

Who was she going to marry?

She headed into the keep, surprised to see the hall empty, but she could hear voices in the solar, so she went down the passageway to the tower room and knocked on the door.

"Enter, please," a child's voice answered.

Lia sat on a stool next to a cradle where the bairn slept soundly.

"Greetings, Lia. Is Maeve here?"

"She stepped out to the garderobe. I'm watching over Grant."

She glanced past Lia and noticed the bookcase behind her. "May I look at the books?"

"Of course. Maeve brought several with her. She loves to read."

Eva stepped over to the books, her finger running down their spines, loving the feel of each tome. She didn't recognize any titles but pulled out one to look at it. After studying a few, she nearly jumped because Grant woke up with a loud bellow.

"He has quite a voice for one so small," Eva said, walking toward him. "Are you going to pick him up?"

"I'm not allowed to lift him without Maeve or Maitland present. You'll have to do it." Lia stepped back and pointed to the cradle, two tiny fists waving in the air.

"Oh, I cannot. I've never picked up a baby." She peeked in at the wriggling bundle, still surprised at the tenor of his yells.

"You must pick him up, Eva. I'll help you. The only thing you have to worry about is his neck. You must support it, though he's pretty strong at this point. He's a sweet laddie, and I'm sure he'll grin at you once you lift him into your arms."

Eva could barely hear Lia's words because Grant's cries were so loud and frantic. "All right. I'll try."

"Put one hand under his head and the other underneath his bottom, then lift. It's quite simple, actually."

Eva did what Lia asked and as soon as she lifted the bairn, Grant stopped his hollering and his eyes locked on hers. "Well, greetings to you, my dear."

She held him in front of her, wondering what she was to do next. She glanced over at Lia for help.

"Tuck him into the bend of your elbow and hold him close. His head will rest on the curve of your arm."

"Like so?" She did her best and the boy finally settled against her, a grin widening on his face and a fist going into his mouth. "Oh my, does it taste good?"

He giggled and kicked his feet.

Lia said, "Sit down with him. He's getting heavy."

"Then what do I do?" She honestly had no idea, having no experience with a child this small.

"Just talk to him. He loves to talk with people."

"He can talk?"

"Not real words, but he thinks he is talking. You'll see. He's quite an amiable bairn."

Eva did as Lia suggested and tucked the boy against her bosom. He locked gazes on her and began to utter the most nonsensical sounds, as if trying to talk with her. "Are you telling me about the day you've had? Are you enjoying your grandparents?"

Lia said, "I'm glad you are enjoying the bairn. You are quite good with him. Are you not hoping for bairns of your own someday?"

Eva stared at the lass, the one who spoke as if she were an elder yet appeared in a body too small to lift a bairn. "I haven't thought on it much." She gave her attention back to the beautiful boy on her lap.

"You should. And Eva, do not believe anything the earl said to you. He was not meant for you."

Eva whipped her head to face Lia. "How would you know about the earl?"

Lia smiled and tipped her head, folding her hands in front of her. "I know nearly everything I need to know."

"But why do you need to know about me?"

Lia pursed her lips and her finger tapped on them, her foot tapping in the same rhythm. "Because. I must help you …"

"Help me what?" She slid to the edge of her seat, afraid she wouldn't hear the soft-spoken lass because of the lad's noises.

"Your husband is near. Do you not have someone in mind?"

"Nay." A sudden anger infused her insides, furious that even this lass spoke of marriage. "Why must everyone insist that I marry? Why can't I live alone my entire life? There's naught wrong with it."

"Unless you were meant to be with someone. Then you would complicate their life's purpose if you refuse your own."

Did Lia know what her sire had wished for

her? "Do you know who my sire chose for me? If you do, I beg you to tell me this instant."

Lia shook her head and took two steps back.

"Please tell me. I need to know who my father chose for me."

"I cannot help you with that. But your soulmate lives nearby. Do not overlook him."

"Tell me who."

Lia shook her head to deny her, but Eva would find out. Unfortunately, it would have to wait because the door opened and Maeve came inside.

Maeve startled Eva, but she kept a tight hold on the boy until his mother approached. "I'm sorry, but who are you? We've not met before. You aren't dressed like a serving lass."

"Eva. My name is Eva MacVey." She stood and handed the babe to his mother. "He was crying, so I wished to calm him down. I hope that was all right with you."

"You did a fine job. Grant, you like Eva? Where are you from, Eva?"

"Clan MacVey, on the other side of Craignure."

"Well, you are doing a wonderful job with him. Do you have younger siblings? You are a natural."

"Nay, he's the first bairn I've held." Saying the words made her realize how much she may have missed in her life. Why hadn't she held a bairn before? There had never been one in the castle that she recalled. Surely there were many among the guards and their families, but they hadn't been around her.

Perhaps she was spoiled in ways she didn't even know.

"I was going to the kitchens. Why don't you bring him along into the great hall? There are more toys there, and his grandparents will be out of the solar shortly."

"Do you mind if I return to borrow a book afterward?"

"Of course. Borrow all you like. I can suggest a couple of titles."

"I would like that. Two books, one for my sister-in-law, if you don't mind."

"Gladly. Come. We can look at the books later." Then she stopped and said, "Here, allow me to show you another way to hold Grant. He likes to see what is going on so if you hold him on your hip just so, he can look about at everyone as you walk."

She did that and the lad bounced with excitement as soon as they headed out the door, Lia behind her.

They reached the hearth where it was much warmer, and Maeve pointed. "When you tire of him, Eva, just set him in his wee boat. It's well cushioned. I'll be right back."

Eva sat down, adjusting the bairn on her lap so he could look about. He kicked like he was about to run across the chamber. The door opened, and she heard the boot falls on the stones, but she didn't look up until they were nearly upon her.

When she looked up, she paled.

Sloan Rankin, his hair unkempt and looking handsomer than ever, stood over her. "Greetings to you, Eva. Could we have a word, please?"

CHAPTER TWELVE

Logan

LOGAN STOOD IN the middle of the forest and scanned the area. His vision wasn't quite as good as it used to be, but he could see more than Gwynie could. Though he hoped her accuracy would be there today. He didn't know this fool who he'd met before, so he didn't trust him either.

Gwynie was hiding in a tree, just in case the piece of slime had other plans.

"I know you're here. I heard you before," he called out. "Dumb arse."

A man stepped out from behind some bushes. "What do you want? This is the last time I'll come when you summon me. I control you."

Logan snorted, the idea of anyone controlling him nearly more than he could handle, but he forced himself to calm down because he needed information first. Maitland was more upset than Logan had ever seen him. Avelina had seen a dark aura on her way over to the isle, something that didn't bode well for any of them.

Logan loved his sister and wouldn't argue with

her because she was right. Something was about to happen, and at present, it was anyone's guess. It was Logan's responsibility to find out exactly what it was.

At present, he had no inkling what was brewing on the isle. Neither did Connor, who counted on Dyna to see things.

But they'd had two other bad indications. First, Tora had told Connor that he couldn't leave because of the bairn. And she told him not to tell Maitland. Even that had made Gwynie pale. Tora had abilities that were just coming to light. Dyna didn't understand her own daughter's special skills. And Sandor was starting to act odd as well. Every once in a while, he would wave at something or someone when no one was there.

Once, Logan had asked him in front of everyone, expecting the lad to tell him he waved at a bird or some other creature.

But instead, he waved with a backward hand and said, "Gweetings, Gwandpapa. I wike yo swowd."

Dyna had gasped, Connor had sat down hard on a nearby stool, and Gwynie had nearly fallen out of her chair.

And then there was Lia, the lass who Magni swore he found under a leaf in the forest. She'd told Avelina and Maitland some things that brought giant tears to Menzie's face, though he told no one what she'd said.

Avelina had taken a hold of Logan's hand and said, "Let it go, brother. He'll tell you when he's ready."

Something bad was coming. He knew it, Gwynie knew it, and so did half the people at Duart Castle.

"What do you want?"

"I want to know why you lied to me."

"I never lied to you."

"The hell you didn't," Logan said, his hand going to the hilt of his weapon. "And don't start lying now. You said someone was attacking Clan Rankin. Naught has happened. So, what's the truth of it?"

"Look, old man. I tell you what I hear. I'm not the one who said they were attacking, so I don't know why it didn't happen."

"You said they were going to take over the Isle of Mull, starting with Rankin land."

"I had it wrong. Someone plans to conquer the isle, but not yet. They are building their forces, and I come over and check on the isle, make sure no one else is trying to attack. When I was here last, I heard another fool say he wished to battle the chieftain of Dun Ara. He's the one you need to fear. The other won't take place for several moons, but I can promise you, it will happen."

"I don't understand someone who is daft enough to tell me their plans." Logan took in the man's dark hair, his smaller sword, but an admirable one, and always searched for a crest or some other sign of his clan, but he never found one. He was tall, but not bulky, half the size of Connor or Alasdair.

He'd never been so confused by someone in all his years of spying.

"Ramsay, you will find out soon enough. What's coming, you'll be unable to stop. I'll never tell you the exact day. I mind my own business and travel here once in a while to keep up with all that takes place. MacQuarie and MacVey both took wives. The Grants have brought a couple score of guards. Little else has taken place. Now I told you what I know. That's all."

"So, there is no imminent attack that you know of? No plan to overtake the whole isle in the next two moons?"

"Nay. None. One fool is spouting out his plans, but no one believes him. He's being driven by the man on Kilchoan."

Kilchoan. MacVey had mentioned Kilchoan. He had to push that.

"Who is he?"

The man shrugged and said, "I don't know his name. He doesn't want land. He wants things he can sell."

Logan's head nearly split in two, but he stayed calm.

"I've told you what I know. You need to return the favor, or you'll never see me again, Ramsay."

He hated that the man knew his name because he had no idea what his identity was, but he was rather well known. "Ask your question. I'll answer if I can."

"Which one is the faery?"

"I answered that question before."

"But they say there are three golden-haired lasses. Are you sure the faery will grant wishes? She's their priority."

Logan could feel the racing of Gwynie's heart at that question. He knew without asking his dear wife that he had to protect Dyna's daughters somehow.

"The one who is the tallest of the three is the faery. We've discussed this before. Golden-haired, not white-haired. Why do you persist with the same questions?"

"And she will grant wishes? That's who they're looking for. If you tell me, they'll just take the one. If you don't, who knows how many they'll take."

"I don't know for certain. I've heard talk of that, but I surely don't know if she grants wishes." *Not really a lie*, he thought.

"And there's a lad. One who has more powers than anyone. Who does he belong to?"

"A lad with powers? I've not heard anything about that. Your sources are wrong. Who told you this?"

The man chuckled and mounted his horse. "A faery under a leaf told me. Beware. Someone wants those two and will pay much coin to find them." He sent his horse down the path and laughed all the way out of the forest.

Hellfire, that was not what Logan was hoping to hear.

Lia was in trouble, but so were all the wee lasses then, Tora and Sylvi especially. But what lad was the one with the powers? Sandor? Or was it Maitland's new son?

Logan glanced over into the trees at his wife, her tears visible from where he stood. When the other was gone, Logan moved to help Gwynie out of the tree. He hated to hear her words. After all their years together, she had the most common sense of anyone he knew, someone who could listen to all kinds of stories and consolidate it into one sentence.

"Logan, nay. They definitely want Lia, and I'm not worried about her. I know Lia can take care of herself, but the laddie cannot."

"Which laddie, Gwyn? Which one are they after?"

"No doubt in my mind. They want Alexander Drew Menzie Grantham."

Maitland and Maeve's son was in trouble.

CHAPTER THIRTEEN

Sloan

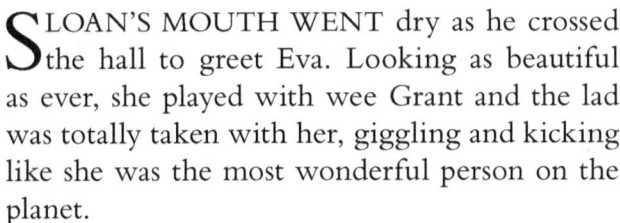

SLOAN'S MOUTH WENT dry as he crossed the hall to greet Eva. Looking as beautiful as ever, she played with wee Grant and the lad was totally taken with her, giggling and kicking like she was the most wonderful person on the planet.

Lucky lad.

"Greetings to you, Eva."

"Greetings, my lord," she said, not making eye contact.

Sloan reached for her chin and lifted her gaze to his, mostly because he was selfish. This close to her, he wished to see her beautiful blue eyes up close. They carried a mystery to them, some parts the color of the bright sky, other sections the shade of the darkest night. Which would it be this day? "I am not my lord or chief or anything to you. I am just Sloan."

She nodded. "Greetings, Sloan."

He noticed how comfortable she appeared to be with the laddie, handling him as if he belonged to her. "You're verra good with the lad. I didn't know you had much experience with bairns."

"I don't, but I'm learning. He is a sweet, happy lad, isn't he?"

"He is. His parents adore him." Sloan couldn't help but wonder if there was ever a day when his father had adored him.

"What exactly do you want, Sloan? I don't think you came here to chat about a bairn." She lifted her chin a notch to let him know that she wasn't going to change her mind, if he were to guess.

He hadn't expected her to. "I had a visit from your brother. Have you spoken to him yet about my offer?"

"Your offer of a betrothal? Aye, I did. I refused. It's just that I'm not ready for marriage yet. Too much has happened. I know it's been two years, but I still miss my sire terribly. I always thought he would be here when I married. Please don't be offended."

He took a seat and rested his elbows on his knees, leaning toward the lad. "Do you have someone else in mind?"

"Nay. I'm just not ready yet." She set the boy in his boat and handed him a soft toy to play with, one that he swung about until he hit himself in the head, then giggled.

"Good thing it's not a wooden toy."

She laughed at that. "He's a wee bit silly."

He wasn't going to drag this out and make it any more painful than it already was. "Eva, I turned your brother's offer down."

"My brother's offer?" She sat back so she could look up at him, the expression on her face one of total confusion. "What was my brother's offer?"

"Your brother told me he accepted my offer for you, that you didn't want it, but he was certain you would change your mind. He accepted on your behalf, and I said I only wanted you if you were willing. I am not interested in a forced marriage."

"He what?" Widened eyes told him that Eva had no idea what Lennox had promised. "He said I *would* marry you? And when was this wedding to take place?"

"Undecided." Sloan held up his palm to her. "No need to panic, Eva. As I told you, I rejected it. I thought we might take the time to see if we do suit, but out of respect for your brother and your blood, I offered a betrothal. I'm sorry you are not interested, but since you rejected me, I want to be clear that I'm not interested in anything unless you are willing."

Her hands kneaded in her lap for a few moments before she spoke again. "My thanks, Sloan."

Sloan watched the woman he'd hoped to marry, the lass he believed he loved, the one he'd hoped to bless them with bairns, the one who would stand on the coastline with him and watch sunsets. But it wasn't to be, something that bothered him more than he cared to admit, the truth of her rejection evident in her lovely features.

Eva was not interested in him, the expression on her face more painful than he'd expected it to be. She had no feelings for him at all.

Her mind was surely spinning with all that he'd told her, and no doubt they were not happy thoughts. "I'm sorry. I assumed you knew of it."

She shook her head, tears misting her gaze, but she was able to contain them.

Maeve entered from the kitchens and said, "Many thanks to you, Eva. I'll watch him. I might take him outside for a wee walk inside the curtain wall, see if we can find his father."

"It was my pleasure, Maeve, but I must take my leave." She nodded to Maeve, then to Sloan, and retrieved her mantle, heading out the door faster than anyone he'd ever seen.

Maeve asked, "Did I say something to upset her?"

"Nay, I did. She's fine. I'll follow her out," he said. "Is Logan here?"

"He left but said he'd be back within an hour. He should be back soon," she said, lifting her son.

"He's a big boy, Maeve. He's growing like the thistles on a sunny day in summer."

"He is."

Sloan took his leave, keeping a distance behind Eva. He could see he'd upset her, and she was probably headed back to yell at her brother, but that was none of his business. How would he have guessed that Lennox would not have told her that he'd promised for her?

Eva motioned to one of her guards and the man retrieved her horse as they readied to take their leave. Just what he'd expected. They opened the gates for her, surprised to hear some bellowing on the other side.

But Sloan was more distracted by what he saw out of the corner of his eye. His brother. "Rinaldo?"

He moved over to the area behind one of the stables, a group of guards discussing something. "Rinaldo. What are you doing here?"

Broc said, "Listen, Rankin. We are not trying to be disrespectful, but we cannot give you any guards at this time. My uncle is considering bringing more Grant guards across the water. We have none to spare with all that is happening."

"I don't understand," Sloan said, his gaze going from his innocent-looking brother to Broc and then the others.

"Rinaldo is looking for guards. Did you not send him here?" Broc asked.

Rinaldo said, "Sloan asked me, but I must have misunderstood. I'm going home now, Sloan."

Rinaldo found his horse and disappeared before Sloan could stop him. "Broc, I did not send him here."

Broc said to the others, "Head to the lists. I'll meet you there." Once the other guards were out of hearing distance, he said, "Your brother changes like the wind."

Sloan tipped his head, confused by Broc's comment. "I'm not sure I understand."

"One moment he is acting seriously about hiring guards, and the next moment he acts like he has no idea what he was just doing. Is he usually that way?"

"Nay." Sloan wished to ask for more of an

explanation, but he caught Logan's voice at the gate. He'd have to deal with Rinaldo at home.

"Is Rankin here? I need to see him."

The guard said, "Aye, by the stable."

Logan approached with his wife. Once they came inside and Eva's group departed, Logan caught his eye and said, "Hold up, Rankin. I have news for you."

Sloan waited, anxious to hear what his news was. Logan helped his wife down and then arranged her new contraption so she could walk inside on her own.

"That's quite a creation. Who made it?" Sloan asked, impressed.

"My niece and her husband. Brigid brought it with her."

"Logan, I'm going inside. Tell Sloan what we've learned." Gwyneth cast a glance Sloan's way and said, "I don't like any of it."

She went toward the keep, Brigid coming around the side of the castle and joining her mother. Logan pointed to an area where they could speak privately.

"The man said you'll not be attacked soon. There's someone not far from Kilchoan who is planning to take over the isle but not in the next couple of moons. They're busy gathering forces now. You need not worry, but then he also said there is some fool, who no one believes has the necessary forces, who plans to attack you first, then battle the other clans, but the man on Kilchoan said he doubts the other has the abilities.

Says the man is daft." Logan crossed his arms and studied Sloan before he finished. "That's not what worries me."

"There's worse?" Sloan couldn't imagine what could be worse, but he needed to hear it, whatever it was.

"Aye. He says there are men who are looking for two things."

"Things or people?"

"More specifically? Bairns. They want the faery who can grant wishes and the lad who has some special powers. Know you who that could be?"

"Obviously, Lia is the faery, but who is the lad? I have no idea. Magni? Rowan? Sandor? Which one has special powers? Could it be Sandor because his mother is a seer?"

"Or is it the bairn?"

Sloan hadn't thought of that. "The bairn? Why?"

"The darkness, the … Oh, I don't know how to explain it, but I think the lad with the powers is Grant."

"Grant? Not Sandor?"

"Not Sandor. I'm not sure why I say it, but I believe they're after Lia and Grant," Logan said. "I'll give you a few coins if you do me a favor."

"I'll do a favor for you without the coins. No need to pay me."

"You won't think so when I tell you what the task is."

"Tell me and I'll tell you what I think," Sloan said.

"Tell Maitland and Maeve there's a group of bad men at Kilchoan who are coming for their son."

Sloan took two steps back. He'd done many distasteful tasks over the years, but not this one. "Nay. Not doing it. See you later, Logan. Thanks for the update. I'll let MacVey know."

One of the lads was also special.

But was it Magni, Sandor, or Grant?

It was Grant. *Hellfire.*

CHAPTER FOURTEEN

Eva

———❧———

EVA PUSHED HER horse too far, ignoring the guards telling her to slow down. Well, they hadn't just been embarrassed and infuriated at the same time.

Embarrassed that the man who offered for her told her he had withdrawn his offer.

Infuriated that her own brother had said he would basically force the marriage.

Sloan did say that he withdrew the offer because she wasn't interested in him, but it still hurt. When coming from his lips, it hurt more than she'd ever admit to anyone. What Sloan must think of her, she wasn't sure, but she tried not to think on it.

And Lennox? She couldn't wait to have words with him.

When she arrived home, she jumped down from her mount, nearly falling on her arse, but she managed to keep herself upright. Lennox stood in the middle of the courtyard talking with Jasper.

"Brother dearest, a word, please."

Her brother gave her a questioning look but held up his hand to let her know that she could wait. Pacing and fuming, she allowed him the chance to finish his conversation, but when Jasper left, she strode directly up to him. "How could you?"

"How could I what?"

"I'm sure you can guess. Think a moment."

"Eva, when you calm yourself enough so you are not making a scene, I'll discuss whatever this is with you." He took her elbow and ushered her off to the side. "If this is about Sloan, I don't think you want every guard here knowing you refused him and that I tried to push you to marry him. We don't need everyone talking about you."

Her eyes misted, but she swiped the tears away. "How could you?"

"Who did you see?"

"Sloan. He told me you accepted, and he rejected me. Now I've been embarrassed too. I've been jilted."

Lennox's jaw did that odd wiggling thing it did when he controlled his temper, but his voice came out in an even tone. "You have not been jilted. You refused Sloan. I tried to accept for you, hoping you would court him for a few moons to see if you suited, but he rejected it as much as you did. It was a mutually agreed-upon refusal. You have naught to be embarrassed about, Eva. No one knows but Sloan and me, so stop panicking. You got what you wanted. There is no betrothal. End of story, so stop being dramatic. It's done as you wished." He looked down at her, then glanced over his shoulder to see who was close by. "Eva, is it not what you wanted?"

"Aye."

"Then why are you so upset?"

How did you explain to someone that it was because Sloan told her he refused her? That he would not marry her if she wasn't willing, which was a perfectly reasonable response. "I don't know." She didn't know how to explain it to him. She needed a female to speak with.

Not her mother. She'd dismiss her feelings.

Not Meg. She wouldn't understand.

She had no one with whom to share her thoughts, her innermost fears.

Lennox kissed her forehead and said, "Go on inside and warm yourself by the fire. You have nothing to be upset about. All is the way you wanted. I'm sure you will find the right person when you least expect it. That's exactly how it happened with me."

She nodded and headed toward the keep, dragging her feet, but nonetheless, going inside, feeling rejected. Yet her brother was right. All was as she wished it to be. No betrothal. No Sloan Rankin.

She sat inside and caught Alycia coming down the staircase. "Alycia, do you have a moment, please?"

"Aye, but outside." Alycia tugged her out the back door and asked, "What's wrong?"

She did her best to explain the situation to her one and only friend but wasn't quite sure how to explain how she felt.

"Are you betrothed to Sloan?" Alycia asked.

"Nay."

"No betrothal. You refused him?"

"Aye. My brother was going to force me to marry, but then Sloan refused because he didn't want to insist ..."

"So, Lennox would force you, but Sloan wouldn't? See, I told you he was a good man. You should have accepted. There are not that many noblemen on the isle."

Eva scowled, not knowing how to explain what she'd meant. "Never mind. I'm fine."

"Good. I have to change two more beds. We can talk on the morrow." Alycia left with a smile on her face.

Shoulders slumped, Eva made her way around to the front of the castle toward the stables. She'd left her horse without brushing her down, so she thought to see how the sweet mare was doing. The stable lads were busy handling the guards' horses, so she slipped inside and headed down the line of stalls until she found the white beauty at the end of the row, which pleased her because she thought at least her horse would listen to her. There was no one else close enough to overhear her words, especially with the chaos taking place at the stable entrance with all the guards and their horses.

"Greetings, Snow Queen. Forgive me for leaving you so quickly." She reached into the apple barrel and pulled out a nice red one for her mount. Opening the stall door, Eva stepped inside and hugged her pet, wrapping her arms around the horse after giving her the treat, the chomping oddly soothing to her. "I don't know how to explain it, Queenie, but I feel so foolish. I should have accepted. He is a fine man and a handsome man, but I'm just not ready. The one insulting Englishman wished to look at my breasts, and I don't wish for anyone to look at them. If I had agreed, would Sloan have asked to see them too? I just don't understand all this marriage and betrothal business. Mama says I'm old enough, but I don't think I am. If I married Sloan, I'd have to leave MacVey land and move to Dun Ara. What would I do on Rankin land where I would know no one?"

The horse pawed the ground as if answering her. "No more treats yet, but you are right. I would know Marta and Sheona, but they're different from me. Marta has two bairns and Sheona is only eight and ten. Younger than I am. She wouldn't understand what I wish to tell her, that I plan to find my own husband, that he should be the man my father chose for me. That I wish for him to be from a faraway land, that we would marry and travel far, far away."

Her horse let out a blow, and she jerked her head up. Queenie didn't blow unless she didn't like something. "What is it?"

A man Eva didn't know stood on the other side of the door to the stall, a smile on his face that she didn't like. "Look, a sweet lass looking for something to do. I have something you can do. Are you not a pretty one?"

"Please leave. Are you a new guard here? I don't

recognize you." She knew most of them, though occasionally one came in who was a stranger. "Who are you?"

"Doesn't matter. I'm here to make you happy, sweet one."

Eva had a bad feeling, so she made her way to the door of the stall, pushing against it to take her leave. Unfortunately, the only way out was past this man. If she could just get by him, she'd run down the line of stalls.

This was not good timing because a large group of guards had just returned from somewhere, keeping the stable lads busy, the sound of horses blocking out anything from this end of the building. The horse in the next stall began to stir as if he could sense her fear.

"I'm leaving. Get out of my way."

He grinned and shook his head, his dirty brown hair sticking to his neck. He grabbed both of her hands and pinned them behind her back, forcing her into the back of the stall. "There's a nice pile of straw here that will suit us perfectly. Relax. You'll enjoy it."

"Enjoy what?"

His mouth descended on hers in a sloppy kiss that she hated. She closed her lips tight, but he stopped and said, "Don't fight me or you'll regret it. Open your mouth." He tried to kiss her again, and she did what he asked, opening her mouth and biting his lip, drawing blood. That infuriated him. "You bitch."

She screamed, hoping someone would come to her aid. "Jasper! Help me! Someone help!"

He slapped her hard, then covered her mouth with one hand while he knocked her legs out from under her, pinning her to the ground, her arms behind her back. He fell on her, his weight knocking the breath from her belly, and she felt as if she were choking, unable to breathe. She shook her head, fighting as much as she could. She bit his hand, and he punched her, hard enough that her vision blurred.

Scream. Fight.

She kicked as hard as she could, tried to free both of her arms, but she couldn't reach anything but air. When she finally had her breath back, she knocked her head against his, giving herself the few seconds she had to scream, and she let out the loudest scream she could.

His hands ripped at her riding skirt, tearing the fabric as his hand scratched her leg while he fumbled with his own trews. He held her head down and she screamed into his hand, her screams now turning to sobs. But then she fainted.

When she came to, the bastard still held her down, panting oddly. Then his weight suddenly lifted from her, and he flew over her horse's back. She found her footing, fixing her skirt and pushing up against the wall in fear, blood on her skirt and her hands. She wiped the blood onto her gown, not knowing where it had come from. What had happened?

Sloan had the man by the throat. "I'll kill you. How dare you touch her!" He let go of him and landed three or four punches to the man's face and belly.

She'd never seen Sloan so mad. Trying to stand, her legs buckled beneath her and her head hit the side of the stable, the sound echoing across the stall. Her poor horse moved about, attempting to rear, unable to understand what was happening. Confused, Eva fell back against the wall again, trying to stand upright, but failing.

"Eva!" Sloan was there in a second, picking her up and carrying her out of the stall. The man took off, heading out the rear of the stables.

Sloan held her tightly, but she fought him, fearing the fool was waiting for her just outside the door. "Don't let him touch me again. He'll hurt me. Please, Sloan. Don't let him near me."

"Hush, he'll not touch you again." Then he turned to Jasper, who was coming down the row of stalls, and shouted, "Go after the bastard!"

Jasper appeared behind Sloan, took one look at the situation, and bellowed, "Chief! You're needed here." Then he told the lads to get everyone else out of the stable. "Who was it, Rankin?"

"I didn't know him. Go after him," Sloan said. "Eva, who is he?"

She shook her head, her hands clinging to Sloan's arms, afraid to let him go. "I don't know. I've never seen him before." She buried her face in Sloan's shoulder just as she heard her brother's voice.

"Shite. What the hell happened to my sister? Who did this, Sloan? Eva, who hurt you?"

She sobbed and sobbed, her hands clutching Sloan because she never wanted to leave his safe embrace.

CHAPTER FIFTEEN

Sloan

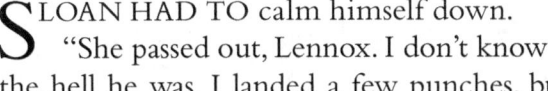

SLOAN HAD TO calm himself down.

"She passed out, Lennox. I don't know who the hell he was. I landed a few punches, but he got away. Your sister hit her head, fainted, her horse tried to rear, and I was more worried about her, so I let him go to catch her. He escaped out the back door."

Sloan settled her in his arms, noticing the blood on her gown at the same time as Lennox did. His friend's face turned furious, and he wisely rearranged her skirts so the blood wouldn't show.

"My thanks to you, Sloan. We'll get her into her bedchamber, and I'll find my mother and have her send for Doiron. Say naught to anyone."

Sloan carried her inside, focusing on her face because she seemed to go in and out of consciousness. Lennox stood behind him, making sure no one got close. "Who, Sloan? Who was he? What plaid?"

"No plaid. Dirty hair and clothing. Never seen him before. Dark tunic and trews. We'll see what

Jasper says. Someone else must have seen him leave."

They entered the keep, Rut's face paling when she saw her daughter. "What happened?"

Lennox said, "We'll update you in her chamber. Get Doiron now."

Meg came out of the kitchens and gasped. "I'll bring fresh water and linens."

Sloan carried Eva up the stairs, then set her gingerly on the bed, kissing her forehead once he took his hands away. He feared he'd get slapped, but he couldn't help himself.

Lennox started right away with his questions. "Eva, who was he? Did you recognize him? Where are you hurt?"

She shook her head, tears misting her gaze, but she controlled it. "I've never seen him before. He came from outside and said he would make me happy. Then he attacked me, punched me, slapped me, knocked me down. The last thing I recall is his hands ripping my skirts. I fainted, I think. What did he do to me?"

"You don't recall the rest?" Her brother took her hand, and Sloan could feel the rage emanating from Lennox as much as from himself.

Sloan's preference would be to set Eva on his lap and hold her tight. She needed comforting more than anything, yet Lennox focused on catching her attacker.

Eva swallowed and whispered, "Nay. I woke up, and he was panting over me and Sloan grabbed him from me and I don't remember anything else. What did he do? How will I know?"

The door opened and Doiron entered with their mother, Meg behind them with a basin of water and a pile of linen squares.

"What happened, Eva? Your face? Someone punched you?" Rut was frantic, grabbing her daughter's hands. "Who did this? Lennox, find him and whip him in front of everyone. How dare he touch my sweet daughter!"

Doiron studied Eva, her hand running up the scratches on her arm, checking the blood on her skirt, her swollen eye, her cut lip. "The blood could have come from many places."

Eva said, "Meg. A wet linen. I must wash myself. I'm dirty. Get him off me. Get him …"

Rut said, "Lennox and Sloan, out."

Sloan took his leave without any more encouragement. It wasn't a place for men. Lennox led him straight to his solar, closed the door, and poured two goblets of his best amber brew.

Lennox whispered, "I'll kill him."

Sloan said, "Not if I get him first. I'll torture him first, then kill him."

Lennox whispered, "I don't think either of us knows exactly what happened, but I'm not going to mention rape. For Eva's sake, I'm going to let it be known that you stopped him before he was able to complete the act, and I pray it's the truth. I thank you graciously, Sloan, for coming to her aid. What made you stop here?"

"I was coming from Clan Grantham a bit behind her. I saw the lone horseman taking the back way to your castle. Didn't trust him, but I had no idea that he was going to attack her."

"Glad you got there when you did. I'm not going to say another word until my mother and my wife update us."

Sloan fell into the chair, his heartbeat finally slowing.

He'd find out who the bastard was, one way or another.

CHAPTER SIXTEEN

Kelvan

KELVAN STOOD ON the parapets of Mingary Castle near Kilchoan in Ardnamurchan, catching sight of the small galley ship headed toward him. It was too small to be from Europe, so it had to be his men near Mull.

As soon as word reached him about the green meadow faery and the wee laddie with special powers, he arranged everything just the way he wanted. He'd arranged to have men on Ulva, Coll, and Mull, all ready to do his work. He'd had Egan at Drimnin and Garvie on Ulva, but some chieftain had taken care of Egan for him. And Garvie had gotten too arrogant, so his death was no true loss either. He'd found someone to take his place in less than a day. A younger man who did whatever was asked of him.

It didn't matter. Egan had been past his prime and had gotten too far along in his years. And Garvie's temperament was too explosive. He'd become more of a hindrance than an asset. The only true loss had been the old couple who'd watched over the bairns. That had upset him because they were harder to replace. The woman had treated the bairns as if they were her own, but when the entire incident with Egan and his men had taken place, someone had located the couple and set them free. This was a huge loss because it wasn't easy finding someone to care for bairns.

He'd have to search for a replacement soon because he already had a plan in motion to abduct the wee ones.

His priority was finding that faery who would grant his wishes. It was the only way to the one missing piece in his life—his daughter.

He and his wife had gone through a difficult time, and while he smiled at the thought of shutting that bitch's mouth finally, he hadn't expected to lose his daughter. Someone had been smarter than he had been, whisking the wee lass away before he could grab her.

He wouldn't stop until he had the lass. His new wife wanted power and revenge against two clans; he just wished to get his daughter back. She could gain him some good coin from afar, though getting her back was more than that. It was revenge against his wife and how she'd treated him. She hadn't liked his ways so he put an end to that by putting an end to her.

He nearly giggled with delight at how easy it had been, but now he had to find his daughter and he didn't care how he did it.

He stood on the parapets as the boat approached, four men getting off the vessel. "Come inside," he shouted down to them from above, pointing to the back of the castle. "Come around and my men will let you in." He'd had to lock up anything facing the water because of the many pirates who dared to try to take over his estate in the past. They couldn't be trusted.

However, whoever was fool enough to try paid the price. He smirked at the last one he'd thrown off the parapets. It had been quite a loud smack when the lying fool's body had landed on the rocks below, his own frame shivering from the memory. The various man's parts were now fish food.

He led the men into the large meeting chamber he kept locked because he had a safe inside, one he did his best to keep hidden. The jewels and the coins nearly overflowed the container, but if he had to, he'd buy another one.

The man in charge of Ulva shoved one of his men ahead of him, cursing at him.

"Problems?" He made a point never to use anyone's name. It was a rule once anyone stepped onto the land around Mingary.

"Aye. The fool decided to try to tap a lass at Dounarwyse and nearly got caught."

"Cut off his cock, and he'll not do it again."

The man's hands went straight to his private parts, telling Kelvan who the culprit was. Men were so ignorant.

"I promise not to touch her again. I was bored waiting for the instructions on when we are to go to Mull. When do we move? I wish to return home to Tiree."

"You'll leave when I tell you," Kelvan said, scratching the stump where his hand used to be. How could he feel his hand when it was no longer there?

His boss, Kelvan's second, shoved the man into a chair. "Sit down and shut up."

The fourth man sat in the next chair.

Kelvan asked, "Have you determined which ones they are and where they are?"

"Aye. Almost certain. The faery girl watches over a wee lad, one still in raggies. I think he's the one with the special powers."

"Almost certain? Are there other possibilities?"

"Aye. The Grant woman who is a seer has two daughters and a son. One has her powers as a seer, the lad has special powers, but no one knows exactly what they are. But he's not the one who is the most special."

"So, you have one who is a faery, a lass who possesses seer abilities, a lad with special powers, and a bairn who might have special powers too?"

"Aye."

"Why do you think the bairn has special powers? He surely cannot use them if he cannot speak or walk."

"Because the faery girl watches over him. They say she never leaves his side."

Kelvan sat down in the large chair behind his desk. "Then we have no choice. We take both lads and both lasses. And …"

"And? Who else could you possibly want?"

"The bairn's mother. Somebody has to change his raggies, unless you wish to, and the last time I looked, I don't have any food coming out of my nipples."

That sent all three men giggling, and Kelvan rolled his eyes. "Get the five of them on the morrow and bring them here."

"Fine, but we'll have to go south with them first. You know there's too much traffic on the sound."

"Go around. In fact, do what you must, but get them to Coll within three days, and I'll visit you there. I'd like to watch the group on my own and decide for myself. And if I have to hurt one of them to get the mother to talk, I'll do it. Get them here safely. Your job today is simple. Make sure you have enough poison for all the rest in the castle. Ready the vessel and the other men. Find enough blankets, raggies, and food for the journey."

"Aye, Chief."

"Get it done on the morrow. No more delays. We need these bairns before my wife gets here. She's headstrong and is determined to take over the Isle of Mull, with my help, of course. I don't care if she does, but I want the bairns before she starts her attack."

"A woman wants to battle? Why?"

Kelvan moved over and pulled the furs back from the window. "She thinks the Grants and Ramsays owe her. And I don't wish to battle those large clans without some extra help."

"Why do they owe her?"

"They owe her for something that happened a long, long time ago."

"A battle?"

"Nay, they killed her grandsire. Specifically, Alex Grant killed her grandfather, and she wants revenge."

His second said, "Going against the Grants is not going to be easy. Why the Ramsays if Alex Grant was the guilty party?"

"She said Logan Ramsay was there too. She wants him dead."

"I know someone who gets close enough to do it."

Kelvan nearly gasped. "Don't be a fool. He has to die in the only way possible."

The man tipped his head at him. "How?"

"At her hand. She has to kill Logan Ramsay herself."

"A woman killing the man who was a spy?"

Kelvan smiled. "You can count on it."

CHAPTER SEVENTEEN

Eva

EVA SAT IN the tub, leaning back so she could soak and think. This was her fourth bath since she'd been attacked the day before. Staring at her pruned fingertips, she'd probably cooked herself long enough.

She couldn't explain to her mother why she needed the third or the fourth bath, she just needed to be rid of the smelly bastard who'd dared to touch her. Opening her mouth, she tested her jaw to see if the pain had eased yet from the punch and the slap the fool had given her, but it seemed worse. The cut on her lip had finally begun to scab over, so that didn't hurt as much.

Eva had gone from having nothing to do to having so many things to do that she couldn't decide which she wished to do first.

Her first two choices dominated her mind. Should she kill the bastard who'd hurt her or kill the bastard who'd hurt her? Unfortunately, she had no idea who or where he was. She could search the isle for him, but her headaches were so bad from being tossed against the wall that she wasn't ready to go yet.

If she just knew the answer to the question everyone asked her, she might rest easier. Had he raped her? Did he complete the act? That whole concept confused her, which is why it was difficult for her to know the answer. She'd found no one willing to explain the intricacies of the act.

As far as she was concerned, he had raped her. What difference did it make if he was able to complete it or not? But her mother had quickly explained, "It makes a difference because he may have gotten you with child."

Her quick remark had been, "Well, you wanted grandbairns, did you not?"

If not for her attack, her mother probably would have slapped her for being so crude, but she couldn't help it. Everyone needed to stop. Asking. Her. Questions.

Because she didn't know exactly what had happened.

"I'm sorry, Mama." Rut had done something entirely out of character. She'd patted Eva's shoulder and said nothing. "Mama, I wish I could answer your question, but I can't. I passed out and don't recall anything until Sloan rescued me."

"Doiron could look."

"I don't want Doiron to look." That had ended the conversation that day, but it came up again.

A knock sounded on the door. "Who is it?"

"It's Mama. Are you even there or did you disappear?"

"I'm about ready to get out, Mama. No reason to come in." She didn't care to listen to her mother's questions and concerns again.

"Fine. I'll see you below stairs after you finish your bath."

"I might stay up here and read the book I brought back with me. Meg found them in the great hall and brought them up."

"Lass, I know you would like to hide up here, but it's not good for you to disappear after such a trial. You must come out eventually. Stay here if you like, but I expect you in the hall for the evening meal."

"Mama …"

"Aye?" Her mother opened the door.

"What if I don't have my maidenhead anymore? Is it possible I could have lost it, but I'm not carrying? Then what?"

"Aye, you could have lost it and not be carrying. If you're not with child, then I don't care, and no one needs to know anything about what happened. That is, unless your brother finds him and brings him back here. If he doesn't find him and you are not carrying, then we will continue on as if nothing happened."

"So, you don't care?"

"I don't care if you lost it or not. It does not change you, daughter. I still adore you and always will. It's just a piece of skin. Foolish, in my opinion, but I am a mere woman." Her mother indelicately snorted, something that made Eva smile.

"So, nothing would change?"

"Nay. If you were engaged to Sloan, I would postpone your wedding for a moon or two so we would know if you were with child. It's only fair to let your betrothed know whether you are carrying someone else's child. Sloan found you, so he is aware of the possibility."

"Then he's probably no longer interested in me."

"I didn't say that, nor did Sloan say any such thing. I think you should rest and come down for dinner. Besides, the last I heard, you were not interested in the man who saved you from a worse attack."

"I'll meet you below stairs for supper, Mama." There it was again, that mention of the fact that she'd refused Sloan.

And her mother was right. Where would she be if Sloan hadn't rescued her? But the most important piece of the entire situation was something no one else noticed or mentioned. Sloan had been so gentle, it had surprised her. He was indeed a kind and gentle man.

Her mother left so Eva finished with her hair and climbed out of the tub. She had a sudden urge to hit something, but she knew better than to attack anything in her chamber. A knock sounded on her door and Meg peeked her head in.

"May I come in?"

"Of course, as long as you promise not to ask me what happened. I'm done talking about it."

"Would you like to go for a walk?"

"I feel like I'd like to punch something. Any ideas where I could do that?"

Meg's face lit up, and she said, "Aye. I have the perfect solution. How do you feel about learning how to throw an axe? I promised to show you once. How about now?"

Eva thought for a moment, the need to hit or strike something so strong that this could satisfy that need. "Aye. I would love to try it."

"I promise not to ask questions, but feel free to ask me anything you like, Eva. You're my new sister, in my mind. Tamsin isn't here, but you are. I'd like to get to know you better, and I hope we can grow closer."

Eva switched out of her gown into the leggings that Dyna gave her to wear during archery, donning the matching tunic. "It's still rather warm, aye?"

"It is. You'll be more than comfortable in that outfit. I love mine. Lennox doesn't like me wearing it around because he said it shows my arse, but I like it."

Eva rolled her eyes. "The tunic hides your arse."

Meg opened the door and led the way down the stairs. "I made the mistake of bending over in front of him once with my leggings on. He nearly had apoplexy."

Eva laughed and had to admit that it felt good to laugh. She followed Meg out, hoping to get some relief from this constant angst that had set itself up in her mind. Angry at herself for not remembering exactly what happened, she knew there was no way to find out, but there was also no way to let it go either.

Meg led her to the small area Lennox had set up for her behind the castle where no one could get hurt by flying axes. "Here are the different sized axes Lennox had made for me. I like the smaller one because it is easier to learn with, but once you get used to what it requires, throwing the larger axes is far more satisfying."

Eva reached for the largest one, but Meg took it back and handed her a midsize one. "Let's see how far you can throw this one first. If you look over there, that's the target, that big piece of wood. If you hit it just right, the axe will stick to it. Here, let me show you how I do it first."

Eva stood back and watched Meg throw the different axes, demonstrating and explaining her technique with each one, then stood behind her. "Now you try but be careful until you get the feel for it."

"All right." Eva picked one up, feeling its weight. "Is it really sharp?" she asked before running her finger down the blade.

"Nay. Lennox had the armorer dull the blades since they are only for practice."

Eva smirked. "Probably a good thing."

She picked up a large axe and held it over her head, almost falling backward because it was much heavier than she thought it would be. "Oh my!"

"It takes a bit to get used to," Meg said, her arms crossed in front.

"I'll try the smaller one." She switched

weapons, then stood back, swinging it overhead and throwing it. She missed the target completely.

"Not bad. You almost hit it. Try again. It takes a while to get used to the weight of each one."

Eva followed Meg's instructions, switching axes, practicing and throwing until her arms hurt, but she was finally hitting the target.

"Great job! Keep going until you feel comfortable with it."

She continued to practice, switching to a heavier one, but then the oddest thing happened. It was as if her attacker were standing in front of the target. She picked up the axe, and as slowly and carefully as she could, she whipped it over her head, right at him. "There. How does that feel, you rotten bastard?"

She picked up another one. "You ugly, smelly troll. How dare you touch me!"

And she hit the target in the center. But that wasn't enough.

She picked up another and another, cursing and hollering at her intended victim. And she sent six axes at the target in quick succession. So much that she was heaving from the exertion.

And she turned to Meg and whispered, "How would I know for sure? Tell me, please."

Meg came over and wrapped her arms around Eva, tugging her to sit on a nearby log. "You would know. You would have been sore between your legs. Inside you would hurt. He forced you, so if he did, you would be torn or cut somewhere, I would think. And you would bleed between your legs, but not like your courses. A light bleed.

But I would expect it to hurt verra much if you were forced."

Eva sobbed against Meg's shoulder and finally declared, "He didn't do it. I never hurt there. And the only blood came from him where I scratched him."

She sobbed until she had no tears left, but now she had a power she'd never had before.

Eva MacVey could protect herself.

CHAPTER EIGHTEEN

Connor

CONNOR APPROACHED HIS daughter as she strode around the outside of Duart Castle. "What is it, Dyna? What are you looking for?"

"Something, but I don't know what. Something is off. I feel strangers around and I don't like it, yet I find no evidence of anyone nearby. I've searched everywhere. I wish I could see into other people's minds."

"You have always said you can only see what happens to people you love."

"Or some kind of connection, aye. But to see someone I've never met before, that never happens. And I don't think I can pick up anything from the bairns. That's my worry."

"But your daughter can, so use her." Connor didn't tell Dyna that he had the same inkling. That his granddaughter Tora had come over to him and said, "*They're coming again. But don't worry. Lia will stop them.*"

Then she ran off and joined the other bairns in their play. Could he trust that a wee lass could stop evil in the world? He didn't know what was happening on the isle. Everything was different here—the weather, the clans, the animals, the seas.

"I've got men all along the roads, Dyna. If anyone tries to attack again, they'll stop them. I've had men search the forest they used before, had them near MacVeys and Rankins. They're all looking, but nothing is happening. It could be something happening at Kilchoan. Sloan believes there is something unscrupulous taking place there. Too many ships about, he says, but I have no way of searching the seas or the surrounding islands. All I can do is protect what's mine here."

"I know, Da," she said, stopping to hug her father. "It hurt so much when Tora and Astra disappeared."

"Astra never leaves your mother's side for more than a minute."

"Even that bothers me, Da. If she hadn't come here, she wouldn't have that feeling."

Her father barked, "You did not cause that fear in her. The bastards who stole her horse and Tora did."

"I know. Mama tells me the same every day. It's getting dark. Let's go in. I'm looking forward to this fine meal. That deer was huge, and Derric caught some fish too. Meat pies, stew, loaves and loaves of bread, fruit tarts, and so many beans. We will eat well. I just worry for that bairn too."

"You think like your father. Lia never leaving the lad's side and saying she'll protect him doesn't make you feel any better, does it?"

"Nay, it makes me wonder what she's protecting him from."

"I've thought the same, and your mother has asked me that three times. Come, let's go inside and enjoy the meal. My men will stay in front so no one will get through the gates like before."

She kissed her father's cheek. "I cannot thank you enough for staying."

She stepped inside, pleased to see evidence of Grant guards everywhere. Once seated at the table, she motioned for the serving lasses to bring some of the food out for all to enjoy. The bairns were already munching on a loaf of bread. Sandor had an insatiable appetite.

The minstrels were arriving, setting up to play their fiddles after the meal. "Aye, I checked them and so did Dyna," Connor said to the man at his side, Logan.

"That one minstrel looks shifty. I think I'll have a chat with him." Logan got out of his chair and made his way over just as more wine came in, the serving lasses handing out goblets to everyone.

Connor's bad feelings were getting worse.

Especially when the minstrel Logan went after disappeared.

CHAPTER NINETEEN

Sloan

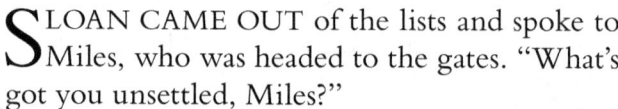

S LOAN CAME OUT of the lists and spoke to Miles, who was headed to the gates. "What's got you unsettled, Miles?"

"Ingelram says he can't find Rinaldo again, so I'm going to look down the coastline."

"You check the stables, see what horses are gone, and I'll find my sisters. See what they have to say." He trudged inside, wiping the sweat from his brow and sheathing his weapon. His men were getting better with their weapons, but he hadn't seen his brother anywhere today. Perhaps his sire knew where he was. He hated having to keep track of a grown man, but someone had to do it.

He stepped inside the hall, noticing his two sisters near the hearth. "Marta, have you seen Rinaldo?"

"Nay, and I have not seen Da either. Have you seen him?"

"Aye, he was watching us at the lists for a while. You know how he likes to watch so he can tell me they aren't strong enough or that I don't work them hard enough, but he left before he could give me his daily criticisms." Miles and Ingelram also listened to the old man's critiques, though Eva's refusal had sent his father into other rages too.

Sheona said, "Go clean up. You're all sweaty and your tunic looks like you rolled in the sheep's pen."

Rowan said, "I'll go look for Grandsire, but I'm not going outside the wall."

"Stay inside the wall," Marta said.

"My thanks, Rowan. I'll return in a few moments." Sloan took the stairs two at a time and entered his chamber, glad to see a fresh basin of water there. The serving lasses knew he came in a mess in the middle of the day. After washing up and donning a fresh tunic, he headed down the stairs and out the door, waving to his sisters. "I'll be back in a bit."

He headed to the gates to confer with Miles, see if he'd learned anything about his brother or if he knew where his father was.

"What have you learned?"

Rowan said, "I can't find Grandsire."

Miles said, "I still have no idea where Rinaldo is, but I did learn something that won't make you happy, Chief."

"About Da?"

"Aye, the old chieftain took a horse alone, told the stable lad he was headed to Clan MacVey. Said he needed to have a chat with Lennox about his sister."

Sloan groaned, not caring that everyone heard

him. "Will the man not leave it be? I'm going after him. Mayhap they've seen Rinaldo." He had a gift to bring Eva, so he attached the wrapped parcel to his saddlebag, then mounted.

"Isn't there a big festival at Clan Grantham this eve, Chief?" Ingelram asked as he joined the two. "If so, I'd bet Rinaldo is there. His horse is missing, and you know he likes festivals."

"Ingelram, I'm going to see Lennox, then I'm heading to Clan Grantham. Aye, there's a party this eve and you're probably right. Let Rinaldo get his fill, but I have to stop Da before he embarrasses me so much that I'll never go outside these walls again."

Miles said, "Everyone knows where your father's words come from. Not from you, but from an old chieftain who is missing his wife."

He patted Miles's shoulder and said, "I hope so. I won't be back for a while unless I have to escort my sire home. In fact, Ingelram, I'll take you with me so you can escort him. He's known you for a long time."

Ingelram smiled. "Longer than he's known you, Chief."

The lads brought out a saddled mount for Ingelram, so the two departed without another word, his mind on what possible situation he was about to find. His life had surely turned into a mess of late. Rinaldo was up to something, but no one had been able to uncover where he was spending his time. His father reminded him daily that he was doing a terrible job with the clan and that he needed to do things differently. Nay, not some things. Everything. Every blasted thing he did of late was wrong. The clan continued to grow and prosper in his eyes, but not in his sire's view.

Then there was Eva. He'd finally had the courage to ask for her hand in marriage, only to be rejected by the lass. He'd loved her for so long that the stake she'd driven into his heart by her rejection was not going to be pulled out easily. And Rinaldo offering to MacKinnis for him nearly put him over the edge. What else could go wrong?

He had an inkling he was about to find out. His father was on the run.

Then he reminded himself that everything on the isle had improved in so many ways that he'd had hope for a fresh start soon. Thane and Lennox were both newly married, both with thriving clans, and Clan Grantham had so many friends from the outside that nothing would ever happen to hurt them.

He loved his land, he loved his clan, he even loved his sire and his brother, adored his sisters, but there was only so much a man could take.

Ingelram asked, "The clan is doing well. Don't let your father convince you otherwise."

"You do a fine job reading my mind, Ingelram, and I thank you for your kind thoughts."

Nothing more was shared between the two men along the path until they approached Clan MacVey. Ingelram asked, "Who do you think he is after—Lennox or Eva?"

"Hellfire, if the man has the gall to go after Eva,

I will be blistering his ears with all my thoughts. Mayhap I'll box them too. It's none of his business, though he thinks it is."

"I'm thinking he'll go after Lennox." Ingelram nodded as if to convince Sloan he was right.

Sloan sighed. "I hope it's Lennox he's after. Lennox can handle him. Eva can't."

On their approach, the gates opened quickly, Sloan looking up at Jasper on the wall. "You were expecting us?"

Lennox approached the gates, a wide smile on his face. "Oh, we knew you'd be here."

"Then why didn't you stop the daft man, Lennox? You didn't leave him with Eva, did you?"

"Hell nay. He's arguing with my mother." He chuckled and said, "I noticed you coming, so I thought to stop and forewarn you, but please don't stop them. I'm loving every minute of watching those two go at it. You have to enter quietly so you can listen before you pull him away."

Sloan could only think of one thing to say. "Hellfire."

CHAPTER TWENTY

Eva

EVA STOOD BACK listening to the two elders argue, and she had no idea what to do. She'd come down the stairs when Dermot Rankin had come storming in, yelling for her mother. And her mother hadn't backed down one bit.

In fact, her mother helped her to stand a wee bit straighter, so much so that she didn't wish to interrupt.

"How dare you insult me and my son, Rut MacVey. Your husband is rolling in his grave over this slight, and you know it," Dermot said, striding across the hall until he stood toe to toe with her mother.

"How dare *you* walk into *my* home and talk to me like that, you old coot. Take yourself back out and enter with a bit of decorum. You'll not yell at me like that."

"The hell I won't. You let your daughter refuse to marry my son? Did you approve of her decision too?"

Eva glanced over as the door opened, and Sloan stepped inside. She'd never been so glad to see anyone. Hurrying around the outside of the hall, she was nearly in tears when she reached him, so she did the only thing she could think of. She launched herself into his arms. "Sloan, I don't know what to do. Help me." He set something down in a chair, then wrapped his arms around her.

Lennox came in behind Sloan, his eyes widening when he saw his friend and sister locked in a warm embrace. Sloan set Eva down but kept his hand at her back as if to protect her.

"Don't worry, I'll end this now."

But Lennox stopped Sloan. "Nay, let them have it out. It's time."

Rut said in a calm, even tone, "She wasn't refusing, but delaying, and since when does your son have to have her brother ask for him? Did you think that mayhap she was waiting for Sloan to come and ask her appropriately? Had that thought ever crossed your old, daft mind, Dermot?"

"That's the way it used to be done, and you know it. There's naught wrong with the old ways. The chieftains made the matches, based on what was best for the clans, just like yours and mine were made."

"Mayhap I didn't like it happening that way. I wished to choose my own husband. I don't like someone telling me what to do." She crossed her arms and swayed her skirts enough to hit Dermot across the legs, an intentional movement. Eva knew her mother's ways well.

"You've always been like that, Rut MacVey.

You gave your husband gray hairs because you speak your mind too much. Women should sit demurely by the fire and do their needlework."

Rut turned to all the servants who stood by watching and shouted, "Get out. All of you. Now." The scurrying nearly set Eva into gales of laughter.

Eva took two steps, but Rut pointed at her and said, "You do not move, daughter, because this man will apologize to you, or I'll spit in his face before I put my fist in it. Sit demurely by the fire. The shite of all the birds on the isle should fall on your head on your way back, Dermot Rankin. How dare you come in here, insult me, insult my daughter after she's barely recovered from the attack. Can't you see the bruises on her face and neck, you old coot? The whole world isn't about you."

Eva jumped and Sloan stepped in front of her, his hand guiding her behind him.

"Sloan, step aside. I wish to see that lass for myself."

"Da, her name is Eva, not 'that lass.'" Then Sloan glared at Lennox and said, "We need to end this now."

Lennox made his way toward his mother while Sloan moved toward his father. "Da, you need to apologize to Lady MacVey, and I'll take you home. You'll leave Eva out of this."

But his father, as stubborn as he was, pushed Sloan aside so he could stare at Eva. His entire countenance changed, and he blushed. "Who did that to you, lass?" Then he looked at his son. "Did you know that happened? You need to settle the score for your betrothed, Sloan. Get your sharpest sword, and I'll go with you. Who dared to touch your betrothed?"

"Da, stop! She's not my betrothed." His voice came out so loud that everyone stared at him. "Leave her be."

Lennox said, "Mother, Dermot, and Sloan. In my solar now."

Dermot turned to disagree with him, but Lennox said, "Don't argue with me, old man. You've said enough to my mother and my sister."

Dermot grumbled all the way over to the solar, casting an occasional glare at Rut MacVey. "My Ailis would never speak the way you do to a chieftain, Rut. And your son should respect his elders."

Her mother, always quick with her tongue, said, "Your Ailis was one of the sweetest women I ever knew. You didn't deserve her. And she wouldn't have allowed you to do what you just did to my innocent daughter."

Dermot hung his head. "Nay, I'll not argue that one."

Lennox stood outside and said to Eva, "I'd like you to sit in the back. I will not ask you to speak, lass."

Eva nodded, doing her best to hold her tears as she found a chair behind the others. The entire clan would be talking about this on the morrow. All her fault. She glanced over at Sloan, seeing him much differently from how she'd ever seen him before.

They'd grown up together but sitting in the solar, looking at the two chieftains standing behind the desk while the two elders sat down, Lennox in his best green plaid and Sloan in his fine-looking purple plaid, they looked so mature, so adult.

They looked like chieftains. Both of them.

And Sloan was far more handsome than she remembered. His skin carried the bronze color from the sun, nearly the same shade as his hair that hit his collar just so. His chiseled jaw was locked right now, if she were to guess, because he was angry with his father. And when she thought of how he'd saved her from the brute in the stables, she nearly teared up.

"Da, you need to apologize to everyone here. You insulted Lennox's mother and sister, yelled at Lady MacVey, and embarrassed Eva. What do you have to say for yourself?"

Dermot got up to face Eva and said, "I do owe you an apology, Eva. My son didn't inform me of your attack. Who did it?"

Lennox said, "Dermot, we don't know who the man was, or he wouldn't have any skin on his back now, but your son stopped it and beat him silly before he got away."

He turned toward the front. "Why did you let him get away, Sloan?"

Eva finally stood. "Because he had to catch me when I passed out, or I would have hit my head and been much worse."

Lennox said, "I saw what Sloan did to the man, and I watched my sister nearly hit the ground, but your son saved her from much worse. I couldn't reach her in time because the fool dragged her into the back of a stall in the stable. You should be proud of Sloan for knowing enough to follow him and stop his attack. He did what he could."

Dermot looked at his son and reached for his hand, staring at the bruised and cut knuckles. "That's how you got those wounds. I wondered. Why didn't you tell me?"

Sloan said, "Truly, you need to ask me that, Da?"

The old man nodded, his shoulders slumping. "Her reputation. Wise. You're smarter than I give you credit for sometimes, Sloan. I'd like to see the bastard's face… Oh … sorry, my ladies."

"Don't be. He was a bastard to dare touch my daughter," Rut said. "He'll get his due before we're done."

"Rut, forgive me. I'm sure it wasn't easy seeing your daughter attacked. But you know I think they'd suit."

"That's our decision, Da, not yours," Sloan said. "Eva's and mine."

The old man sighed and moved over to the door. "Forgive me, MacVey. I'll take my leave now."

CHAPTER TWENTY-ONE

Sloan

SLOAN ESCORTED HIS sire out to where Ingelram waited. "He's ready to go home. I'm going on to Clan Grantham."

"Mayhap I should go with you," his sire said, looking at him with hope in his eyes.

"Da, it's nearly dark. You won't be awake for but another hour. Go eat your evening meal. You look tired. It's been a long day."

"You staying more than an hour?"

"Aye, Da. And it's an hour away from MacVey's, so I have a bit to travel home too. I may stay at MacVey's if it's late."

"I'll see you on the morrow, son."

Hell, his father never called him by that name.

Once they left, two more guards going with them, Sloan headed back inside to speak with Lennox.

And to say goodbye to Eva and give her the gift he brought. He'd set it aside somewhere in the hall. He had to admit his heart had sped up when she'd launched herself at him. Damn, but she fit his arms perfectly. How he wished she would reconsider his proposal. He had to settle for small pleasures, having her softness and her sweet scent in his arms if only for a short time. He'd savor that memory for a while.

He stepped inside and strode straight for Rut. "Lady MacVey, my sincerest apologies to you and Eva for my sire's rudeness."

Rut waved a hand at him. "Your father misses Ailis. Your mother was the sweetest woman I ever had the pleasure of knowing, so I understand. Forget it, Sloan. But let me take the opportunity to thank you for helping my daughter."

"It was my honor." He gave her a short bow. "My father sorely misses your husband too. They were fast friends."

"They were," she said, her eyes misting briefly. "I miss him too."

Lennox and Meg came down the stairs, dressed for the festivities if Sloan were to guess. Lennox said, "Heading to Grantham land?"

"Aye. I was hoping to go. I sent my old man off with Ingelram and he went willingly. My apologies to you too, Lennox. Meg, you look lovely, as always."

Meg blushed, whispering, "My thanks." He could tell she was not accustomed to compliments.

Lennox said, "I think Eva is considering going with us. She's readying herself and should be down shortly."

Sloan forced himself not to get excited over that possibility. A moment later, her door opened, and she descended the stairs, wearing the leggings and tunic that were probably a gift from Dyna or Eli. And she wore them well.

"You aren't going?" Lennox asked her. "I'd hoped you'd come along. Get out of the keep."

"I am, but I feel the need to be completely covered. Dyna won't mind."

Rut said, "Nay, she won't. And I don't either. You are prepared to ride your own horse, lass?"

Eva blushed, something Sloan rarely saw. "Nay, I was hoping I could ride with you, Sloan. Are you going? Would you allow it? I'm afraid …"

Lennox glanced over at him, and Sloan did his best to hide his surprise, but he said, "Say no more, lass. I'd be happy to escort you, and just a ride. I understand."

"My thanks, Sloan. I do need to get out of the hall. Mama and Lennox are right."

Meg said, "Tamsin and Thane are going. I'm excited to see everyone. I heard there will be minstrels."

Lennox added, "And Connor Grant already has over a hundred guards around the castle and in the forests. I'm not worried."

Rut gave her daughter a hug and a kiss and said, "Go and enjoy yourselves. I'll be waiting for you here."

Eva glanced up at Sloan with those blue eyes that had a way of squeezing his heart and said, "I'm ready, Sloan."

"Lennox, we'll be right out. Eva," he said, grabbing the wrapped parcel. "I brought these for you. If I recall, you used to enjoy reading when you were young. Marta and Sheona helped me choose them for you."

Eva, excited to open a true gift, took the package over to the nearest table and set it down, untying the twine. "Sloan, you didn't need to bring me a gift." She pulled it open and nearly teared up. Inside were two books, both in lovely bindings. "These are exquisite." She thumbed through the first one, skimming in spots, and was surprised at how interesting it looked. If she stayed home, she'd have something to do.

"This was unnecessary."

"I thought it might help keep your mind off other … things."

Her mother turned her back and moved over toward the fire. Eva stood up on her tiptoes and kissed his cheek. "Many thanks to you. It's a lovely gift, and I will treasure both."

Then she smiled, and it took every bit of control he had not to lean down and kiss her the way her rosy lips should be kissed, but he knew she was not ready for that. So, he set his hand on her back and ushered her out the door, Lennox and Meg following.

"Bye, Mama!"

If Sloan turned around, he was certain he'd see tears in Rut MacVey's eyes. It was on his honor this eve to escort Eva, treat her well, but mostly, help her get past the nightmare that had happened but a few days ago.

The horses were all saddled and ready, so he said, "May I lift you or would you prefer your brother?"

She pointed to his chest, which nearly made it explode, but he did as requested and lifted her onto his horse and mounted behind her. They set out for Clan Grantham, Eva settled in front of him, and he was pleased to see that she did indeed trust him because she didn't hold her back rigid like some lasses do, instead leaning against his chest, taking in his heat, if he were to guess.

"Don't worry, lass. I'll protect you with my life. You'll be safe with me."

He had a sudden inkling that made him question the truth of that statement. What the hell could happen?

As soon as they approached Duart Castle, Eva tipped her head back to Sloan and said, "Oh my. There are so many guards in red plaids. Are they all Grant guards?"

"I see a few Ramsay guards. They are in blue plaids, and the other plaids? I believe those belong to Clan Menzie. I heard Maitland's parents had arrived with a number of guards too. It's quite a group."

"Is that your brother?" Eva pointed to a man standing by the stables, helping with the horses as more arrived.

Sloan couldn't believe his eyes, but there was Rinaldo fiddling with the horses. Hell, the fool couldn't help his own brother, but here he was assisting strangers. And he was as polite and sweet as ever. "Greetings, Rinaldo. I wondered where you were." He waved his brother over, though

Rinaldo made the mistake of reaching for Eva, who quickly denied his request to help her down, instead waiting for Sloan. He dismounted, handed the reins to his brother, and lowered Eva to the ground as carefully as he could.

"Greetings to you, my lady." He nodded to Eva, smiling that innocent Rinaldo smile. "I'm glad you came after the troubles you've had."

"Enough, Rinaldo." Sloan hated to have to plant his fist in his brother's face in front of a crowd, but if he said one more insulting comment to Eva, he would, brother or not.

Eva nodded and walked away from him, something Sloan needed to do more often. Glancing around, he was glad to see more guards posted on the wall than usual and a number checking all guests. They were waved on, so he ushered Eva into the great hall as quickly as he could.

"Eva, if you need anything from me this eve, please let me know."

"My thanks, Sloan. You are forever the gentleman, and I do appreciate it. I think I may choose to visit with Maeve and the bairns for a bit. And I may have a chat with Dyna, though she's probably busy at the moment."

They stepped inside, Lennox and Meg directly behind them. Meg swooned. "Oh, the decorations are lovely, are they not, Eva?"

Eva looked at the greenery over both hearths, at the blue ribbons on the staircase, and the flowers on the tables, all multicolored, just as their summers were. "It is beautiful."

Meg saw her sister, so she took Eva's hand and said, "Come, I wish for you to chat with Tamsin and me."

Eva went with her, a smile on her face. Lennox moved closer to Sloan and pointed over to a table. "Look, I see a lass with my favorite amber liquid. Alycia, I'll have two of those."

Alycia joined them, curtsying to Lennox. "Here you go, my lord. Many thanks for allowing me to work here this eve."

"That's up to my mother, lass, but there are so many here that I'm sure the Grants appreciate your help. Make sure you speak with Eva. She's over by the fire with Meg."

Alycia headed in that direction.

Connor and Maitland both joined them. "Good eve to you both and many thanks for joining us," Maitland said. "You'll be eating fine this eve. Dyna and Eli took a huge deer down together. Alaric and Derric had a time getting it back here with just the two of them."

"Meat pies?" Sloan asked.

"In three flavors. Lamb, venison, and a few beef. And Derric went fishing with my father, so we have a delicious fish stew. It's terrific."

Sloan lowered his voice, but he had to ask, "Have you seen anything or anyone questionable?"

Maitland said, "Nay, have you?"

Sloan shook his head but then said, "Nay, just an inkling."

Connor said, "You and my daughter and my wife. I don't like all these inklings one bit."

"And Maeve," Maitland said. "I wish I could make the fear leave her."

As if on cue, Maeve headed straight for them, wee Grant on her hip with a grin as he watched all the activity in the hall. Lia and Magni were on either side of her while Tora and Sylvi ran over to visit with Alana and Tamsin.

Sloan said, "With a protector like Lia, I think you should worry less."

"Why do you say that?" Lennox asked. "I thought you didn't believe in seers and all that, Rankin?"

He took a swig of his drink and said, "The only one who has ever been able to sway me is that lass coming toward us. Her devotion to the lad, the words that come from her tell me she is different."

Maitland said, "Say more. I like to hear the opinion of someone on the isle. Do you have faeries here?"

"After hearing everything about her finding Magni, and with Thane's parents and Kilchoan, Lennox, I've begun to think differently. I don't know exactly what she is, but I'll tell you one thing."

"What?" Connor asked.

"Whoever dares to touch that laddie of yours, Menzie, better run as fast and as far as they can. And she'll still get them."

Maitland wiped the sweat from his brow. "I can only pray you are correct."

Connor clasped Maitland's shoulder. "I agree wholeheartedly with Sloan. Have you truly watched the lass? Look at her now. She's not much larger than a toddler, yet she's standing next to Grant and studying every person in the hall as if they were an imminent threat. My sire would tell you she's like the most well-trained guard he's ever seen."

Sloan took a swallow of his drink and nodded. "Interesting point of view, Connor. And I'll make you feel even better about it, Maitland. When that lass decides to hurt someone, it's not going to be with a fist, an arrow, or a sword. It'll be a force unlike any we've ever seen."

And if she ever did, Sloan hoped he'd bear witness to that power.

CHAPTER TWENTY-TWO

Kelvan

———⁂———

"K, EVERYTHING IS ready." His second-in-charge, known simply as O, answered. Kelvan didn't allow anyone to call him by his real name, so Kelvan became K.

K sat in the boat on the far side of Duart Castle, a spot well hidden from anyone watching from the curtain wall, though he doubted they'd be seen because of the dark night. Better to play it safe. "You have the ones inside all ready to pass out the poisoned brew?"

"Aye, it's being circulated through the hall as we speak."

"How long before you send the men in?"

"Less than a quarter of the hour."

"Good. We wait." He nodded to O, who had the six men masked and ready to go with their weapons. He decided he had to send six to grab four bairns and the mother. The mother and the wee lad would take one, then the golden-haired lasses, all three if they could get them, and finally, the other lad. He was to be left behind if they couldn't get them all. Wee bairn, mother, and the golden-haired lass were his focus.

He glanced over at the other two boats awaiting transport, one to head to Ulva and one to go across the sound to confuse anyone following them. His boat would head back to Kilchoan until he received word of the successful transfer of the captives to Coll, where he would meet up with them again. First Ulva, then Coll.

Then his wish would come true. The faery would have to grant his request. He'd threaten to kill the mother of the wee one if she didn't, so all would be done as he instructed.

First, he would find his daughter, then, a thousand gold coins. Next, a golden castle of his own wherever he decided to have it. And lastly, a successful attack for his dearest wife. He wanted the faery to allow an easy takeover of the Isle of Mull. That would require many dead Ramsays and dead Grants.

His wife was angry with the Ramsays and the Grants for killing her grandfather. He had his own crosses to bear. He would settle up with the Menzies, especially the one known as Avelina, the one who stole the sapphire sword.

O asked, "How did you know about the tunnel into the cellars?"

"I have my ways. I paid MacDougall to tell me all the secrets of the castle. The tunnel entrance, the place in the cellar, and the best places to hide during an attack. My wish will be complete soon enough."

He'd thought to grab the bitch Avelina, but he decided she had too many powers. He had no idea where that sapphire sword was at the moment, but when he learned the faery that had the ability to grant wishes had arrived, he dismissed the idea of the sapphire sword. If he was right, the faery could grant him the secret weapon made from gems. All he had to do was wish for it to come from her hands.

Mayhap later. He took three steps and stared up at the curtain wall. No movement. The men who'd been given the brew had passed out. Now was the time to move.

O looked at him and waited for approval.

"Aye, send them." K rubbed his hands together, a wee sense of glee coursing through him.

The bairns would be his soon enough.

CHAPTER TWENTY-THREE

Eva

EVA STOOD NEAR the hearth taking in everything in the hall. She made sure that she always knew where Sloan and her brother were. Now she knew, without a doubt, that Sloan Rankin would always protect her, and it gave her more comfort than she would ever tell anyone.

Riding with him to Duart Castle had been the nicest experience she'd had since the attack. No matter what happened—rain, thunder, another attack—she knew he would protect her.

Thoughts of that brute who assaulted her never left her alone for long. Oh, she could converse with others, carry on conversations without fear, but once she stopped, the man appeared in her mind.

His dirty hair, his stench, his cruel eyes.

His touch.

Would she never be free of him?

Alycia appeared in front of her. "New wine for everyone and it is a fine one."

"My thanks, Alycia. How are you? Where is Elvard?"

"He's here somewhere. First with Alana, then with Sylvi and Sandor. Bouncing about. I have to get moving. Have fun, Eva."

Eva nodded to Alycia, Eva's eyes darting to every man on the opposite side of the hall. She took one whiff of the wine in her goblet and decided not to drink it. She handed it to Tamsin who had finished one goblet already and gladly took hers.

Maeve held the bairn and stood next to Maitland, Dyna moved around the hall checking on things, Eli and Alaric groped each other, and Connor and Sela stood close to the bairns. Everyone sipped their wine or their brew. Sela never took her eyes from her three grandbairns, Astra standing next to her. Surprised to see Sela hand Astra a goblet, Eva was more surprised when she drank it down with one sip. Eva had heard the kidnapping had affected the poor lass terribly.

That's when it started. She glanced away from Astra only to see someone's head fall and hit the table, then another, and another. Lennox went for Meg, just catching her before she fell to the ground. Lennox went next. Tamsin fell after that, Thane catching her just as he collapsed.

Sloan called out to her. "Eva, don't drink it."

She hadn't, but he had, and before he could reach her, he fell to his knees and then crumpled onto the hard stone floor.

Eva screamed as the others began to fall so quickly. It was horrible.

Connor, Logan, Dyna, Derric, Gwyneth, Eli, Alaric. Fall after fall. Maitland tried to take the bairn from Maeve, but he dropped next.

And then the chamber was full of masked men. Six? Eight?

One man grabbed Maeve and the bairn, another went for Lia. Eva reacted without thinking, grabbing Alana who was now crying, and then ran to an alcove near the tunnel passageway. She passed one masked man, the stench of him hitting her so hard that she nearly stopped but then kept going. He was headed toward Sandor. Sylvi raced by her screaming, so she grabbed Sylvi and picked her up, taking her with her to hide in the alcove.

Once behind the curtain, she grabbed both girls and shushed them. "Hush, we cannot let them find us."

Alana cried, "Mama fell down."

Sylvi mumbled, "I saw Papa fall too, then Mama, then Grandpapa. Where's Tora?"

The men were yelling at one another to grab this bairn and that one, so Eva put a finger to the girls' mouths as the chaos continued. Someone yelled out, "Where's the other white-haired lass? He decided he wanted all three of them."

Sylvi looked up at Eva, tears in her eyes, gripping her hand as if she were the only one who could save her. She didn't know what to do, hadn't brought a weapon, but the three of them were safe.

When all seemed quiet, she peeked out of the

curtain and scanned the area. No one moved. Then Magni came in from the tower chamber and began to scream and yell.

"Magni. Hush!" she called out, pulling the curtain aside a wee bit.

Magni saw her and rushed over. She tugged him inside the alcove and made room for him. He rambled on and on, "What happened? Where is my sister? Your mother, Sylvi? Where are Thane and Tamsin? I'm so scared again."

"Hush. Listen carefully, but you must be quiet. Everyone started to pass out and then six masked men came in and took Maeve and the baby. I think they took Lia too. I don't know who else, but I saw Sylvi and Alana, so we hid in here. Did you see anyone with a mask?"

Magni shook his head. "Nay." He chewed on the tips of his fingers and whispered, "Not again …"

Eva closed her eyes and said, "Listen. See if you hear anything. We cannot go out until we hear a voice we recognize."

It seemed like forever before some people began to awaken. Gwyneth's voice was the first one they heard. "Logan, wake up!"

Sela called out to Connor, but he didn't answer. Then Eli and Alaric. Voices grew louder and louder, searching for their loved ones.

Tamsin screamed, "Alana!"

"Can I go?" Alana peered up at her, but Eva was doubtful.

"In a moment." Eva stood and peeked out, holding Alana's and Sylvi's hands, Magni clinging to her. By now, half the people were up and looking around. She stepped out and after gazing around, said to Alana, "Go."

"Mama!"

Dyna woke up screaming. "Sandor, Tora, Sylvi! Where are you?"

"I'm here, Mama," Sylvi screamed.

Eva took her over to Dyna who immediately asked, "Where are your brother and sister?"

Sylvi began to cry, and Dyna looked at Eva, who shook her head. "I don't know. I grabbed these two and hid."

In the middle, a man moved from person to person, searching and searching, then ran into the kitchens and up the stairs calling out, "Maeve! Where are you? Maeve!"

Finally, he shouted, "Who saw anything? Anyone? Who stayed awake?" From the balcony, he yelled, "Someone must have seen something."

Eva said, "I did." Magni hugged her.

The hall quieted as they all turned to her. "I saw six men with masks come inside after everyone passed out. They went straight to Maeve and grabbed her, the bairn, and Lia. I grabbed Sylvi and Alana, and we hid in the alcove. Magni came out of the tower, so I tugged him in."

"Who were they?" Maitland shouted, his face filled with a fury unlike she'd ever seen before.

Eva began to cry, and Sloan appeared next to her, climbing up off the floor and wrapping his arm around her shoulders. "Stop yelling at Eva," he barked at Maitland. "She saved three bairns."

Then Dyna said, "Stop your shouting, Menzie.

She saved one of my daughters. She didn't do anything wrong. And right now, she's the only clue we have to what happened." Dyna had a tight hold on Sylvi who had her head on her mother's shoulder, tears running down her cheeks.

Maitland said, "Forgive me. I know. I'm sorry, Eva. I just … I cannot bear …"

Then Maitland's head fell back, and he let out the most haunting moan Eva had ever heard.

Four bairns were gone. And so was his wife.

Dyna said, "Da, go to the gates and see what they know. Broc, you and Logan, check the cellars. Derric, you and Maitland search all the chambers above stairs. Alasdair and Alaric, go to the men on the wall and find out what they have to say. How did the attackers get in? Where did they go? Then meet back here. We'll find them. Everyone else, stay here!"

Magni ran over to Thane and hugged him. Then Thane and Tamsin approached Eva, Tamsin hugging her. "My thanks for saving Alana." Her face was covered in tears. "My word, poor Dyna and Maitland."

Thane thanked her, then said, "You leaving or staying, Sloan?"

He looked at Eva who shook her head. "Not yet. Please."

Lennox and Meg joined them. "Eva, you are hale?"

"I'm fine. Just shook up. But please don't make me leave yet, Lennox. I think one of them was the same man. The man who attacked me."

Sloan had to keep his hand from turning into a fist. "Why would you say that?"

"The stench. When I rushed past one of the men, he smelled the same. Disgusting. It's a verra distinctive odor. I can't leave yet. Please."

Sloan said, "I think we should stay and find out exactly what happened. Come sit by the hearth and get warm. See what the others say when they return. There could be men still outside, Lennox. I wouldn't take your leave yet."

Eva grabbed Sloan's hand, never wanting to let go. He found her a chair, set it near the hearth among the others, then settled a fur on her lap. He kneeled in front of her and said, "Look, Eva. You are possibly the only one who saw them. Everyone else seems to have passed out. Try to remember everything you can about the men. Forget the one bastard, think of the other five. Recall everything you can, how tall they were, color of their hair. Their boots. Anything could help us find them."

Logan came over and sat down near her, still wobbly in the legs. "Alaric said all the men on the wall passed out. It was some brew, possibly the wine we were given. Did you drink it, Eva?"

"Nay, I gave mine to Tamsin. I didn't want it."

"Well done, lass. You are the only one who could help us. Think of anything at all about them. Was there anything different about the masked men? Their clothing, their boots, their weapons. Anything unusual?"

She thought hard, then said, "Aye, one thing. I don't know if it matters, but I do recall something."

"What?"

"Their boots. They were all wet."

Logan grinned and said, "Well done."

"What does it mean?"

Sloan squeezed her hand. "They came by boat. They must have come in through the cellars. We'll go look. Is there a doorway in the cellars to the outside? Through the curtain wall?"

Logan answered, "Not that we're aware of, but we need to do a more thorough search. This wouldn't be the first castle with a hidden tunnel to the outside."

While the men headed down to the cellars to search for any clues, Eva couldn't get one thing from her mind.

One of the kidnappers was the same bastard who tried to rape her.

CHAPTER TWENTY-FOUR

Maeve

MAEVE GRABBED ONTO her dearest son so tightly that he finally squeezed against her until she let up her grip. The men shoved her through a door in the cellars into a damp, dark tunnel, no one speaking. "Leave us be. Maitland! Maitland, help us. Wake up, please!"

She'd seen everyone change from vibrant conversationalists into sleepy-eyed people who fell to the ground in less than a few moments. It had happened so fast that she didn't know what to do.

First Logan, then Dyna, and when Maitland's eyes fluttered shut, he'd reached for her and mumbled her name just before he crumpled onto the floor. What was happening?

Then the men came rushing in from the cellars, all carrying swords and wearing masks. One man pointed, and the others grabbed whomever he pointed to. She was first and Grant was second. Lia was third.

Maeve cried and screamed until the head man slapped her and said, "The next one I hit will be the lad." She shut up after that. They shoved her into the cellars, Lia hanging on to her gown. Lia had grabbed two extra plaids from the baskets as they'd been pushed toward the staircase. How the lass could be so wise at her age, Maeve didn't know.

They dragged her and Lia along and shoved them into a galley ship, pushing them below deck with the rowers, probably to keep them hidden from any onlookers along the way. Within a few moments, Sandor and Tora were shoved in behind them. Maeve took one of the plaids and wrapped it around Lia and Tora, then wrapped the other one around herself and Sandor leaning against her, Grant in her lap.

Oh no, poor Dyna, Maeve thought, but said nothing and tugged the two wee ones closer.

There were already six men getting ready to row, while four in masks set to other tasks. The one in charge came over and said, "You'll keep your mouths shut and no one will get hurt. We'll feed you and keep you safe."

"Where are you taking us?"

"Doesn't matter, does it?"

Tora looked at Maeve and said, "To Ulva and then Coll."

"Who told you that?" the man demanded, lifting Tora into the air.

Tora, unbothered by the man, pointed to her forehead and said, "I see it here. But now I can see things here too. He's Kelvan." She pointed to another man not far away, causing him to drop her as though she'd burned him.

The man Tora had pointed to behind him said, "She's the seer we wanted. Leave her alone."

The men took several steps back from them all, and Lia leaned in to whisper, "Do not worry. We'll be saved, eventually."

"Another aventuwe," Tora said. "And this time, you awe with us, Sandor. We have fun."

Sandor didn't seem to be overly upset, so she set Grant facing the bairns so they could entertain one another. The men were busy giving orders, two other boats nearby. The one in charge got off the boat and then said, "I'll see you in Coll."

So, Tora had been correct. Maeve didn't know much about Mull, only what she saw when they traveled across on arrival, but Maitland had tried to explain about the surrounding isles. One must be Coll. Ulva was where Tamsin had come from, very small, if she recalled correctly.

When the galley finally left shore, their boat headed in the opposite direction from the other two, away from Craignure. The opening to the upper deck was right next to her, so she had to take one last chance. She waited until she had a good view of Duart Castle, then handed Grant to Lia and said, "Hold him."

Then she bolted up the stairs and leaned over the railing, screaming up toward the curtain wall where she could see men walking. "Ulva and then Coll! We'll end up at Coll!"

Then she fell back onto the lower deck, the hand tugging her hair as ruthless as any she'd felt before. "Shut your mouth, or I'll knock out your teeth, lass."

She glanced up, pleased to see one person had shot out from the bushes and run to the end of the coastline as if they'd heard her. How she prayed that person had caught what she said. For now, she had to behave, or her son would never survive without her.

"Keep your mouth closed if you want to live. We don't need you. K only wants the laddie and the faery. You're expendable." They didn't realize it, but she'd never leave her wee bairn.

Never.

CHAPTER TWENTY-FIVE

Sloan

S LOAN RUBBED HIS head, the headache from whatever brew they were given unrelenting. Eva looked as though she was trying not to fall apart, Maitland was about to succumb to sheer panic, and Dyna sobbed, Sylvi in her arms while she leaned against Derric.

"Not again, Derric. And Sandor too."

Derric said, "But Maeve is with them. And Lia too. I don't know what faeries can do, but I'm going to believe that she stayed by his side for exactly this reason. She knew someone would come for him, and she wasn't about to be left behind."

Magni said, "And Tora scares them too."

"What? Explain that, Magni," Dyna said.

"Because she sees things. Tells them what she knows just like she does here. Then they get scared and leave her alone. She told the other man before that she knew what was in his pocket. He never touched her again."

Derric smiled. "That's our girl, Diamond.

They'll be fine. Maeve and Lia will protect them all."

Maitland came over to take a seat as soon as Connor returned. "Get everyone together so we can plan our attack."

Maitland's parents had come down the staircase, their eyes wide. He filled them in on the details, and his mother hugged him. "Nay, Maitland. Not Maeve and Grant." He switched seats, giving his mother the chair. "But do remember what the lass told you. That light would prevail over the darkness. She knew this was coming."

Drew said, "We should have come down for the meal, but we were both overtired."

"Da, I'm glad you and Mama were above stairs. I didn't have to worry about you two, and Mama can help. Have you seen anything about it, Mama?"

"Nay," she whispered. "Has Dyna?"

"Not yet. Once we discuss everything, we're going to make a plan."

Avelina lowered her voice, but Sloan could still hear her. "Remember, I believe Lia is an angel so she will protect all of them. And once the discussion ends, I'll speak with Dyna."

Eli let out a shrill whistle and everyone came running in to gather around Connor in the center. Maitland said, "Please. We have to do something, Connor." His parents stood behind him. "I cannot do nothing and wait."

Avelina said, "Once everyone calms down and I find out what we've learned, Dyna and I will go on the parapets to see what we can uncover with our visions."

The last two to enter were Broc and Logan from the cellars. "Quiet, everyone," Logan said. "We've uncovered how they were able to get inside past the guards. They came by three galley ships. There's a door to a tunnel in the buttery. We followed it out, but we were too late. However, we learned a few things. Broc, tell them what you heard."

Broc stood in the center of the hall. "We could hear sounds from a boat but couldn't see it. Then at the last moment, two boats left shore and headed down the Sound of Mull, both toward Craignure and Kilchoan. Logan followed them to see what he could find out, but I could hear another boat. I ran in the opposite direction and pushed through the bushes until I could see the vessel. It was a good-sized galley ship—I would guess eight rowers. As it shoved off, I heard a scream, and a woman, who had to be Maeve, ran to the edge of the upper deck and shouted, 'Ulva and Coll. We'll end up at Coll.' Then she was grabbed and shoved below."

Maitland grinned. "That's my lass."

"But she said *at* Coll. What does that mean?" Lennox asked.

"She doesn't know Coll is an island. Probably thinks it's a village."

Connor said, "That makes sense. So we need how many groups?" Then he stopped and said, "Maitland, I hope you approve, but I'm going to pass this over to the three men who know the area best. Lennox, Sloan, Thane. Tell us about the isles and how best to go about this."

Maitland nodded, his face more hopeful.

Lennox looked to him, so Sloan explained, "Imagine Mull is a big rectangle, then Ulva and Coll are both islands off the opposite corner from where we stand in Duart. Since Loch na Keal is in the middle of Mull, the best way to those isles would be to head toward my land, and there are a couple of routes between MacVey and Rankin land to take you toward Ulva, which is almost due west of where we are now. Ulva is a short boat ride across Loch Tuath while Coll is a much more difficult boat ride across the rougher waters of the sea. They are taking the long way around, or the way least traveled, and will probably stop at Ulva for a night or two before attempting to cross over to Coll. Then, from what I've learned, they could go to Kilchoan or be sold directly from there."

"Sold?" Maitland asked.

"Bairns can be sold to Mideastern groups or Europeans."

Maitland ran his hand down his face and began to pace. "Boats, Rankin. Who has them? How many groups do we need?"

Sloan looked to Thane, who said, "The first group should head straight to Ulva. I have three boats to take us there. It's a small isle with less than a score of livable buildings on it. Coll can be reached from my land or from Rankin land.

Definitely weather dependent, though, as it's imperative to check the roughness of the sea. Ulva is more protected and much closer to Mull."

Sloan said, "Take one group to Ulva, another to Thane's to be ready for the boats, and one to my land to watch. Have two of the groups ready to head to Coll when the weather is right. But the group from Ulva can also report back and assist at Thane's. Hopefully, we'll never have to travel to Coll. If we can find them on Ulva, it will be ended quickly."

Lennox said, "I've heard mention of three groups. What say you, Ramsay? Grant? Any input?"

Connor looked to Maitland and said, "What do you wish to add, Menzie? Or Dyna?"

Dyna looked to Derric, who said, "We'll go along with any advice. One of us will stay here, one will go to Ulva. Doesn't matter who we go with."

Logan said, "Send Dyna. We'll need archers. Derric, you can defend here, especially now that we've found the tunnel. Odd no one discovered it before, but MacDougalls are wise."

Connor crossed his arms in front. "What say you, Maitland?"

"I've asked my mother and Dyna to try to see what they can learn, then I'll go with the first group to Ulva. My lass told me where she was headed, and I need to be there. I don't wish to waste much time—I'll be ready to leave in half the hour. I'll be in the first group because I cannot sit and do naught. Thane, you'll give us a boat? I'll take Dyna and whoever else wishes to go with me."

Thane said, "I'll go. I know the isle best. Only two more, one archer, one swordsman."

Logan said, "Eli and Alaric. Ready yourselves. The rest of us will plan the other two groups and the one to stay here. One more to MacQuarie land and one to Rankin land. We'll gather over here to make our plans."

Connor said to Logan, "You decide. I'll go wherever you send me. Sela, Astra, and I will go to the kitchens in the meantime to prepare food to send along. I want to speak with the serving lasses too. We have to be prepared."

Sloan moved along with Lennox, Eva between them. He couldn't have been more surprised when she said, "I'm going to Ulva."

Sloan said nothing, waiting for Lennox to speak. "Eva, you have no skills to help."

"Is Meg going?"

"Aye, the way she throws her axe, I want her with us. We'll go to Rankin land with Sloan. She's proven her value."

"But I learned how to throw an axe too."

Lennox took his sister's hands and said, "Eva, I love you dearly, but you are too emotionally involved to go with us or with the other group. Do you know how to get to Ulva? Know you anything about the isle?"

"Nay, but it's small. Thane said it was. I'm not asking to go to Coll. I wish to go to Ulva."

Eva's fury was not hidden at all. Sloan ran his

hand up her back but said nothing. "Lennox, could she travel with us? Or she could be in my group that will head to Coll once we see the activity there?"

"Nay, I forbid your involvement at all, Eva. I'll drop you off along the way. Meg and I will go to Rankin land, so we'll see you home."

"I'm going to lie down. I feel dizzy all of a sudden," she whispered.

Lennox turned to Gwyneth who was seated by the fire. "Is there a place where Eva could rest for a wee bit until we head back to our land?"

Gwyneth said, "Our chamber. It's the door next to the kitchens."

"My thanks," Eva said.

Sloan followed her along and once she was at the door, he said, "I apologize for your brother, Eva. But mayhap a rest first is a good idea. Is there anything I can get for you?"

She shook her head and said, "Many thanks. I'm tired."

She stepped inside and closed the door.

Sloan turned around and looked at the group and all that was being planned. Yet he had the oddest feeling that Eva wasn't happy with her brother's decision.

He'd wager she was going to follow along behind her brother's group once they left MacVey land. But he had another sudden question.

Where the hell was Rinaldo?

CHAPTER TWENTY-SIX

Avelina

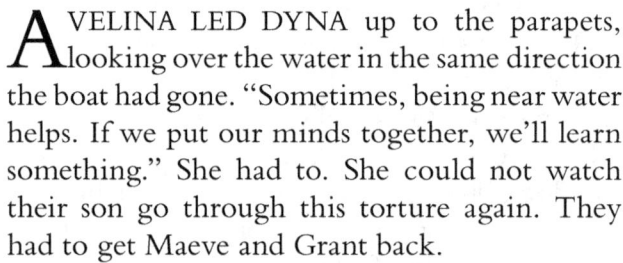

AVELINA LED DYNA up to the parapets, looking over the water in the same direction the boat had gone. "Sometimes, being near water helps. If we put our minds together, we'll learn something." She had to. She could not watch their son go through this torture again. They had to get Maeve and Grant back.

Maitland, Drew, and Derric stood behind the two, Derric with a tight hold on Sylvi who'd not left his side since the attack. "I miss Tora and Sandor."

Derric said, "We'll find them. Mama and Lady Menzie are going to help us now."

"Papa, if I see anything, should I tell you?"

He arched a brow and looked at Dyna who nodded. "Anything at all, tell us, Sylvi."

Avelina and Dyna faced the water, Avelina taking Dyna's hand in hers, then said, "Sylvi, would you like to hold Mama's hand?"

Sylvi nodded, and the three stood together while Maitland moved to his mother's side,

Derric on the far side next to Sylvi, Drew behind Avelina.

Avelina glanced at her son, her heart so wounded for his pain that she vowed this had to work. She said some quick silent prayers, then began her favorite chant that she'd learned from a friend long ago.

"Close your eyes, Sylvi, and think while Lady Lina chants," Dyna said.

Avelina saw the boat in her mind as soon as she finished her chant, the vessel nearly rounding a bend, indeed headed to Ulva as they had thought. "I see Maeve in the lower deck, eight men rowing. Grant is on her lap laughing with Sandor who is huddled next to Maeve. Lia is on the other side of Maeve huddled with Tora. They have blankets wrapped around them. They are all hale, Maitland."

"Praise God for that much."

Dyna added, "The men are all afraid of Tora."

"Why, Diamond?"

"Because she told Maeve where they were going, and they overheard her," Dyna said. "She was right, and they wanted to know how she knew. That's my girl!"

Sylvi said, "Hush, Mama. Lia is trying to talk to me."

Avelina and Dyna both opened their eyes, the group glancing among themselves, the hope in the group heartbreaking. Avelina said, "Listen and tell Mama everything she says, Sylvi. Good job."

Sylvi kept her eyes closed, squeezing her mother's hand. "Lia said they'll be at Ulva for one night. Then the morrow's eve, they'll take two boats to meet one big boat in Loch Tuath not far from Thane's land. She said to be ready for them there."

"Anything else? Be patient, lass. In your mind, ask Lia why we can't get them at Ulva."

She concentrated, then replied, "Lia said you'll never find them. Be ready for the boats." She stared up at her mother. "Did I do good like Tora?"

"Aye, lassie. You did a great job." Dyna kissed the top of her head.

"Wait, Mama, Lia is calling me again." Sylvi closed her eyes. Then she said, "Someone wishes to steal Rankin land from Sloan. Someone he knows. In three days. From Kilchoan."

Sylvi smiled and looked up at her mother. "Am I like you *and* Tora?"

Dyna, teary-eyed, picked her up for a big squeeze. "Aye, you did a great job. And Derric? She's staying here with you so we can relay any messages."

Avelina turned to Maitland and hugged him. "Lia said to tell you to be at Loch Tuath on the morrow and all will be well. You may have to swim."

Derric said, "Tora is a decent swimmer, but Sandor is not."

Maitland's eyes widened because Lina knew that was one of his worst fears. Maeve couldn't swim, and their son surely could not either.

"We have to trust that Lia will help them all."

CHAPTER TWENTY-SEVEN

Eva

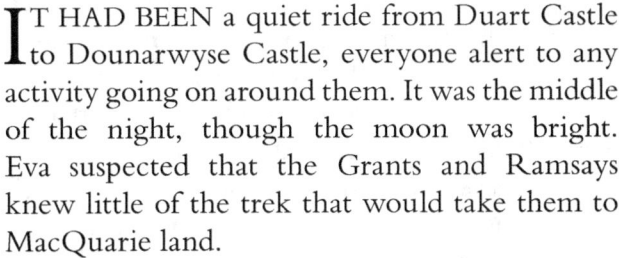

IT HAD BEEN a quiet ride from Duart Castle to Dounarwyse Castle, everyone alert to any activity going on around them. It was the middle of the night, though the moon was bright. Eva suspected that the Grants and Ramsays knew little of the trek that would take them to MacQuarie land.

But Thane knew how to get there the quickest.

Once they arrived, the group stopped to make adjustments and water the horses briefly before the next leg of their various journeys. Sloan helped Eva down, and she said, "Many thanks for your assistance."

He gave her an odd look but said, "We'll get him for you, Eva."

"Well, if you do, please bring him to me so I can put an axe in his private parts."

Sloan arched a brow but said, "I can agree to that. If he's still alive. You realize Maitland might choke him with his bare hands."

"Understood, but there are six of them. I have just due for that troll."

He leaned in to kiss her cheek, but whispered, "What have you planned, my lady?"

Hellfire that he understood her that well. "Naught." She turned away so she wouldn't have to look him in the eye. "I don't know what you mean."

"Then I'm going to change the subject on you since you won't tell me your plans. I wish for you to know that I know you refused my betrothal offer, but if you ever change your mind, the offer is still there."

Eva immediately thought of what Lia had told her, that the one meant for her was not far away. Could it be Sloan? He was a handsome man, and he would protect her with his life. "Many thanks, Sloan, but I'm still not ready."

"You have too many things on your mind. I understand that, but I think we would make a good couple. I would take care of you and we could travel wherever you wish to go. I love boating and I've always wished to see more of the Highlands. Edinburgh is lovely this time of year. We could shop for gowns or just look for books."

Eva nearly teared up at how hard he tried to please her. "I must focus on what is most important now and it's finding those bairns. I became quite fond of wee Grant when I met him and the thought of some evil person holding him doesn't sit well with me. But I will consider your words another time."

Sloan sighed and his disappointment showed in every one of his movements. He nodded and turned away. "I'll take my leave and see you soon, I hope."

"Oh, Sloan, look. Ingelram is here to speak with you. I'm going inside now. I'm verra tired."

He nodded, escorting her toward the keep and not turning to Ingelram until she opened the door and stepped inside.

Damn him. Why did the man have to be so kind and thoughtful? No matter. She'd go upstairs and settle her saddlebag, then sneak out the side entrance.

She was going with the group, no matter what Lennox said. At first, she'd thought to just head out on her own, but that would have been foolish because she had no sense of direction. With her luck, she would have ended up lost in the middle of the forest with no idea where to go.

Smart enough to recognize her weaknesses, she'd get a fresh mount while the stable lads were busy brushing down the returned horses, then she'd head out without a word, hide in one of many places she knew of, and follow the group to Thane's castle. That much she could do, and as long as they didn't notice her until they were nearly there, they'd not send her back, especially since her dear brother and Sloan would be with the other group on Rankin land.

In fact, she decided to take Shadow along, plus a large supply of axes. Meg would never know because she was headed to Rankin land with Lennox already.

Before she left, Eva looked everywhere to talk

with Alycia, to see if she'd heard anything, but they said she'd left for the evening. That didn't surprise her because she was probably worried sick about Elvard and getting him home. She usually traveled with one guard for protection, so they'd likely left already.

Eva would tell her everything when she returned.

Finally ready, she headed down the staircase, stopped at the dog pen, giving Goldie a kiss, though she was still sleeping, then picked up Shadow. He was big enough to run on his own, if necessary, and could protect her if she was attacked. At least she hoped he would.

One stable lad noticed her saddle a horse after everyone else had left, but she said, "I'm just going to catch up with my brother and Meg."

"Aye, my lady." They ignored her so she moved along. Stable lads were never in on Lennox's special instructions.

She had no trouble staying behind the group because it was such a large one. Three groups that would split at the fork, two headed west and one group to Sloan's land. She had to admit that she'd grown quite fond of the man, something that surprised her.

How to explain to him that she wasn't ready to marry yet, that after the situation with the creepy earl she may never marry, that she still missed her sire, that he'd chosen someone for her but he'd never said who, that she'd dreamed of traveling the world, taking boats to Europe. Riding to London. A trip to Edinburgh to shop for the finest gowns. She'd dreamed of all the things that most lasses wanted.

Eva had the sudden realization that she wasn't like most lasses. She had some wonderful role models to thank for that. Meg had found her own way and was living her best life, even if it was with Eva's brother.

Eli with Alaric, a lass who could fire an arrow and hit someone in the heart with one try. Dyna, also a great archer, a lass chieftain of her clan, a seer, and probably the woman Eva admired most. Although she had to admit, her mother had impressed her when Dermot had attacked her verbally.

Mama had fire in her blood too.

But something else had surprised her at Duart Castle. She'd learned to love bairns, their innocence, their smiles, even their trust. Protecting Sylvi and Alana had given her so much pride in what she'd done.

Eva MacVey had proven herself useful, with her mind, her heart, and thus was not about to allow the bastard who attacked her to get away.

She was after blood. The blood of a man who dared to touch her, who had hit her and treated her like she was the dung on his boot or the smallest insect crawling in the dirt.

Perhaps the earl was untouchable, but the foul man was not.

He was going to pay for that mistake, and she'd not stop until she found him.

CHAPTER TWENTY-EIGHT

Maeve

M AEVE SAT UP, brushing her wild strands back from her face and searching for light to tell her where she was, but there was nothing but a small tallow burning somewhere down the passageway. The soft rhythmic breathing of her son calmed her immediately, so she leaned over to kiss his head, watching him smile in his sleep in reaction to her tenderness.

Her memory came back. They'd arrived at the Isle of Ulva and been led into a building. Then at the very back of the manor home, under a chest that was pushed aside, a piece of wood was lifted by one of her captors and they were hurried down a staircase that took them into what looked like a dungeon in a small castle. A cold passageway with four doors that locked, two off to each side, was not the least bit welcoming. Their abductors had shoved them into the farthest chamber, a room with four pallets, a pot to pish in, and several blankets, all disgustingly dirty. They were given one loaf of bread to share along with a pitcher of water and then the men disappeared, leaving

Maeve and the children alone in the cellar, the wooden door with one small window now locked by a key on the outside.

Thank the Lord for small favors that wee Lia had the foresight to grab the two thick woolen plaids on the way out of the great hall. The two were plenty large enough to cover the five of them. She lay on one pallet with Grant and Sandor tucked up against her, covered with one plaid, while Lia and Tora slept on the pallet next to them, snuggled under the other clean plaid Lia had grabbed.

How long were they going to be stuck there?

Maeve had to admit that seeing how well-hidden the staircase to the cellars was had not made her feel any better. If Maitland entered, he'd never know the cellar or the staircase existed because with the chest replaced, it was so well hidden the door would never be seen. Even though Lia persisted in telling her that they would be saved, and that this all needed to happen for a reason, she couldn't shake the fear deep in her belly.

Her worst fear could come true on the morrow. If they were headed to Coll, they'd be back on another boat in the sea, and fear would have its fingers in the deepest parts of her body.

Especially when their only path to safety might mean swimming. She couldn't swim and neither could her son. It was possible Tora and Lia could, but probably not Sandor. Three of them would drown if forced to swim anywhere or if their boat capsized.

The tears welled in her eyes, but she did her

best to keep them inside. Sleeping would be the most pleasant way for the bairns to pass the time. They'd be less afraid that way, though Sandor persisted in thinking they were on an "aventuwe," as Tora had said.

Sandor opened his eyes, his back up against Maeve, a little beneath wee Grant. He smiled and waved, though she had no idea why.

"Who are you waving at, Sandor?" she whispered, not wishing to awaken the others.

"Gwanda. He o'er dare." He pointed into the corner, one thumb in his mouth.

She had to give that some thought. Sandor's grandfathers were Connor and Derric's father; neither were dead, so who could he be seeing? "Gweetings to you, Gwamma. See Gwamma too." He pointed to a spot next to the first place he pointed. "Her hair like you."

What was the boy seeing? He must be dreaming and not awake yet.

Tora woke up and explained to Maeve as if she read her mind, "Nay, not Gwandpapa Connor. Gwandpapa Alex is watching over us. He said to tell you not to wowwy. Maitland will save us on the morrow in the boat. Maitland, Sloan, and Eva."

Maeve's insides nearly burst. She wished to jump off the pallet and beg her dearest mother and father to help them get out now. If she could believe their ghosts were truly here watching over them and communicating with Tora and Sandor, she had so many questions.

"Gwamma says be patient. She says we will

all be fine. She says my mama is coming on the morrow." Then Tora sat up and said, "Gwamma, I'm cold."

Maeve couldn't imagine the lass would warm, but she had to ask. "What's happening, Tora?"

"Gwamma told Gwanda to warm us up." Then she giggled.

"What?" Maeve didn't wish to miss any of this, whatever it was.

"Gwandda says she's always cold. And she said, 'Alex.' And he said he fix us."

A sudden blast of heat came from the ceiling as if a hearth sat above them. "Tora! Do you feel it?"

Tora said, "My thanks, Gwandpapa." Then she settled back under her blanket.

"Da? Mama?" Tears misted her gaze as Maeve stared into the darkness. Alex and Maddie Grant had adopted her long ago and treated her as their own. She'd been their youngest, and once she arrived on Grant land, she'd never left until she had fallen in love with Maitland.

Suddenly, the aroma of apples overpowered her, the same scent she had enjoyed whenever she and her father had picked apples in the orchard they'd planted long ago. She gasped and tipped her head back, inhaling to cherish the moment, the memories so strong that she could revisit the experience of running in the meadow, the scent of lavender from her mother now cascading over her.

"I'll be patient, Mama. But please don't go." When the scent dissipated, she whispered, "Sandor, are they still there?"

The wee lad said, "Aye, Gwanda and Gwamma stayeen. I seepy." His thumb returned to his mouth, and he closed his eyes.

Maeve breathed a sigh of relief and said a quick prayer of thanks. That was just what she needed to continue to be strong for these bairns.

CHAPTER TWENTY-NINE

Sloan

S LOAN COULDN'T HELP but smile. The lass had more gumption than he'd ever given her credit for. He knew she had something planned, so he'd hung back after the group left, sending Ingelram ahead with instructions for Lennox and Miles, then hid off the main trail at the fork in the path where the group split.

Sure enough, Eva waited long enough, popped out of the forest with her dog on her lap, and followed the others.

So Sloan followed her. He waited until they were halfway to Thane's castle before he ventured up behind her, startling her a wee bit, but she'd traveled alone for long enough.

"Sloan?" she asked, a little nervous.

"Don't worry, I'm not going to escort you back. I didn't agree with your brother. After training as an archer and then working with Meg, you've got enough skills to help us, Eva. And you have a good reason to wish to see this whole situation finished. I don't know where these men are from, but we all hope to see it come to an end."

She let out a sigh and said, "My thanks, Sloan. My brother is overprotective."

"He is, but don't be too harsh on him. These men are ruthless and dangerous, but you demonstrated the amazing ability to be quick on your feet, lass. I don't think he gave that much consideration."

"I did?"

"Most people save themselves when confronted with an outright attack. Verra few can think enough in that type of situation to save two bairns. And even after you saved two, you saved Magni when he came along. He was risky. He's been abducted by them before."

Eva nodded and said, "I didn't really think, Sloan. I have to admit it was just instinct. I love bairns, and I didn't wish to see any more taken. Poor Dyna and Maitland."

"And Derric. He acts strong for Dyna, but he's writhing inside, I would bet. Not one but two of theirs. I'd be beside myself."

They rode in silence for a bit, then she asked, "Do you think they'll send me back?"

"Nay. You can be helpful in some way or another. Or were you going to try to go before the first group goes? You wouldn't be foolish enough to try on your own, would you? Against eight rowers and six masked men?"

"Nay. I need some rest first. Even a corner in a servant's chamber would suit me right now. I'd forgotten how tiring it is riding a horse. But I will be there with the others at first light. I'll do whatever I can to help. Does Lennox know?"

"Probably by now. I told Ingelram to go on ahead and tell Lennox I'd be there in a few days. I told Ingelram only that I suspected you were going to try to follow along. He's not to tell Lennox anything about you unless someone comes from his castle for you. Ingelram will tell your brother that I decided to go with this group, but I'd be back on my land the day after the morrow."

"My thanks. I just wish to be helpful. I don't like sitting around and watching others while I do nothing."

"You're maturing, lass."

"I guess I am," she said, a bit wistfully.

Once they arrived, he covered for her and said the two of them had decided to assist this group for now. No one questioned them, and Eva asked Tamsin if she could find a bed for a short respite. Sloan was glad to see her go with Tamsin.

Eva was a stubborn woman, but even that didn't change how he felt about her. If anything, his feelings for her were becoming stronger.

He followed Thane and Maitland outside, and at the last minute, he decided to go along with the group. As they rowed over to Ulva in two boats, he took in the view from Thane's land. Nearly as nice as his own.

"Have the inhabitants changed much since Garvie's death, Thane?"

"Nay, not that I'm aware of. There were verra few who lived there because Garvie chased them all away. As far as I know, the structures had not been kept up, so no one was interested in staying.

There were no vendors or markets on the isle. Too few people to buy. The one baker I spoke with said Garvie forced them to come once a fortnight. Said he'd never come back if Garvie hadn't forced him. He preferred Mull."

"Why would one prefer to be isolated if you had a choice?" Maitland asked. "Mull has more resources, better hunting. True, the views might be better, but at what price? I'd stay on the larger isle."

"Thane, what about his men? Second-in-charge? Any guards of his. Could they be part of this group?"

Thane thought for a moment and said, "Surely, it's possible. They had nowhere to go and no coin, though they probably took everything of Garvie's they could. Tamsin didn't take anything of his." He held up his hand as they approached the isle. "See, this is eerie to me."

"Why?" Dyna asked.

"Because there are no signs of life. No boats, no torches lit anywhere. No animals. It won't take us long to search the isle. There were only four or five structures and they're all close to this side. The other is all forested coastline. Uninhabitable. If no one is here, no one is on Ulva."

Maitland asked the question everyone was thinking. "Then where would they be?"

Thane's gaze searched the surrounding sea, off toward Tiree and Coll especially. "I don't think they would cross to Coll at night. They would have had to stop somewhere along the way, especially with bairns. They have to feed them somehow, give them liquids."

"Another place on Mull? MacClane is building on this side of the isle." Sloan looked back onto Mull for any sign of life past the area where most of the fishermen kept their boats.

Thane followed his gaze, but didn't see anything either. "True, but I don't see him harboring bairns. He hires some guards that are questionable, and has fired some because of that, but you can't hide bairns. Grant is still at the breast. He won't be quiet because some bastard tells him to." Thane looked to the others for confirmation.

"My son can be quite loud when he's hungry. Probably why they are keeping them in such an isolated place like this. Maeve said Ulva, so they have to be here." Maitland did his best to convince everyone. "I'm thinking back on what Sylvi said. I didn't look that closely, Thane, but the view of the trip to Coll is right in front of your castle, aye?"

"Aye," Thane said.

Sloan added, "Or from my land. If we miss it, Lennox will see them. I fear they are not here. Just another odd inkling."

"It's possible they didn't make it this far. There is a fine area of beaches on the far coastline, but no inhabitants that I'm aware of. All forests. If we don't find them here, then we man the boats on the morrow looking for any activity on Loch Tuath or near Coll. I'm telling you, Maitland, what Sylvi said was the best advice. They'll be waiting directly in front of my land to meet the larger boat. If they are there at low tide, we could walk halfway out to them, and I have four boats total, enough to hold us all. We'll get them soon enough." Thane looked confident and Sloan had to agree with his reasoning.

"Does Coll have more inhabitants?" Connor asked.

"Aye, one castle that I know of and several cottages in the village near the port and probably more on the far side. It's larger than Ulva."

They approached Ulva, so Sloan and Thane hopped out to pull the boats onto shore. Thane pointed to a path up to the buildings.

Two hours later, the group stood on the beach in front of MacQuarie Castle, discussing their alternatives. Alasdair and Broc joined them. Thane said, "Most everyone is down for the night. We've only got a few hours left. Why don't we all go in for some sleep?"

Maitland said, "I'll never be able to sleep with my wife and son missing."

Dyna shook her head, leaning against her sire, his arm around her shoulders. "Me either. What do we do now?"

They'd searched every building on Ulva and found them all deserted. A couple structures held evidence of recent activity—dust missing on a hearth mantle, footprints in sand—but they found no evidence of any person still there.

Dyna had searched for raggies outside every structure. Not a bairn or raggie in sight.

"Gwyneth told me that. Look for smelly raggies tossed out the door. That's how they found Gracie and Ashlyn. But there were none," Dyna said. "I looked everywhere."

Alasdair said, "You all have to get something to eat, or you'll be of no help on the morrow when the boats are out there. Some of us could be swimming and that takes a strength you may not have without food or sleep. You'll not do it without some food in your belly. Come inside and find a bite and an ale. Mora left bread and meat pies out. We all heard what Sylvi said. I'm confident in our team waiting for the boats on the morrow, but I need you all strong enough to help."

Connor said, "Alasdair is right. I've got to eat something, Dyna. And I need a couple of hours of sleep."

The group agreed, so Thane led them all inside. Sloan held up the end of the line, still looking around for anything. At the last minute he heard a dog's whimper. He said to Alasdair, "I'll be right in. Going to relieve myself."

He followed the sound, surprised to see it was Shadow, Eva's dog. And he was doing his best to tell him something. "All right. I'll follow."

Shadow led him back to the spot across from Ulva where all the fishing boats sat. The closer they got, the more the dog whimpered.

Sloan sighed and said, "She went on her own, didn't she? All right. Get in the boat. I'm going to borrow this one and take you across. We'll find out where she is."

The dog's whimpering was like a fist to his gut. Sure, Eva had gone inside, but that didn't mean she hadn't snuck out on her own. Or that she woke up an hour later and took her leave.

Eva must be missing, or Shadow wouldn't be acting the way he was. Where the hell could she be when they had just come from Ulva and found the isle deserted? And they hadn't passed her along the way anywhere.

The dog's tail wagged as they crossed, so Sloan was convinced he was headed in the right direction. Once he landed the boat, the wolfhound leapt off and began sniffing all around until he found her scent. Sure enough, the beast stopped and turned to look at him as if to ask him what was taking him so long.

The hound was off, following the scent to the middle of the small isle where they'd just been. They passed a set of trees, Sloan's focus on the dog, but that was his mistake.

Someone brought a boulder down on Sloan's head and the world turned black.

CHAPTER THIRTY

Eva

THE DOOR OPENED and two men carried a man inside, the chamber so dark that Eva had no idea who it was. But she recognized one of the villains as her abductor just by his odor. Fortunately, he ignored her this time.

Their captive's hands and feet were bound, so they dropped him on the floor and left, locking the door on their way out.

Sloan!

Eva moved over next to him, grateful that she wasn't bound as he was. "Sloan?" she whispered, hoping he would awaken. If anything happened to him, she would feel responsible. Surely, he'd come looking for her.

Sloan didn't move, so she leaned over and kissed him softly on the lips. "Sloan, please wake up. I'm sorry I brought you here." She ran her fingertips down his strong jawline, surprised at how stubby his beard had grown already.

Sloan's eyes fluttered open and his gaze searched the chamber, finally falling on her. The smile that emerged made her heart sing a wee bit. He would be fine.

"Eva, where are we?"

"I don't know. In some cellar on Ulva."

"You are hale?"

"Aye, they didn't hurt me. They were too busy doing other things, though I'm unsure of what they have planned exactly. I did see piles of swords being moved about as if they were going to battle. That's all I saw."

"Have you seen the bairns anywhere?"

"Nay."

"We were just on the isle about two hours ago, searched all the buildings, but found nothing. Do you know what building we are in?"

"Nay, but the entrance to the cellar is well hidden. It's a wooden door under a chest. You probably walked right past it."

"Where are the men? Or where did you come ashore? We saw no men at all."

"I came on the south side. Found a fisherman to take me across for a coin and he dropped me into a cove on the south. Right after he left, another boat came along with the swords, and they saw me. That's all I recall."

"Did you recognize them from Duart?"

"Aye. They are the same ones. I could smell one man. He's the one who attacked me. I'm sorry, Sloan. I thought I could get close enough to hide somewhere and throw my axe. A foolish lass. Now I see that."

"A brave one who kisses verra sweetly."

"You were awake enough?"

He nodded, then wiggled. "Can you help me lean against the wall? With my hands bound, it's difficult. Have you anything to help me break my bindings?"

"Aye, my small axe. They took your sword, I'm sure."

"Aye. If you release me, I'd be forever indebted to you."

She pulled the axe from the bag hidden inside her tunic but dropped it to the floor because the door opened again.

Her attacker entered. "I'd like a few moments with you, my sweet."

"If you hurt her, I'll kill you," Sloan said.

The man chuckled. "I don't think you'll be hurting anyone all tied up like that." He grabbed Eva by the arm and yanked her to her feet. "Let's go. I'll leave your boyfriend here so he can listen to us."

"You touch her, and I will kill you. There will be men all over here on the morrow and we'll be rescued."

The man laughed as they headed down the passageway. Over his shoulder, he called out, "They already came and went."

Eva struggled to follow along but stayed upright, her eyes taking in everything as they moved into a passageway and through a door at the end, then into a small area at the base of the stairs and through another door in the opposite direction.

There were two separate sections off the staircase. Perhaps the bairns were on this side.

He stepped into the next passageway and shoved her into a cell with one pallet on the floor. "I'm here to finish what I started before, and let me give you a fair warning," he said, pinching the underside of her upper arm. She refused to react, glaring at the ugly brute instead.

"If you ever tell anyone about me, I'll come back and slice your face. You noble whores are all the same. Flaunt what you have but don't allow anyone close enough to touch you. Well, I'm taking what you taunt men with before you give it to a fool like the man in your cell."

He gripped her arms and attempted to tear her tunic, his tongue licking her cheek. "You are a sweet one. I felt your tits before. I'll see them this time."

She spit on him.

His hand swung out in a wide arc and slapped her hard just as a door slammed down the way.

"What the hell do you think you are doing, D?" a man asked.

"O, I was just getting a little taste. I'll let you go first, if you wish." The man backed away, though he kept his hand on her arm, pinching tightly.

She kicked him and he raised his clenched hand to punch her, but the man named O caught his fist. "You do not touch any of the merchandise. She will earn us a good price because of her beauty. I'll cut off your sac if I catch you with her again. Understood?"

The man paled but nodded.

"I'll take her back. You get to work. We don't

have much time. Dawn is upon us, and we leave at high sun."

The man took off, not saying another word, while O marched Eva back down to her cell, unlocking it and tossing her inside before locking the door again quickly.

Eva fell onto a pallet next to where Sloan leaned against the outside wall. The man had touched her, licked her cheek, nearly attacked her worse. She was so disgusted that she couldn't speak.

"Eva, you are hale? That wasn't the same man who took you. What happened?"

Eva shook so hard that her teeth chattered. She closed her eyes to rid the view of the evil bastard from her mind but failed.

Sloan rubbed his wrists. "I managed to get free of my bindings, thanks to you, so here is your axe back." He set it near her, but she shied away.

"Sloan, don't touch me. Ever again. I'm so soiled." Tears slid down her cheeks, the shame overpowering her because of all that had happened. Grateful that O had come in, it didn't stop the feeling of being sullied by the malodorous brute who took her away.

"Eva, what can I do to help you?" Sloan moved over and sat on the pallet next to her, his soft tone beginning to make its way through the cobwebs that possessed her mind, tangled webs of the past fighting with the present, seeming to tie up tighter and tighter.

"Eva, I know you can hear me, so I wish for you to listen. I don't know where this fear of *my* touch comes from, but you need to try to rid yourself of it."

She shook her head, her tremors continuing, not abating at all. If he only knew what she'd gone through back in the stable, and in the other cell, perhaps he would understand, but she would not tell him. She couldn't. Her embarrassment, the shame, wasn't something she wanted to deal with now. She could still smell the man, and the pain in her face from the brutal slap ached more than she would admit.

"Eva …" Sloan moved closer. "Whatever happened, I'll help you deal with it. This has naught to do with my offer of a betrothal, this is an offer from one person who cares for you as a friend, who wishes to help you get past whatever is tormenting you. I believe you can. You are a strong woman, and you can deal with it."

Eva opened her eyes at what she'd heard. Had Sloan called her strong? No one had ever said she was strong. Lennox was. Meg was. Eli, Tamsin, Dyna, and Marta all were strong, but not her.

Never Eva. She was invisible.

But Sloan saw her.

"Why?" she whimpered, wishing anyone would help her to get past her fears. Could Sloan do it?

He moved a touch closer to her on the pallet. "Because our captor knows your weakness now. He'll continue to taunt you every chance he gets. Until you can show him touch doesn't bother you, he'll continue. He has one of those sick minds that loves to torture people, in any way they can. They enjoy it."

"What do I do, Sloan? I hate him. He hits and pinches me, and I can't forget how awful I feel when he's close." Her voice came out in the lowest whisper as cold began to course through her. The cold of the cell, of their situation, reaching its tendrils into her deepest parts until she shivered from the inside out. A new form of torture she'd never experienced before.

"Help me, Sloan. What do I do?"

"I'll tell you, and I'm going to do it, but you have to trust me."

"Anything but touch."

"I have to touch you."

Her head shook involuntarily as she thought of all the touches she hated. "Nay, nay, nay."

He set his hand next to her, not touching her, but close.

"Don't touch me. Please. I'm disgusting."

"Nay, you are not disgusting. He is. Do not allow him to get into that beautiful mind of yours. Allow me to hold you so we can get through this together. Can you promise me you won't scream, lass?"

She didn't know if she could contain it, but she had the odd feeling that if she didn't stop, she would shake herself to death. Her continued trembling brought on a cold shivering that frightened her. It was Sloan Rankin or die.

Sloan said, "You're shivering with cold. I promise not to hurt you, but I'm going to lift you up, settle you on my lap, and wrap my arms around you. Please don't scream or they'll return and that won't be good for either of us."

The cold inside her gripped deep, something she'd never felt. Oh, she'd shivered and trembled and shaken before, but this shuddering? This could kill her. There was a time when she would have allowed it, back on that day in the stables, but no more.

Eva made a new vow. Thinking of the bairns who'd been stolen away, of Magni who'd told her how frightened he'd been, her resolve changed to a commitment to herself. She had to trust Sloan.

She nodded. "I'll agree." If there was one thing she knew about Sloan Rankin, it was that he gave off heat like a giant hearth. She had to fight, or her captor would win. Never.

Sloan lifted her up and set her on his lap, and without thinking, she began to shove at him, but the blessed man didn't stop her or drop her. Her hands held little force behind them, so she inflicted no pain. It was reactive because, in her heart, she couldn't hurt Sloan.

"Well done. Don't scream, Eva. I'll not leave you alone." His voice came out in such a warm tone that it wrapped around her and soothed her like a blanket. "Hush, and you'll be warmed. I'm reaching around to pull you in close, so you'll take my heat. I've got too much."

She tensed, every piece of his body touching her so painful that she wished to shove him away. But in between the stabs of pain were sensations of heat, sudden gushes sweeping through her, flowing from his hands to every part of her.

An amazing thing happened—her tremors slowed.

Sloan spoke in her ear. "I'll not walk away from you, Eva. I vow never to hurt you. Never to touch you without permission, without letting you know I'm near. You're doing great and your tremors are slowing. I'll get you there. I'm going to lower my head next to yours so my breath will warm you too. That's all I'll do."

His warm breath brushed her ear, and she jerked away.

"Nay, trust me. You must trust me so we can escape. Once we're gone, you can slap me all you like. Just not now. Come back, lass. You're too far away in your mind."

And for some odd reason, she finally gave in to all of Sloan's ministrations. Leaning back against him, she sighed and sank into his warmth. Gave control to him, let hers go, soaked up his heat, his tenderness, the calmness of his soul overpowering her until her shaking slowed.

"Why did you follow me, Sloan? How did you know?" What would have happened to her if he hadn't come along?

He chuckled, his hand rubbing her back lightly. "You don't recall all the times I followed you when you were just a wee lass? The time you thought to follow us to Loch na Keal to swim and fish? I knew you were coming. I told Lennox and Taskill I forgot something, and sure enough, there you were on your pony trying to sneak out the back."

She laughed. "I do remember. My pony wouldn't fit through the door."

His hand rubbed her neck. "Or the time you

chased us back to Rankin land, running down the hill so fast that you were headed straight into the frigid water?"

"But you caught me. You've always been there for me, Sloan. Why?"

She felt his shrug against her shoulder. "I always knew what you were thinking, I guess. Your brother was too old, and Taskill was busy flirting with anything in a skirt."

"I'm sorry I insulted you."

"Nay, you did not insult me."

"I didn't like my brother telling me what to do."

"Strong women have that tendency. You're forgiven for any hurt you thought you caused me."

"If we ever get out of here, could you court me secretly? Not tell my overbearing brother?" She had a sudden warmth inside just for Sloan Rankin. When she thought about how much he'd done for her, how much that meant to her, how he'd followed her here, putting himself at such risk for her.

And now, the tenderness he showed was something she wished to have in her life forever.

Forever and ever. She'd made a huge mistake rejecting this man, and she prayed he would forgive her folly.

"I would like that." His hand reached up and cupped her cheek. "And I wish to tell you something else. I would never force you to do anything. And I will wait for you forever, if that's what it takes."

They sat in silence for a few more moments until her tremors stopped.

Completely.

"Good job, lass. Now we need to focus on getting free. Tell me what you learned. Did you find out where the bairns are?"

"Nay," she said, forcing herself to recall the trek she took. "But there's another set of locked chambers in the other direction from the staircase. I would wager the bairns are over there."

"Good. Do you recall enough that you could lead us there?"

"Aye."

"Not yet. You need to warm up. Just soak up my heat, then we'll talk."

She sat there as if she were in her own private heaven, no one to bother her. Closing her eyes, she willed her body to stay that way, absorbing Sloan's quiet tones and warm embrace, his relaxing voice taking her to another place. A place where men didn't hurt her, where she had friends she could trust, a place where she was loved for who she was. Never threatened and not hated for her noble blood, for being the chieftain's sister.

Where people didn't hate her for who she was, for her name, or for where she was born.

A place of hope.

"Eva," he whispered a few moments later. "You're doing much better, but now I can tell you that I've seen him twice and I'll never forget him. I will make you a promise, lass."

She turned her head a touch, just enough to

gaze into Sloan's eyes, her lower lip the only part of her still trembling.

"I will make him pay, whatever his name is."

The tightness in her chest seemed to lighten. The cold, hard covering she kept it in broke just a wee bit.

Sloan Rankin had fractured the ice encasing her heart.

CHAPTER THIRTY-ONE

Connor

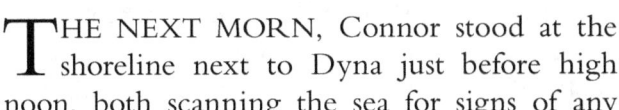

THE NEXT MORN, Connor stood at the shoreline next to Dyna just before high noon, both scanning the sea for signs of any boats.

Dyna asked, "How much longer, do you think?"

"I honestly have no idea. But do you know something odd?"

"As if there haven't been enough odd things, Da. You have to give me another one? Make sure Mama doesn't hear you."

Connor smiled. "Nay, this is a good thing."

"Then please do tell."

"I woke up this morn and felt like I'd been with Mama and Da."

Dyna said, "Oh, praise God above. I felt the same way! What were they doing? You first."

"They were sitting together watching something. Every once in a while, Da would get up, walk in a circle, his hand on the hilt of his sword."

"Mama would chat, but he would quiet her?"

"Aye! You had the same dream?"

"I did, Da."

"What were they watching? I couldn't see."

Dyna's eyes misted. "The bairns. They were watching Sandor and Tora. They are watching over them, Da. I know it."

Maitland and Alasdair joined them, Maitland heading directly to the beach. "What the hell is that?"

"What?"

"In the water," Maitland said, pointing. "Is that a person? It's coming directly this way."

Thane joined them and headed straight to the shoreline. "Nay, it's a dog. Coming from Ulva."

"It's Shadow! That's Eva's dog," Dyna said. "Has anyone seen Eva?"

Thane shook his head. "Sloan never came into the hall last eve. He's missing."

Alasdair said, "He said he was going to relieve himself after we all headed in. I didn't think anything of it, but I never saw him enter, now that you mention it."

Thane said, "Eva snuck out and went after the bairns on her own is my guess."

"Why?" Maitland asked.

Thane sighed. "Meg told Tamsin that Eva was attacked in the stables a few nights ago. The man who attacked her was one of the masked men. Tamsin was afraid that Eva followed along for that reason. Lennox refused to let her come with either group. She snuck out after he and Meg headed to Rankin land. Sloan followed her."

"What the hell am I missing?" Connor asked.

"Sloan's requested a betrothal to Eva, but she

rejected him. He would never let her go anywhere alone. He's loved Eva for a long time." Thane rubbed his hands together. "So, the good news is I would wager they both found the bairns. Let's hope they are all together and they'll be on the boat with Maeve and the bairns."

Connor said, "I doubt Eva can be much help, but having Sloan aboard could be extremely helpful. I'm feeling better about the day. Are you sure that's Eva's dog?"

Maitland moved to the edge just as the puppy came out of the sea, shaking the water from its fur all over Maitland and Dyna, who'd moved closer, Dyna squealing when she got soaked. She kneeled and Shadow ran to her. "Did you come to tell us that Eva needs help, Shadow? Is that it?"

The dog wagged its tail and whimpered, running in a circle, then running in the direction it came from.

"She's there, isn't she? You've come to let us know, sweet puppy."

Maitland let out a big sigh and Thane smiled.

Connor crossed his arms. "I don't understand why Eva being with them makes you feel better, Menzie. Do tell. She's not an archer, is she?"

Dyna said, "She has trained a bit with me, but unsuccessfully. And I'm sure she does not have a bow or quiver with her."

Thane chuckled. "Nay, she's been training with Meg to learn axe throwing. She probably has a couple of those with her."

"And Maitland," Dyna said, "you need to remember what Lia told you. All will be well. I believe it. We must have faith that she is truly a faery. Avelina saw it, so that is proof enough for me."

"You are correct. And now that I think more about Eva, I'm feeling better." Maitland chuckled, clapping his hands together. "Growing up on an isle, I would wager Eva's a hell of a swimmer. True or not, Thane?"

"Oh, Eva is a hell of a swimmer. She'll get the bairns off the boat," Thane said. "Things are definitely looking better."

Connor said, "I'm surprised Sloan came this way knowing his land is about to be attacked in a few days. You told him, didn't you, Dyna?"

Dyna looked from Maitland to her father, her eyes wide. "Nay. Logan said not to, said he'd tell him when he needed to."

Maitland let out a deep sigh, his hands on his hips. "I forgot completely. I was too worried about Maeve and Grant."

"He doesn't know?" Dyna asked. "Does anyone on Rankin land know?"

Connor said, "Just Logan. I told him, and he went with Lennox."

CHAPTER THIRTY-TWO

Sloan

———————

W HEN SLOAN FINALLY had Eva warmed up and calmed down, he said, "Come. We have to try to find the bairns. We need to go wherever they go. Maeve will never be able to save them on her own. We can help."

"Aye. Give me my axe and I'll tuck it away."

"Only if you promise me not to use it here unless it's saving a life. We'll need it on the boat. You know we can swim to shore, and the group will be watching from the coastline somewhere. Sylvi told them to, so all will be well. No trouble until we are on the boat. Then we'll have plenty of help when the two boats wait to meet the larger boat."

"Agreed. But I would feel better if we could find them. Let's see if we can. But how are we going to get out?"

"The key is on the wall. We'll have to find a way to get it off the nail." Sloan got up and wiggled the wooden door to test its strength. "This is a weak door. I could probably kick it in rather than waste time trying to get the key."

"But will the noise draw them down the stairs?"

"Nay, when they brought me in, no one was upstairs or down here. They were all near the boats with crates of different weaponry. That's all I saw."

"We don't have much time," Eva said.

Sloan smiled and took Eva by the waist and set her aside. "Then allow me, my dearest."

And with one kick, he broke the door, giving them the ability to turn the handle and get out. He took her hand and escorted her out, then said, "Wait here while I look through the windows of the other doors." There appeared to be four separate chambers or cells, whatever they were used for. They could be sleeping quarters or prisoner cells.

"All empty. Show me where you went."

The underground passageways were dark and very damp, and they had no idea what time of day it was. They crept as quietly as possible, closing two doors behind them without making a sound. The other passageway was exactly like the one they'd come from.

Sloan pointed to one side. "You look in those windows, and I'll look into these."

But as they drew closer, they both heard movement and whispering in the last cell. Sloan held up his hand to stop Eva, then crept down and peeked in the window.

Sandor waved to him.

He found the key and unlocked the door, Eva joining them. "Oh, thank the Lord," Maeve said. "Are we free? Is Maitland behind you?"

Sloan sighed and said, "Nay. We were both captured for sneaking around outside, but together we will make a stronger force against them. Let me tell you what we learned, Maeve. Avelina and Dyna saw that you were being held on Ulva. Lia told Sylvi that you would be moved by boat and told Maitland to be in front of Thane's land to watch for the boats midday today. They will be there."

Maeve closed her eyes and whispered, "I hope so, because I cannot swim, and small boats scare me. If we tipped over, I wouldn't be able to save Grant, and Sandor can't swim either."

Sloan and Eva both sat on a pallet. "Then let's think of how we can do this. I have no weapons, so I can't fight with anything but my fists. Eva has one axe that we are saving. So, let's say this. If you think the boat is going over, come next to me, Maeve, and I will hold both you and Grant up. Eva can handle Tora and Sandor. Lia, can you swim?"

"Of course."

Eva said, "I can tie these blankets on me in such a way that I can slide one of the bairns inside. Sloan can wear one too. We're both strong swimmers, Maeve."

"I can swim too," Tora said. "Maeve, do not fear. Eva and Sloan belong togethew so they will save us."

"What?" Maeve asked.

Tora pointed to Eva and Sloan. "They are one. Stwongew togethew so they work togethew, and all will be well."

The wee lass delivered a punch in his gut unlike any he'd ever received before. Sloan stared at Eva to gauge her reaction, but Maeve spoke first. "They do belong together, I think."

Eva peeked at him with a look that nearly did him in. He'd known his feelings were strong for her, but her next words sealed his fate.

"Sloan does belong with me, Tora. You are right."

Sloan fell in love with Eva all over again, just from the smile she gave him. It was a smile of hope, of promises, of certainty. She'd faced down a nasty earl and a cruel attacker and yet she could still smile in the middle of adversity. He loved her with all his heart, so pleased with her that he nearly burst with pride. But he forced himself to focus on the important events at hand.

Maeve nodded and said, "I think you should tie one on me too in case I go over with Grant. I won't have to worry about him if he's tied to me." Maeve began to cry, but her tears stopped quickly when the door opened and three men entered.

The man known as O said, "You found your way here. Makes it easier for us. I'm moving all of you, splitting you up into two boats. Then you'll be moving to a larger boat in the middle of the sea. Then we're off to a much bigger island. If anyone fights me, I'll throw the bairn overboard."

Maeve gasped and tugged Grant tighter to her. Sandor climbed up on Sloan's lap and Tora found her way to Eva's lap, neither saying anything.

O looked at Sloan. "In fact, I thought of killing

you, but I could use an extra man with some strength. The lass I can sell with the bairns, but you? I'll keep you for your brute power."

Sloan was about to respond to him about selling people but thought better of it. He feared they might leave him behind or put a sword in his belly, and he surely did not want either.

O crossed his arms and tipped his head to the group. "Which one of you is the faery?"

Lia smiled sweetly and said, "I am. I will go with you willingly if you free the others."

"You will grant me my wish when I am ready. And nay, I'm not letting the others go. What power does the lad have? And is it the wee one or the other one?"

He looked from Maeve to Sloan and then to Eva. The two other men snickered. Sloan was glad to see that Eva's attacker was not one of the three men in front of them, or he would have had to use his fist on the fool. No one spoke.

"Fine. You don't wish to answer, then I'll find out myself." He reached for Grant, but a flash blinded them all and his hand jerked back. "What the hell! Something burned me. It was like a bolt of lightning shot through me."

No one said anything except Grant who giggled uncontrollably.

"You wee piece of shite. Give him to me."

Maeve said, "Nay. Leave us be."

O moved over next to Maeve and said, "Fine. Then I'll take you, you whore. You two are both coming with me, then I'll figure it out on my own."

He touched Maeve's arm, grabbing her, but Grant let out an urgent squeal.

O jumped back, the skin on his hand smoking from the burn. "You bitch. You burned me!"

He swung his hand up in an arc aimed at Maeve, but Sloan caught his wrist, and Lia said, "I wouldn't do that if I were you. The laddie burned you twice. If you touch any of us again, it will be worse. Can you not see it in the lad's face?"

Grant scowled, his gaze locked on the man's hand that had stopped in midair. O's hand turned a deep red, and he shoved at Sloan, then the other two, and all three ran out the door, locking the door behind them.

"I'm never touching either one of them again. Get me the hell out," O said. "Leave them here until we ready the boats. Then we'll return for them."

CHAPTER THIRTY-THREE

Logan

JUST PAST DAWN the day after they'd split into groups, Logan stood on the point past Dun Ara Castle, overlooking the sea, his gaze traveling from the Isle of Coll and back to Kilchoan over and over again.

Lennox came up behind him. "I don't understand why Sloan isn't here. He was supposed to be part of the group guarding his own castle. Would he not wish to be on Rankin land?"

Logan said, "He would be if we'd told him what Sylvi had told us, but I told the others to keep it quiet until we got the bairns back."

"You didn't tell him about his own castle being under attack? Why the hell not?"

"Because he had something more important to do."

"What could be more important than protecting his own castle?"

Logan sighed and shook his head. "You are dense sometimes, MacVey. Why did you go to MacKinnis Castle in such a hurry not long ago?"

"When I chased Meg? What the hell does that have to do with Sloan?"

"Sloan is protecting your sister."

"Eva? Why would she need protecting when she's at home?"

Logan arched his brow at MacVey. "Are you sure about that?"

"Hell's ashes! She left? Where is she? I'm going after her. Hell with this watch. I'm going to kill her!"

"Calm your arse down. Don't you think it's time that you recognize your sister is an adult?"

"She's not. She doesn't think like one. Our father spoiled her and …"

"One of the men who stole the bairns was her attacker. She listened to all the tales, said naught, and left after you did. She hid and followed the other groups to MacQuarie land, and Sloan knew her well enough to wait for her to leave so he could follow. And they're way ahead of you, so there's no sense in you going after Eva. There are two score Grant guards at MacQuarie Castle as you know. Thane and Sloan will both watch over her."

"How the hell do you know all this, Ramsay? You've been here from the start."

Logan smirked.

Meg approached and Lennox turned around, looking bewildered. "Did you know that Eva was going after her attacker on Ulva?"

"She did? Go, Eva!"

"What the hell does that mean? She'll be attacked again, Meg."

Logan said, "Nay, she won't. She's got the fire in her eyes this time, MacVey. You'll not stop her until she gets her just due. And she deserves a slow one." He smirked and said, "I know a few others who got it when they needed it. Let her go. Sloan's following her."

"But she can't protect herself! And how do you know Sloan went after her?"

"You are blind, MacVey."

Meg laughed, then kissed her husband's cheek. "Do you recall the other day when I asked you for a new target board for my axe throwing? It was because your sister destroyed it. I taught her how to throw axes, and she ended up being pretty good at it."

"But she doesn't have any axes with her."

"There were a few missing when we left for Duart."

Lennox stared over the water. "Eva? An axe thrower? What the hell!"

Logan laughed and said, "Don't feel bad, MacVey. Gwynie did the same to me when we were first married. Enjoy it and let Sloan take care of your sister. I promise you he will. Then he'll come flying back here when Dyna tells him his castle is under attack."

Lennox set his hands on his hips and said, "That explains where Sloan is, but where the hell is Rinaldo?"

"That's my question," Logan replied, his gaze scanning the sea again. "I don't trust that man. He's naught but trouble."

CHAPTER THIRTY-FOUR

Maitland

———◆◆◆———

" BOATS! I SEE two of them coming from Ulva. They have to be in them." Maitland paced back and forth on the beach in front of MacQuarie Castle. They'd seen a few small fishing boats, but there had only been one or two men in each.

Thane moved over to the edge of the water and peered across. "I think it is them. I would say stand back so they don't see us here watching. I don't want them turning around and waiting until it's dark."

Alasdair moved back, then asked, "Aren't we getting in the boats? I say we meet the bastards in the middle of Loch Tuath. I'm not afraid to fight in a boat."

"Naaaay!" Maitland bellowed. "You step in that vessel, and I'll drag you off it, Grant."

Every face turned to stare at him, and he could feel himself blushing. "Maeve can't swim, and if you jar that boat and scare her, our son could go overboard. He'll drop like a stone."

Alasdair paled, scratching his scruffy beard.

"Sorry, Menzie. You're right. What about Sandor and Tora? Can they swim at all, Dyna? This is an aspect I hadn't considered."

"Sandor could keep his head above water for a few moments. Tora could swim from here to that rock over there, but neither one could swim from there to shore. Maitland's right. We can't tip the boats over. Eva and Sloan can't go for four bairns and an adult. And any battle between men on boats will threaten one or the other to capsize."

Connor said, "Thane, you know the water better than any of us. Your suggestions?"

"Get Eli out here. We need archers. I'd let Dyna and Eli in the water—two lasses won't threaten them or draw any attention. Keep the quivers on their backs, and they'll never see the bows until it's too late."

"That's a long way for accuracy, Thane. And we have six people we don't want to hit."

Thane said, "Listen. I know Sloan well enough to know he's one of the craftiest men around. If he and Eva are there, and I think they are, then let them make the first move. They can both swim, and they'll help the others. My guess is they didn't return last eve because they were both inside and found the bairns. Even if they had gotten them away from the captors, they didn't have the boats to row all of them back. Their only hope is for us to see them and attack from here. Both can easily swim from that distance and that's on both of their minds. They know we have the archers and the men. We just have to plan our approach carefully and be ready to assist them."

"A long way out, and the larger ship is on its way," Connor said, pointing off into the distance. "Quite a ways away yet, but I see it."

"Shite," Maitland said, tugging on his hair. "Dyna, can you see anything with your visions? Anything at all?"

Connor moved back to the curtain wall with a few of the others. "Aye, let's allow you some peace to see if you can discover anything through your visions, Dyna. We need to know how many are on the boat, and I'd like to know with some certainty if Eva and Sloan are there."

Maitland stepped back, moving over to a shaded tree on higher ground, peering across the water and praying that his wee son and wife would be safe soon. He had to have faith in what everyone else advised and not do what his reactions told him to do.

He was prepared to swim to the boat on his own and grab Maeve and Grant before they saw him, but it was too risky.

Dyna sat down on the beach and closed her eyes, trying to reach out to Tora. A few moments later, she said, "Eva is with Tora and Sandor in one boat and Sloan is with Maeve, Grant, and Lia in the other one. And Tora said not to worry. Eva and Sloan will fix everything."

"Eva?" Maitland asked, stunned by the reply. "How is Eva going to fix everything?"

Thane smiled when he peered through an odd-looking piece of glass. "I'd wager that she has a great idea."

Connor said, "Eva's the one who fixed Gwyneth's contraption. Give them a chance."

Thane held an object in his hand and stared at the far grouping. "In fact, I believe she just went overboard with Tora and Sandor, and they're swimming this way. It's nearly low tide, so they may only have to swim about half the distance, and she'll be able to touch."

"How could you know that from this far away, Thane? And what is that you're holding?"

Thane handed it over to Alasdair. "It's something we found on an abandoned Viking ship. It oddly makes anything in the distance appear larger."

Alasdair held it up to his eye and whistled. "I agree. That is Eva in the water with Dyna's two. Get ready, Chief," he said to his uncle.

Connor grabbed Dyna and held her back. "Not yet. Let them get a little closer, lass. Eva's got them. And I see no ruckus on the ship yet to indicate they've noticed their departure. Don't give them away." Then he looked at Alasdair and nodded toward Maitland.

Maitland couldn't stop his tears from falling as he ran toward the beach, but Alasdair pulled him back, though it took Thane's assistance to hold him tight.

"She's got them, and Sloan will handle Maeve. They are both excellent swimmers."

Maitland muttered, "You don't know how hard it is to stand here."

Alasdair said, "Alaric, Thane, and I will man

the boats. Be ready to move. Archers, stay back. Connor, you can swim too, to back up Dyna."

Maitland said another prayer, wiping the tears from his eyes.

CHAPTER THIRTY-FIVE

Eva

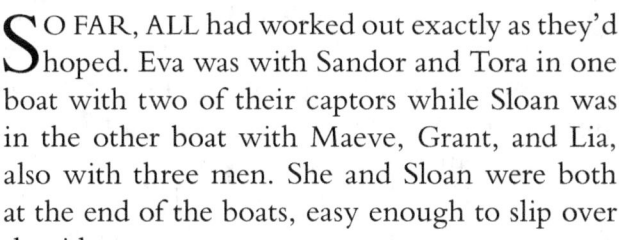

SO FAR, ALL had worked out exactly as they'd hoped. Eva was with Sandor and Tora in one boat with two of their captors while Sloan was in the other boat with Maeve, Grant, and Lia, also with three men. She and Sloan were both at the end of the boats, easy enough to slip over the side.

Their captors busied themselves with the view of the large galley ship in the distance, which helped their escape plans because they paid them no mind.

Sloan had fashioned two loops of cloth from the dirty blankets to hold Sandor and Tora close to Eva's body when she climbed into the water with them.

Tora said, "I can swim. Sandow swim with you, Evie."

She prayed Tora could keep herself above the surface until she was able to get in the water with Sandor. She noticed people on the beach, praying they were from Thane's castle, but Sloan, Maeve, and the children blocked the view of Eva in the water, something she needed, before the men in the boats noticed them. Dyna was on the far bank observing, if Eva guessed right.

The plan was for Sloan to start a disturbance to distract the men so Eva could slip over into the water. Maeve was petrified of a rocking boat, but she'd tied Grant to her chest the same way Eva would do with Sandor.

As soon as the boat stopped to await the approach of the larger boat, Sloan pointed to the farthest boat and told them it was sinking, his planned distraction, and then nodded to Eva. She set Tora in the water and grabbed Sandor, slipping him inside the tight loop and climbing over the edge to drop into the sea, her breath hitching at the temperature change.

She took Tora's hand and pulled her close, slipping the loop over Tora's head and chest, then Eva rolled onto her back, swimming for all she was worth, one arm after the other reaching over her head and keeping her kicks underwater as fast as she could, hoping she had enough time before the men noticed.

The boat erupted into chaos, men shouting and arguing, about to jump after her when Lia shouted, "Do not dare go after them!" She stood in the boat and raised her arms, a giant black thundercloud appearing out of nowhere, lightning shooting through the air, one bolt hitting a tree not far away.

O bellowed, "Let her go. We have the faery and the lad. We don't need them!"

And all the men sat down again, but the boat rocked, and Maeve screamed.

Eva kept swimming, talking to the bairns. "We'll be fine. I bet someone is swimming straight toward us."

"Watew wocking," Sandor said, enjoying the swim. "Wawm too. Gwandda comeen."

"Just keep your mouth closed, Sandor. I don't know who is swimming this way, but I bet you know them. Mayhap it is Grandda."

Sandor waved at some unknown person, but Eva ignored him. "Can you see, Tora? I hear someone swimming from behind us."

"Aye, is Mama. She's coming."

Eva swam as hard as she could, another boat approaching that she guessed would be Thane and his men, so she kept her strokes steady. When she heard Dyna's voice, she nearly cried. "Eva, Maitland and I are coming up behind you. Keep swimming until we are next to you."

Eva waited until they sounded closer, then she stopped and treaded water, knowing she was losing steam, but she stayed strong, pulling Sandor out of the fabric loop just as Maitland approached and took the lad from her.

"I have him." Maitland grabbed the boy who didn't seem the least bit bothered by the situation.

But the men on the boat saw them, and arrows flew across the water, missing by a great deal. Eva was pleased when she caught sight of Eli firing back, hitting one of the men who then fell into the water with a loud splash. She managed to get

Tora out of the loop and handed her over. "Dyna, take Tora, and I'll go back for Grant."

Maitland said, "Nay, you take Sandor, and I'll go."

Dyna grabbed his shoulder. "Nay, Maitland. You know a female would be safer. They are watching you now. They'll kill you on your approach. They aren't paying Eva any attention at all."

Connor approached from behind them and shouted, "She's right. They aren't watching Eva. She's a stronger swimmer than I am, and she's nearly back at the boat already. Get the bairn in, Maitland, before an arrow hits him. That's my grandson!"

Maitland did as he was told, so Eva continued to swim wide, heading to the other side of the boat where no one was. She still had the loops around her. She couldn't handle both Maeve and Grant, but she could get the bairn away while Sloan handled Maeve.

Thane's boat was nearly there just as all chaos broke out, one boat rocking so that it nearly tipped over. Maeve screamed again, but that helped Eva to know exactly where she was. Reaching the side, she tugged on Maeve's gown and whispered, "Hand him to me. Maitland's coming. Until then, stay near Sloan. He'll save you."

No one paid them any mind, because Thane's boat had connected and the sounds of swords clashing and grunts of pain rang out over the water, sounding like the largest battle ever. Maeve sobbed but handed Grant to Eva, helping her to get him into the loop on Eva's chest. She kissed her son's head and said, "Go, before he slips from my hands. There's water in the boat, and we're going over."

Eva kicked away, struggling with Grant a bit until she calmed him, but then Lia handed Maeve something and said, "I found it. The Norse use it to keep their head above water. Hold on to it and go, Maeve. I'll take care of the rest."

Maeve glanced over the boat's side and froze. "I can't."

Eva treaded water, holding Grant's head next to hers with no problem. "You have to. If the boat tips over, you'll get knocked in the head. I'll keep you up, and Maitland will be here soon. I promise. He and Connor are nearly here."

Maeve shook her head. "I can't. Go with Grant, and tell Maitland I love him."

Eva kicked away because she saw Lia come at Maeve with a force, and Grant's mother flew over the edge, landing in the water with a splash and a scream, but she held the device tight and came bouncing up.

"Get her!"

O stood in the boat and ordered men to jump over, but Lia raised her arms above her head and a creature rose from the depths below. It scared the hell out of Eva, its body sluicing through the water faster than any ship she'd ever seen. She moved closer to Maeve so the poor woman wouldn't panic and managed to grab her gown, tugging Maeve along next to her the best she could. They moved around the side of the boat and toward shore, kicking so hard she nearly cried.

The creature's head looked like a giant snake and its tail cut a wide arc next to the boat, finally whipping into the vessel and overturning it, sending all its occupants into the water.

Eva swam and swam as men shouted, swords clashed, fists crunched, and blood stained the waterway. What the hell was she seeing? Maeve sobbed but kept her head above the surface.

And to scare the hell out of Eva even more, Sloan's face popped up from underwater, but she'd never been so glad to see anyone.

"Eva, do you have him tight?"

"Aye, but grab Maeve, she's panicking."

With two strokes, he was next to her. "Maeve, I'm here. I'll support you."

Sloan took one arm and wrapped it across the top of her chest, sliding his body underneath her to lift her head above the water. "I've got you, but don't fight me or you'll take us both down. Relax, Maeve."

Connor's voice called out, "We're coming. Dyna and Maitland are almost to you. Hang on."

The creature came up out of the water again, and Grant laughed, waving to the reptilian monster.

What the hell was happening?

Maitland appeared between Sloan and Eva. "I'm here, Maeve. Who shall I take?"

Sloan said, "Neither one, Maitland. Grant is safely tied to Eva, so swim next to her until she can touch. Maeve is calm with me, and I'd rather not move her. Too much fire and chaos to stop."

Maeve said, "Maitland, I'm fine. Sloan and Eva saved us both."

Connor and Dyna swam on either side of them and Dyna said, "Da, are you watching your nephew and the creature?"

Connor said, "I noticed. He's enjoying this, is he not?"

Dyna said, "A wee bit too much, I think."

Maitland looked around and asked, "Where's Lia?"

Eva said, "She was still on the boat when we left."

Dyna whirled around in all directions before continuing. "I don't see her in the water, but I wouldn't worry about her. I think she's controlling everything."

Maeve said, "She pushed me in the water before the creature appeared. I haven't seen her since."

Grant pointed at the creature and said the first word they'd ever heard from him, "Wia." Then he giggled again.

"Wia."

CHAPTER THIRTY-SIX

Sloan

A SHORT TIME LATER, Sloan sat on the small hill in front of the castle wall, Eva settled between his legs, leaning against him. "You are a strong swimmer, lass. You did well, especially with the two bairns together."

"They were easy, but I tired quickly. I've been thinking about it all, and I've decided I know one thing for certain. I don't think anything is ever going to hurt Alexander Drew Menzie Grantham."

Shadow spun around and yipped at Sloan as if to agree with her, then launched himself at Eva, right onto her lap. She laughed and tickled her dog. "I know, I know. You are such a good lad. You told them all where I was. And you told Sloan about me traveling there too. You deserve a treat!"

He barked so Eva pulled a piece of dried meat out of a nearby sack and handed it to him. "Here. I knew you deserved some, Shadow, so I grabbed you a wee bit of Thane's last batch of venison."

The pup ate his treat, then rushed off toward the beach, running in the grassy area.

Thane and Tamsin sat next to them, Maitland on the other side, leaning back on his elbows and chewing on a blade of grass. Maeve and Dyna had taken the bairns inside to wash up and to feed them. They'd all been through an ordeal.

Maitland glanced over at Sloan and Eva. "I don't know how to thank you properly for saving my wife and son. Both of you. Incredible how well you timed getting Eva off the boat and distracting the men, Sloan, so they never noticed her until it was too late."

Eva said, "I know we all believe Lia is Grant's protector, but I wish she would return."

As if she'd heard them, Lia stepped out from behind a tree, looking as fresh as ever.

Mora had come out to join them, and she rushed over, wrapping Lia in a huge hug. "There you are. I missed you so much and I was worried about you. Will you stay with us for a few days, Lia? Please? And we have to get Magni back, so it feels like it used to. Promise to stay with us?"

Sloan glanced over at Thane, both men smiling at Mora's exuberance and her inquisitive nature. How she adored Lia and Magni.

Mora stepped back and declared, "Lia, you are not a bit wet. Did you not get thrown into the water with the others? How did you get back here when the boats are out there still? Well, two of them are gone, but one was destroyed with that monster's tail, and what was that, anyway?

Was it a snake or a giant fish? Mayhap an eel of some kind?"

Lia joined them and said, "You know, I'm a bit tired so I think I'll go inside for a nap. Well done, everyone." She brushed something off her arm, and it fell to the ground.

Maitland said, "Maeve has Grant inside, feeding him."

"I do indeed need to take a nap first." She smiled as she glanced up at the clouds overhead, pausing, then stopped near Maitland. "I let Sylvi and your mother know that everyone is safe so your father and Derric won't worry. I'll be back in a few hours."

Maitland sat up, peering at her oddly. "Don't you wish to follow Grant?" She'd never been away from him since he'd arrived on the Isle of Mull. Not even for a few moments.

Lia stared at the clouds for a moment longer, but then said, "Nay, he doesn't need me now. I promised Magni I'd come home for a bit. And Mora too. Pardon me all."

Mora chased after the lass. "Lia, did you not wish to ask if the bairns all made it back? They could have been hurt by that creature, or the fire, or when the boat tipped over. Or what about when all the swords and the men were punching everyone? I've not seen anything like it. Don't you wonder how everyone is?"

"Nay, Mora. I know you would have told me if there were any problems." Then she yawned and waved as she moved into the keep.

Mora whispered, "Does anyone else think Lia is a wee bit odd?"

Thane snickered. "We'll talk later, Mora. You've missed a bit."

Mora reached down and picked up whatever it was that Lia had brushed from her arm. "What is this, Thane?" She handed it to him. "It's a different color of green, or is it gray? I've not seen anything like it. Where do you suppose it came from?"

He studied it for a few moments. "It looks like a scale to me."

Maitland said, "I'm not asking any more questions about her because I don't think I wish to hear the answers. I'm just grateful to all, Lia included."

Tamsin got up and paced closer to the beach. "Thane, did you recognize any of the men? I swear that when I stepped out here, I recognized the man who was bellowing all the orders to the other man. Voices carry so across the water, and I thought he sounded familiar. Did you know any of them?"

"Nay, but one did seem familiar …"

"Which one?" Connor asked.

"He had a name. I heard them call him something."

Eva said, "O. One is K, one is D, and the other was O."

"Oh my word, Thane. Odart! It's Raghnall's second. That's it."

Sloan asked, "From Ulva? Odart, the fool who assisted Garvie?"

"Aye," Tamsin explained. "He ran everything when Raghnall was traveling. He's the one who drove the boat when Raghnall tried to drown me. He knows the isles verra well."

Sloan said, "So, in other words, Odart just took over Garvie's business of selling bairns like Mora, Brian, and Thane?"

"And Magni."

Sloan thought for a moment, thinking about all the evil the bastard had caused everyone on the isle. "Eva and I will be taking our leave in about an hour."

"Back to Rankin land?" Connor asked. "Because we forgot to tell you that Sylvi said your castle will be attacked by someone on the morrow or the next day. Sorry, but we had to focus on this first."

"Dun Ara? On the morrow?" Eva turned around to look at him, but Sloan knew what he had to do. She'd never be right until they settled the issue with the bastard who attacked her.

"Nay, not returning yet. Those are words from a wee sweet lass. If it turns out to be true, then I'll be there by the morrow. Lennox, Miles, and Ingelram will protect Dun Ara in my absence, but I have something more important to take care of, and it is sitting on the Isle of Coll." He squeezed Eva's hand. "I will escort Eva there. Anyone care to join us?"

Maitland said, "I'm sorry, but I cannot help you. I am presently incapable of leaving my dear wife and son. I'm staying here."

Connor looked at Alasdair and tipped his head while Alasdair gave him a subtle nod. "Alaric and Eli will join you. They went in to eat. Anyone else wish to go?" Connor asked. "Dyna will stay here. The bairns need her."

Thane said, "Oh, I'll be there. You and Eva have just due for one man, Rankin, but I get Odart. We have a score to settle."

Connor asked, "The man they call K. Is he from Kilchoan?"

"Aye, so they said," Sloan replied. "Why?"

"Ramsay and I are looking for the man who killed Magni's parents."

"*If* he killed them. You heard about my parents, did you not? They told me they killed them, but in truth, my mother and father were stolen to take care of the bairns. Every time my sire tried to escape, they would make him watch as they beat my mother."

Connor said, "Sounds like the man we're looking for. If we find him, he's mine. And I want him alive. He's tortured this isle for long enough."

"He's yours."

"And those three all escaped? Did anyone see any of them go over into the water?"

Eva whispered. "O survived. And I know D is still alive. I heard him when he made it to the big boat."

Sloan said, "He'll not be alive for long." He kissed her neck and helped her up. "Come, we need to eat something before we go."

Eva said, "And I need to find a couple more axes to bring with me."

Connor smiled and said, "So O is for Odart. K is in charge. D is the man you're after. What's it stand for, Rankin?"

Sloan drawled, "D for *Dead man.*"

CHAPTER THIRTY-SEVEN

Eva

EVA WAS READY to go, hoping they'd soon have the opportunity to put this all behind them. The bairns had come through it as if it were nothing, though Connor had gone directly up to Tora and asked, "Are you going anywhere soon, lassie?"

Tora had given her grandsire a hug and said, "Nay, I staying here to play. We go home on the mowwow."

Connor had looked at his daughter and rolled his eyes. "I'll just ask her from now on. She tells all."

Dyna had smiled and kissed her father's cheek. "Staying put for one day, Da."

At the last minute, just before they were to head out the door, Tora had run over to Sloan, lifted her arms so he would pick her up, then whispered something in his ear.

Eva asked him what she said, but he'd replied, "Naught that I understood. Something about an apple orchard."

Then the wee lass had shoved away from his chest to be let down before running off to play with the others.

Thus, the group consisted of Sloan and Eva, Thane, Connor, Alasdair, Alaric, and Eli.

As they approached the isle, Alasdair asked, "How many buildings should we search? Or is any building more likely to hold the scavengers?"

Thane said, "We're headed to the village of Arinagour. That's where we're going ashore. It has several merchant buildings because the ferry boats land here. There is a castle on the southern end on a loch, but we're not going that far. It's MacClane land and no help to us. We'll go to the market, and I'll be direct and ask for Odart. Bastard should be well known by now."

Eva huddled close to Sloan, the breeze cool. "Do you think we'll find them?" she whispered.

"I do. Where else would they be? I bet they are all discussing the creature from the sea at the moment. I don't understand any of it, so I'm not mentioning it to anyone."

"What about my brother? Would Lennox believe us?" Eva asked.

"Nay," Sloan said. "I wouldn't believe it if anyone told me."

"You don't believe in seers, so that's not a surprise," she drawled. "Have you changed your mind about Dyna and Tora yet?"

"I almost did when we were told that Dyna could see us in the separate boats, but anyone with good vision could have guessed that. I'm not convinced yet, but …"

"There's doubt, isn't there?" Eva squeezed his arm and smiled.

He cast a sideways glance at her and said, "There is. I'll admit it. I'd believe it of Dyna more than a child."

"And Lia?"

"I will not discuss Lia. Nay, will not discuss. And that thing she gave Maeve? What the hell was that? I've never seen anything like it."

"She said it was from the Norse, but it worked. Maeve clung to it and her head popped right up in the water, and she had a gown on. I don't know how that didn't drag her under, but it helped because I could pull her along easily."

"And the oddest part? Once we got to shore, no one could find it."

"I know. I looked for it. If she'd left it in the water, it should have floated."

"But it wasn't anywhere to be found."

They found themselves pulling up to a long dock, the only boat there. A couple of fishermen nearby shouted over, "Welcome to the Isle of Coll. Who are you looking for?"

"A man named Odart. Know of him?"

"Sure do. Ugly bastard just went up the hill to their land. What business have you with him?"

Sloan looked to Thane, who said, "The kind that will put him out of business. How can we find him?"

"Glad to hear it. Straight up ahead, take the path to the right and down to the end. You'll find two buildings, a house and a stable that are not kept up. Abandoned buildings they took for their own use."

"What use is that?" Connor asked.

"Anything questionable and Odart will do it. I like to keep my neck attached so I don't ask. Hoping someday he'll cross the wrong person. Who are you?"

Sloan drawled, "The wrong persons."

The man grinned, showing a missing tooth. "Then we'll have an ale for you on your return."

Once they exited the boat, Connor approached the men and said, "Connor Grant of Clan Grant. How many fools are there?"

The man looked Connor up and down before answering. "Only five got off. They tossed two overboard and two headed on to Kilchoan. There was a hell of a battle on Loch Tuath or so I heard. They sounded daft, talking of lightning and faeries and snakes in the water. Know you anything about that?"

Connor grinned and waggled his brow, then drew his sword out of its sheath in one smooth move. "I might. We'll be back in a few moments for those ales. Then if you want a house or a stable, there will be two available."

The men chortled for quite a while after the group moved on.

Connor, Sloan, and the rest headed in the direction the fisherman gave them, finding the manor home not far down the right-hand path. The group gathered to plan their attack and Connor said, "I'll stay here. Thane and Alasdair, go in the front, Alaric and Eli into the stable,

Sloan and Eva around back. Whoever finds them, let me know and I'll get us all together, if we need to."

Sloan took Eva's hand, and the two headed around back, finding a small path in the thick forestry to the left side of the house. It would be dark soon, but there was enough light to see the way without much trouble. Just before turning the corner, Sloan said, "Stay here for a moment. Let me see how many there are first."

Eva nodded, tiptoeing carefully behind him, then stopping as he took a few steps ahead. Just as she was able to admit to herself how much she loved Sloan, he disappeared from view. She vowed to tell him on their journey home, or mayhap later this eve once the evil bastard D was dead. How she prayed they would find him.

She was just about to worry when a sound caught her attention in the bushes. A split second before she was grabbed, the odor hit her. She knew that smell. The cruel man who'd attacked her before was here.

A moment later, D grabbed her from behind and put a hand over her mouth, muffling her scream.

CHAPTER THIRTY-EIGHT

Sloan

———❧———

"THERE'S NO ONE here, Eva," Sloan said as he returned to her, except she wasn't there. "Eva?"

He moved back down the path and ran into Connor. "Eva come back?"

Connor shook his head. "The other four are dealing with Odart. Thane is thrilled to have found him, and he'll be dead soon, if he isn't already. I'm here to help you find the others. Odart has three with him, so there is still one missing. Where could Eva have gone?"

"I don't know, but she's gone. I just went to the end to see how many men we would be facing, and she disappeared," Sloan said, an icy grip settling in his belly. He spun in a circle, searching the entire area.

"She can't have gone far, Sloan. But we're moving together. Let's follow this path because I came from the opposite way."

Sloan's insides tortured and twisted with various fears, but only one stood out. He finally had hope that perhaps something was developing between

Eva and him. Hope that she was beginning to develop feelings for him. He wished for nothing more than that—an opportunity to learn more about her, to learn all the little things about her to love. The way her eyes narrowed when she focused on a villain to center her strength, the way her eyes danced before she laughed—even the way she looked at him had given him hope.

Before, she'd always looked at him with disdain or disgust or something he didn't wish to know. But that had changed. She hadn't looked at him like that in a long time. And he loved the way her tiny hand would reach for his, her fingers curling around his when she needed his support.

Eva MacVey was teaching him how to love and he didn't want her to stop. Ever.

After all they'd been through, his love had only grown stronger, and he knew without a doubt that he would do anything for her.

He would die for Eva MacVey, and he'd kill anyone who touched her wrong.

They hadn't traveled far when something caught Sloan's eye. He bent down and picked up one of Eva's axes. "Shite. He's got her, and she wasn't able to use this. There's no blood." He tucked the weapon in his belt and took his sword out of its sheath, Connor doing the same.

They searched the entire area and found nothing. Sloan rubbed his forehead, searching his mind for any clue as to where he could have taken her.

Connor said, "I wish Dyna or Tora were here. We need help."

Sloan gave him a doubtful glance. "I think Dyna could help, but do you truly believe Tora is a seer?"

"Tora has warned me of every bad event since coming to the Isle of Mull. If she pulls you aside, you better listen. Because of her age, she doesn't explain things clearly, but the clue is always there."

Sloan thought for a moment, rubbing his chin. "She approached me right before I left. I dismissed it as bairn drivel."

"What exactly did she say to you? Hellfire. Think, Sloan. She was warning you. And she ran away as soon as she said something, didn't she?"

"Aye," he mumbled, forcing himself to recall Tora's words. "Something about … apples. That's it." He searched the area with renewed hope. "She said to look for the apple orchard."

"Then that's where Eva is. Way over there." Connor pointed to a grouping of trees far off in the distance.

"Truly? You believe her?"

"You have any other ideas?"

"Nay." The two headed toward the orchard, not slowing until they approached, Sloan in the lead and moving his hands to tell Connor to slow down. He'd heard something.

A male voice carried through the trees. "I see the way you look at me, bitch, and I'll make sure you never forget me."

Eva screamed, then they heard a slap before he bellowed, "You bit me, bitch! If you do or say one more thing, I'm cutting your tongue out, then I'll slice an eye in two. They pop open like an egg. Did you know that?"

"She's fighting him, that's good," Connor said.

They crept through the trees, staying away from the path in the middle of the orchard, until they reached a huge clearing. At the farthest end, D was busy tying Eva to a tree. Her chest was already tied, and he worked on her legs while he continued to berate her, his mouth going nonstop.

Alaric and Eli came up behind them quietly. Connor pointed to two separate spots and the three spread out, keeping themselves well hidden in the trees.

Sloan stepped out and stood directly across from her until her gaze finally locked on his, and he did his best to tell her with one look that he would save her. That he'd never give up.

That he loved her.

Her gaze never left his, and then her lips moved. *I love you, Sloan.*

Had he seen her correctly? Had she just said she loved him?

His heart soared, so locked in on the small lass in front of him that when Thane touched his shoulder and said, "Give us a moment to arrange ourselves," Sloan ignored him.

D hit her again, and that was all the motivation he needed. He dropped his sword because this battle needed to be physical, personal, not at the end of his sword. Sloan raced directly at him, grabbing him by the throat, his fist striking him hard in the face before the brute could even lift his sword. Sloan threw him on the ground and straddled him, pummeling the man's face, shouting loud enough for the entire isle to hear him.

"Never touch her. Never, ever touch her."

It was Thane and Alaric who took him by the shoulders and pulled him back while Connor set his sword at the man's throat to keep him in place, the villain now covered in blood.

Sloan heaved and said, "Let me go. I'll kill him." But then he looked up at Eva as Eli released her bindings. Once Eva was free, Sloan held out his arms, and she fell into his embrace. He held her close, inhaled her sweetness, and swore he never wished to let her go.

Connor said, "You have first rights, Rankin. I just wanted her free before you finish him."

Sloan kissed Eva's forehead and said, "Nay, I don't have first rights. She does." With tears in his eyes, he stepped back, wiped his hands on his trews, and lifted her chin, her eyes misting as much as his were. "Your choice, love." He took the axe out of his belt and handed it to her.

Eva thought for a moment and nodded to him.

Eli said, "May we have a word, Sloan? I know what she needs. Eva, if you please?"

She nodded. "Aye."

Eli pulled her back, and the two whispered a distance away.

Sloan had to turn away from the man on the ground, his whimpering changing to his usually bold threats. "I have other men here who will be looking for you. Then I'll teach you and that bitch who's the strongest."

Eva called Sloan over where she stood, so he approached while Eli waved to her husband. "Come, Alaric, help me tie this slimy piece of shite to this pole so he gets what he deserves."

D said, "Another bitch. I'll take care of you too once my friends save me."

Eli said, "Where the hell are they now, fool?" Then she pulled her fist back and struck him in his nose, an odd crack ringing out.

Sloan turned back to Eva, still at the back of the clearing, and said, "I'll help you in any way I can, Eva."

"Sloan, did you read my lips?"

He looked at her and moved back to her spot, wanting this to be as private as possible, given the circumstance. His gaze drank in everything about her, shocked that she was still able to stand tall after all she'd been through. He took a moment to tuck a stray strand of her hair behind her ear. "I did, but I must ask you. Is it true in your heart or do you think it might be due to all we've been through together?"

"Nay, it's because of you, Sloan. Your heart, your quick mind, your tenderness, your devotion. All of it is special, and I'm so fortunate that you love me. I love you with all my heart, Sloan Rankin, and I am grateful for all that you are and that you chose me to love."

He didn't try to stop the tears from falling, but he swiped them away once Eli called out, "He's ready when you are, Eva."

Eva took Sloan's hand and placed him next to her, then lifted her axe over her head, but then lowered it. "Eli, wipe the blood from his eyes. I want to make sure he can see me."

She lifted the axe and fired it, hitting the exact spot she'd planned.

Eli rejoiced. "Grandmama would be so proud."

Eva strode forward, taking Sloan's hand in hers. Her victim lived, but was bent over in pain, gagging. She said, "I needed to make sure you'll never hurt another lass."

She walked away, stopping to kiss Sloan on the way out, and Sloan had never been happier.

Life was wonderful.

CHAPTER THIRTY-NINE

Eva

THE GROUP TRAVELED back to the opposite side of the isle the next day, one group heading to Duart Castle and the other toward Dun Ara Castle. Connor, Alasdair, and Thane had come along in case there was any truth to Sylvi's prediction.

"Do you wish to stop and see your mother, lass?"

"Nay, Tamsin gave me enough clothes, and I'm sure Lennox is on your land. I wish to be there for you if there is an attack." Then she patted the bag tied to her saddle. "I have my axes."

Sloan said, "Off we go."

Connor came abreast of the two. "I'm to meet Logan on your land. He was bringing Magni with him."

Sloan said, "I have to say I love seeing Magni with his new adopted grandsire."

"Logan wants to find out the truth about Magni's sire. What think you about this man K who got away?"

Eva said, "K definitely got away. I think he was the one who operates from Kilchoan."

Sloan agreed with a nod. "He's the one in charge, so they say. They're all afraid of him. It all fits with what Lia learned at Drimnin with Lennox."

Connor nearly snorted. "Neither Logan nor I are afraid of a cruel man at Kilchoan."

They moved ahead, Connor bringing a score of Grant guards with him. Sloan had left without any of his guards because he'd followed Eva.

"Sloan, you'll tell me if you see anything unusual?"

Sloan glanced over at her and said, "Do not worry. I'll protect you forever, Eva. No one will hurt you."

She wasn't worried about herself. "But I don't want you hurt either."

Connor laughed and Thane said, "I wouldn't worry about Sloan, Eva. After the way he tore across that clearing and lifted D like he was the size of a squirrel and pummeled him, no one's going to hurt either of you."

"But the prediction? Do you all believe it?" Eva asked. "It was Sylvi's comment about the alleged attack, was it not?"

"Aye, but I'm still doubtful," Sloan said.

"You believe Tora after that hint about the orchard, do you not? The lass was correct, Rankin," Connor said.

"She was. Who is left to attack my castle? We just took out five of the evilest men around. Who is left beside K? He's going to have to reassess and get more men. If there is any truth to it, he'll have to delay his plans."

Eva said, "I hope you're right. I've had enough battle for a time."

Sloan moved his horse closer to Eva's as a few horses approached them. She recognized the first to be Logan with Magni in front of him, and the two behind him were Lennox and Miles.

Logan stopped and Sloan moved ahead of Eva's horse, but she could still hear everything. "All is well with you?"

"Aye, more than well," Sloan said.

"How many did you take out?"

Thane said, "Odart, along with his two friends, and the man who attacked Eva will never attack another, thanks to Sloan and Eva."

Lennox said, "I'd like to hear those details."

"We'll fill you in over an ale," Sloan said. "But first, please apprise me of all that has happened in my absence. Is there any truth to the attack?"

Logan said, "I have a score of men planted in various locations, all checking for anything different. Nothing seen yet except for a big ship readying to leave Kilchoan, at least I think it's loaded with men."

Lennox said, "We have seen a few men about who we don't recognize. I've sent them away, but your brother has been uncontrollable in the courtyard. Your sire is there with both of your sisters, trying to calm him. He's afraid you've been hurt. But …"

"But what?"

"Sloan, he's doing his best to act like the usual

Rinaldo, but he's different. I can feel it, yet I can't explain it. Go see him for yourself."

Logan said, "Do not trust him, Rankin. He's a liar."

"Rinaldo? I doubt it, but I'll go see what he is doing." He reached for Eva's hand, but then said, "Eva, I do not want you next to me. I have a sudden inkling too."

"Eva, what's this? You've had a change of heart?" Lennox asked, wide-eyed.

"Aye, I'll explain later, brother dearest. Let Sloan see to Rinaldo."

"Meg is inside on the steps of the keep. You can sit with her, but if things get rough for whatever reason, the two of you should go up on the parapets."

Sloan said, "I think that's wise."

They approached the gates, and Eva was surprised to see they were closed.

Rinaldo's voice carried to them. "Where is my dearest brother? I'm so worried, Da. I hope he's unhurt. I don't want anything to happen to him. What will I ever do if I lose him?"

Dermot Rankin said, "Please end the sniveling, Rinaldo. We've all heard enough. He'll be here soon. Sloan is a fierce chieftain who has many duties. He'll be here as soon as he can."

The group entered through the gates and headed toward the stables where they dismounted, everyone except Logan and Magni.

Sloan escorted Eva over to the steps where she took a seat next to Meg. As soon as she did, Alycia came from around the side of the building and sat next to her while Sloan approached his brother.

"What are you doing here, Alycia?"

"I wished to watch the show," she said, smiling.

Eva frowned, wondering what she meant by that comment. She opened her mouth to ask her friend more, but Dermot yelled at Sloan, so she turned back to watch the activities between poor Sloan and his brother.

"I heard you had some pressing issues, but there are issues at home too. I'm worried. I don't like that ship out there. Do you not realize you belong here? We've all had to listen to Rinaldo's whining all day." Dermot looked worn and confused, and Eva's heart softened for the man she loved.

But Sloan didn't lose his temper, staying calm. "Da, I had business to attend to. Rinaldo, I'm here. Calm yourself. Go get Da an ale."

A collective gasp erupted from the group of onlookers when Rinaldo pulled his sword out and said, "Shut your mouth, Sloan. You'll not be telling me what to do again."

Eva had never heard Rinaldo speak in that tone.

His brother continued, "I've lived a poor life because you were born first. I am the smarter one, the wiser one. No one respects you, and all your men would prefer to have me as chieftain. Take out your sword so we can end this. I could lock you in a cell, but I'd prefer to see you dead."

Rinaldo held his sword in front of him as if he were about to attack Sloan while a small group of men came in from the now open gates to stand behind Rinaldo. Eva didn't like this turn of events one bit. She stood and reached for Meg, the two heading for the staircase to the parapets, but Eva never made it.

Someone grabbed her by the hair and tugged her back. "You aren't leaving. You'll stay for your just due." Alycia set a dagger to her neck.

"Alycia? What the hell is going on?"

Rinaldo said, "I'll tell you. I love Alycia and she loves me. We deserve to be in charge, and our son should be heir to the castle. But Sloan won't go away. We tried to get rid of his chance of marrying by shoving Gormal over the cliff, but nay. Then he had to fall in love with you, Eva. We tried to sully your reputation, but Sloan would not give up on you, so you forced us to take action. There will be no lads coming from Sloan's loins at all. I've had enough of your games, Sloan. I've been planning this for a long time, and you'll not stop me."

Sloan stepped back, nearly running into their sire. "You? It was your fault Eva was attacked? And you killed Gormal? Rinaldo, you've lost your mind."

"I didn't kill Gormal, Alycia did. I am innocent, and I deserve to be chieftain. Draw your weapon."

Logan rode forward on his horse, nodding something to Connor who hurried through the gates. Then Logan interrupted. "Innocent, Rinaldo? Hardly. You're a lying bastard. I saw you at Duart Castle that night. You're the one who poisoned all of us. You and your sweet little girlfriend were the ones who served the goblets of ale and wine, are you not?"

Rinaldo challenged Logan, his eyes black with fury. "Aye, we did. I let the men in the tunnel and helped with the boats. I wanted everyone in Duart Castle dead, but we clearly did not give you enough poison. Why? Because I needed coin. My brother never gave me enough to use as I wish, so I traded the faery and the lad for extra forces. A boat just came from Kilchoan full of men who will fight for me. They are all here now to assist me in this endeavor. Any guard who stands behind you, dear brother, will be slain. Any who choose to stand with me will be well rewarded."

Logan laughed, something that made Rinaldo even angrier, if possible. "I don't fear you, Ramsay."

"You should, laddie," Logan drawled. "Whenever you see me coming, you should run the other way."

Alycia said, "Rinaldo is doing what's best for the clan, and I was honored to assist him. Rinaldo is smarter than all of you. He's going to be chieftain, and I will be his wife. Our son will be heir to Dun Ara." She yanked on Eva's hair again. But then she whispered in her ear, "I even sent Dante just to hurt you. You are such a fool, Eva."

"Why, Alycia? What have I done to you?"

"Because you're so spoiled. You were given everything, just like Sloan. You have all the servants wait on you. Well, you'll be kissing my feet if you wish to live. Kill him, Rinaldo. Do it now. We need to end this."

Rinaldo growled, "Draw your sword, Sloan."

Sloan shook his head. "Rinaldo, you're my

brother. I'm not going to kill you." His sisters stood off to the side, gripping each other tightly.

"Rinaldo, please stop this insanity," Marta cried. "Sloan can't kill you."

"I can," Eva said, stomping on Alycia's foot, causing her to scream, then she put her fist into Alycia's face, knocking her to the ground. Yanking her axe out, she raced toward Rinaldo.

Sloan caught her by the waist, stopping her. "Nay. We're not going to kill my brother. There's a better way."

To everyone's surprise, Dermot took Sloan's sword from its sheath and said, "You don't have to, Sloan. I should be the one to kill him. I created the evil seed."

CHAPTER FORTY

Sloan

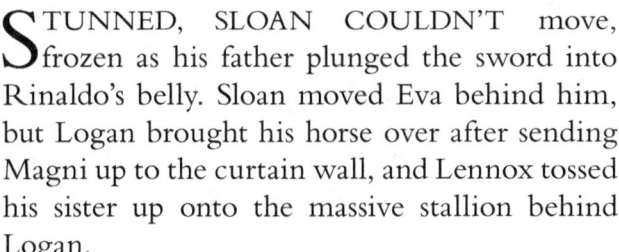

STUNNED, SLOAN COULDN'T move, frozen as his father plunged the sword into Rinaldo's belly. Sloan moved Eva behind him, but Logan brought his horse over after sending Magni up to the curtain wall, and Lennox tossed his sister up onto the massive stallion behind Logan.

Weapons were drawn around the courtyard. A whistle from Connor brought two score of guards rushing through the gates along with Sloan's men who went after the paltry group Rinaldo had assembled. The battle was on.

But Sloan couldn't let it end so easily. His brother fell to his knees, his hands gripping the sword. The dying man stared up at his father. "Da, why? You always liked me better." His brother had reverted to his childish voice, the one he'd used on them for so many years.

But something broke inside Sloan. The secrets that had just been revealed overpowered his thinking. He grabbed his brother's tunic and pulled him to his feet, the sword still embedded deep in his belly. He had to know before his brother took his last breath. "You're the one who wished to attack Dun Ara? You've planned this for moons? My own flesh and blood? And you poisoned everyone at Duart Castle so the bairns could be stolen away? Just to take over the castle? *And* you and Alycia killed Gormal? Why do you hate me so?"

"I did it all, and I'd do it again." Rinaldo tried to spit at him but couldn't get the breath to do it. "I hate you ..."

Their father grabbed Rinaldo from Sloan, held him up enough to spit in his face, then said, "This is how you deal with traitors! My own son is a traitor. I deny you, Rinaldo!" Dermot dropped him to the ground and yanked the sword out, only to plunge it deep into the man's chest, Rinaldo gurgling before his eyes closed. "I deny you and your wife and son."

The battle ended a short time later, so Eva jumped off Logan's horse and ran to Sloan, hugging him tight. "I'm so sorry, Sloan."

Sloan couldn't speak. He held onto Eva with such a force that he feared he'd hurt her. Lennox and Miles came along and ushered him inside, Eva with him, while Magni took care of their horse. The two settled him at his desk in his solar, then got him a goblet filled with the amber brew. Miles stepped out as soon as Dermot came inside.

"Miles, throw my son's body in the water. Or find a faraway spot to leave him to the animals. He doesn't deserve a decent burial."

"Aye, Chief."

Dermot said, "Nay, I'm not your chieftain any longer. Sloan is the only chieftain here, and he is a damn good one."

Miles left and Dermot stayed. Still stunned by all that had taken place, Sloan didn't know what to say to his father. He could hear the tears of both sisters in the hall, but he couldn't move.

Their brother was dead. Somehow, he felt responsible, but he knew that in some twisted way, it was Rinaldo's fault.

His father took a chair opposite his remaining son. Lennox gave him a goblet of the fine brew, and the older man threw it down with one gulp. It was a long time before anyone spoke, and finally Sloan brought his gaze up to his father's. "Did you know, Da?"

"Nay. He fooled me." He poured himself another swig of brew and said, "I just wish to say that I've never been prouder of you, Sloan."

"Why? My own brother hated me."

"Och, Ailis would tell you the lad was never right in his head. He was always off, killing animals with a smile, playing tricks on his sisters that you would never do. I tried to make up for any mistakes I might have made, but when I watched him out there, I knew the evil was deep inside him. And after causing all that tragedy, there was only one solution. It was right that it was at my hand. I created him."

His father hung his head, but then said, "But I've never been so proud of you. You did the right thing not drawing your sword. And you made the correct choice following Eva to MacQuarie land and making all the allies you have. Why, there were more Grant and Ramsay and MacVey guards around than our own. And then you brought MacQuaries with you. And when the renowned Logan Ramsay came on his stallion to back you up? I've never been prouder. Well done, Sloan." He held his head in his hands. "I don't know why I've been so blind to everything."

Eva stood right outside the door, not wanting to interrupt, yet she hated to walk away from Sloan. He'd never deserted her during her troubled times, so she wouldn't leave him.

"My thanks, Da." Then Sloan stood and held out his arm, so Eva walked to his side and he tucked her in tight.

Dermot grinned and said, "And you've chosen well. She put that big bitch down flat faster than I've seen anyone go down. I'm banning that woman from the entire Isle of Mull, she and her son. You'll not have to do that, Sloan. I'll do it. I'll have them on a boat on the morrow. My apologies, Eva, for any pain Rinaldo caused you."

Eva kissed Sloan's cheek. "I love your son, Dermot. It took me a long time to figure it out, so I was not about to allow anyone to stop our love."

"Looking at you two gives me hope. Getting married on the morrow?"

Eva said, "Nay, I think I need to tell my mother first."

Dermot waggled his brow and said, "Och, sweet Rut." Then he left.

Sloan and Eva just stared at each other, slack-jawed.

CHAPTER FORTY-ONE

Eva

LATER THAT NIGHT, Eva hurried into the keep, rushing over to her mother and giving her a giant hug and giggling, Sloan directly behind her. Then she leaned down to pick up Goldie, who was barking at her feet. "Oh, I'll hug you too, sweet thing."

Her mother assessed her daughter carefully. "Lass, is that blood on your tunic? Where the hell have you been?"

Lennox and Taskill strolled in behind her. Lennox said, "Entertaining me and everyone else. Shall I tell her or you, Sloan?"

Sloan said, "Go ahead. I'm exhausted, but before anyone else says a word, I respectfully request your daughter's hand in marriage, Lady MacVey. I love her with all my heart, and I vow to protect her with my life."

Eva chuckled and looked at her mother. "I'm in love, Mama!" Then she hugged her mother again, twirling her around. "Say aye! I'm marrying him!"

"Aye!" Her mother finally laughed but then

pushed her away. "What the hell do you have all over you? You're ruining my gown."

"Then get another!"

"Lennox, would you please explain a wee bit? After the poisoning?"

"Nay! Me!" Eva paused to take a deep breath, then began, "I snuck away, and Sloan followed me. We were both kidnapped near Ulva and then locked in a dungeon where we found the bairns. They took us on two boats headed for Coll, but I jumped in the water with Tora and Sandor and got them to shore while Sloan got Maeve and Grant to safety. Garvie's man Odart was one, and he's dead, along with his friend. The bastard who dared touch me will never touch another lass, and …" She paused to gather her breath. "We came back, and Rinaldo tried to kill Sloan because he wanted to be chieftain so he could marry Alycia and their son could be heir to Dun Ara! And they poisoned everyone at Duart and let the men kidnap the bairns. Dermot killed Rinaldo and Alycia's been banned from Mull and …" She spun around. "Did I miss anything?"

Meg came in and joined Lennox, who stood with the largest smile she'd ever seen on her brother's face.

Sloan tucked her next to him and said, "You covered it well."

Her mother asked, "Alycia? She wished to marry Rinaldo? Our Alycia? She helped him poison everyone?"

"Aye, Mama. I thought she was a true friend,

but she said she hated me. She was as evil as Rinaldo. But I know where I'm meant to be. I love Sloan and we belong together."

Her mother began to cry, then said to Lennox and the others, "May I speak with Sloan and Eva alone?"

Eva looked at her mother, confused. There was no need to send the others out.

Lennox came and gave his sister a kiss on the cheek, then his mother, and escorted the others out.

Sloan asked, "Should I take my leave?"

Her mother said, "That is entirely up to your betrothed." Then she strode over to a chest and pulled out a box, unlocked it, took out a folded piece of parchment, and brought it over to Eva.

"Mama, what is this?"

"Please sit down and read it. It's time."

Her mother smoothed her skirt and took a chair in front of the hearth, pointing to a seat for Eva to take.

"Mayhap I should leave," Sloan said.

"Nay, stay, Sloan. I have no secrets from you. I'll read it."

Rut explained, "It's from your father. He asked me to help him pen it for you the day before he passed."

Eva's hands shook as she unfolded the parchment, looking at the careful strokes on the page she held.

She began to read aloud:

Dearest daughter,

I'm sorry I'll not be with you when you are ready to marry. If I were, I would choose a certain man for you. You are my only daughter, my sweetest lass, with a quirkiness that I love. It will take a special man to take care of you, one who will allow you to be yourself—a beautiful girl who has a strength inside her that she has yet to discover.

But that day will come.

The man I have chosen I have studied from afar. He has an impeccable character. A man of honor who is the only man I've seen who deserves you, who will love you and also guard your tender heart.

Sloan Rankin …

Eva stopped because the tears burst like they'd been kept inside for years. She reached for Sloan's hand and continued:

Sloan Rankin is an honest, hardworking chieftain who takes his responsibilities verra seriously and manages his clan and its members as if they were all part of his family. A fierce warrior, he will pick up the tiniest bird in his hands and set it back in its nest with such care that I know he will always treat you with kindness.

I can ask no more of any man, but I'm convinced that you and Sloan Rankin are destined to be a truly happy couple who will have several fine bairns.

How do I know? From deep in my heart, I know he is for you.

But also, the small golden bird sitting on my window edge chirping is telling me so.

I wish the two of you all the happiness in the world.
I love you, my sweet princess Eva.
Love the man with all you have,
Papa

Sobbing so much that her mother grabbed a linen square for her, Eva hugged Sloan first, then her mother. "How did he know Sloan was right for me? It had to be something more than a bird."

Her mother smiled, leaning back in her chair. "Many moons ago, you snuck out the back door when your brothers and the other lads went down to fish in the sound one summer. Your sire and I were arguing about something, so we never noticed that you disappeared. I never would have guessed that you would do such a thing, but half the hour later, Sloan came up and handed you to me. You were soaked, had jumped in the water after the others had climbed into a boat and rowed to the middle. Sloan told your father that he saw you coming so he stayed back, but you jumped in before he could stop you. Poor Sloan thought we were going to yell at him for allowing you to get all wet. But your father had nearly fainted with fear, thanking Sloan for saving his wee lassie for him. Once Sloan left, your father told me that Sloan was your person. He always believed it."

"Mama, why did you never tell me? I knew he chose someone."

Rut kissed her daughter's forehead, brushing the wild strands of Eva's waves back from her face. "Because *you*, not your father, needed to choose your husband. But I'll also tell you something else that has haunted me since I helped him write that letter."

Her mother brushed the tears away. "That golden bird never left until I finished the last word."

Eva looked out the window. "What did the bird look like?"

Her mother smiled, her eyes misting.

"Oddly enough, she reminded me a wee bit of that Lia."

CHAPTER FORTY-TWO

And the others

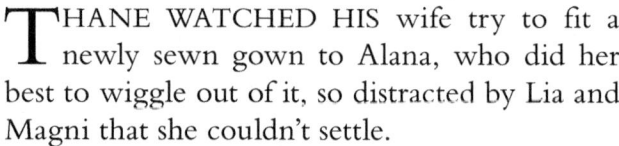

THANE WATCHED HIS wife try to fit a newly sewn gown to Alana, who did her best to wiggle out of it, so distracted by Lia and Magni that she couldn't settle.

His mother stood next to him from afar and whispered, "She hasn't figured it out yet?"

He suspected Tamsin was carrying their first bairn, but he wasn't certain. "Mama, I think she does, but she was so afraid that Raghnall did permanent damage to her insides that she feared she'd never be able to carry again."

"She's had her courses since you married, though. I know it because she asked me a few questions once."

He wrapped his arm around his mother's shoulders and kissed her forehead. "She'll come to it on her own. Her belly is growing, but I ignore it."

"Da and I are so proud of you, Thane. I don't know how you were able to keep your brother and sister alive living in the forests."

"We had help. Artan admitted he used to leave us food every week. He was the fisherman who rowed his boat here with that wicked bitch. Said he came back to check on us and when he discovered the cave we slept in, he left us what he could so we wouldn't starve. The man even left blankets once and an extra tunic for each of us."

"How did you find Artan?"

"We didn't. He found us. Eventually, he convinced us to come here and help build the castle. We gladly joined him and the others."

"I'm glad I didn't know. I would have worried every night."

Mora approached and said, "Mama, look at these tarts I made. Do they look all right? Will you taste one, please? I think I burned a few, but are they still edible? And the berries? Are they sweet enough? I used the honey, but I may need to put more in."

Thane watched the two go back into the kitchens, so pleased to see how Mora had improved since their parents' return. Much of it was also due to Tamsin, Alana, Lia, and Magni. Mora had gone from being a sad lass to one who was blossoming into quite the young lady.

He'd stared at his lovely wife for long enough, knowing he had work outside, so he headed to the hearth, leaning over to kiss Tamsin's cheek. "I think I'll go out to the lists, then I have some repairs needed for the stable. Magni, join me?"

"Aye, Chief. I'll help."

"Lia, how long do you plan to stay with us?" He agreed with everyone else about Lia, though none of them had decided exactly where she came from. Under a leaf just didn't answer enough questions for Thane, though Magni believed it with all his heart.

"I'll be here for another moon, my lord. I may have one other place to visit on the isle. Will that suit you?"

Tamsin's head jerked up quickly. "Grant does not need you for a moon? What about after that?"

Lia laughed and waved her hand in dismissal. "Grant won't need me again until he's nearly grown."

"Then who is next?" Tamsin asked, frozen. Thane knew she feared it would be Alana, but for some reason, he was quite certain Alana would not be bothered again.

"I think I'll go into the forest for a wee bit. I'll meet you in the stable later, brother Magni."

Lia disappeared without answering their questions, something she excelled at. But Magni grinned with pride. "She is my sister. I tell everyone she is, yet no one believes me. She just had to find me in an odd way."

Thane ruffled his hair and said, "I'm heading out, Tamsin."

"Me too?" Alana asked.

"Nay, Grandmama and Mora made fruit tarts for you."

"Yum!"

Thane reached the door, Magni running along behind him, and he knew the boy would ask him the same questions he always did.

Magni ran in front of him and spun around.

"Tell me about Odart again. He was a mean bastard."

Thane arched a brow at him.

"Sorry, Chief. I meant he was a mean man. Grandpapa Logan lets me curse. Sorry, I forget."

Thane grinned. Logan had adopted Magni as his grandson, and Thane considered it one of those endearing things most people wouldn't understand. But Logan was exactly what Magni needed. He gave the lad undying love, something Magni often doubted he deserved.

Logan was just the person to convince him of his value.

Magni hadn't been distracted from his purpose, so he carried on. "Odart was a mean soul. He tried to kill Tamsin before. What would Alana do without her mother? What did Odart say about it all? Was he in charge?"

Thane answered Magni again; he was sure it was the fifth time he'd told him the story of finding Odart on Coll. "Odart said he only drove the boat for Raghnall with Tamsin in it. Said he had no idea what his boss had planned to do. He said he liked Tamsin, but he hated Garvie. After Garvie died, he said the man on Kilchoan informed the group left on Ulva that one of them had to manage the business. If they didn't, they'd die, so Odart killed the other one who wished to challenge him."

Magni chuckled, his hand going over his mouth. "And tell me again what he said about hating bairns and what you did …"

"But I already told you this, Magni." Thane had

never thought a lad could be so entertaining, and their little conversations brought a smile to his face daily.

"But one more time. Please?"

"I asked him how many bairns he'd sold—"

"And he said five and ten, and then you said—" Magni waited, staring up at him.

"I was going to knock one tooth out for each one he sold. And then I started—"

"And you hollered for everyone to hear that this is for Magni and Lia! And you knocked out five teeth for us!"

"Nay, only three," Thane corrected as they made their way into the stable.

"But I think you said five once …"

"Nay, three."

And Magni slapped his legs again and broke into gales of laughter. "Three teeth. You knocked out three teeth because they were so mean to us."

Thane's father stood next to their new stallion, a gift from the Grants, brushing the animal down. "You're telling the O story again, son?"

"Aye. His favorite tale. Is that not so, Magni?"

"I wish I'd seen it," he said. Then he stepped away so he could swing his fist in a wide arc. "I think you looked like this, Thane. And this would be for my sister Lia, and this one is for Tora and Sandor." He swung his fists, bouncing around the stable. "And this is for Magni. Is this the way you did it?"

His father said, "I fixed that hole in the wall."

"My thanks. That's why I came out."

"No need. Thought I'd brush Midnight Specter

down for you. I don't think I've ever seen as fine a horse as this one. He'll be quite a stud for you."

Thane grabbed an apple and moved over to his newest pet, feeding him the treat and running his hands down his withers and over to his nose. The animal finished its delicacy, then nickered at him. "Don't worry, Midnight. I've got a lady almost ready for you. Be patient." Then he chuckled when the beast tossed its mane. "He's a fine one. Da, I don't know why I got so lucky. Tamsin, Alana, finding you and Mama, the Grants and MacVeys and Rankins."

His father stopped and stared at his son. "Because you deserve a good life now. After all you've done and accomplished, you deserve the blessings you've gotten."

He clasped his father's shoulder and said, "So do you and Mama, Da."

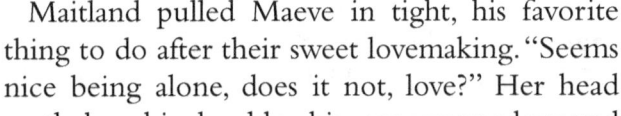

Maitland pulled Maeve in tight, his favorite thing to do after their sweet lovemaking. "Seems nice being alone, does it not, love?" Her head nestled on his shoulder, his arm wrapped around her.

Maeve laughed. "I know she wasn't paying us any mind, but she was often in the same chamber with us. It wasn't until we got Grant in the other chamber that I could convince her to leave us alone."

He rubbed circles on her arm.

Maeve said, "Maitland, can I confess something strange?"

"Go ahead."

"I can't decide if I'm glad she's not here to watch over him, or if I fear more for him that she's gone. She truly was his protector."

"That she was. I'm confident that if Grant was ever in danger again, Lia would be here for him. I think it's a good thing. I think it means that he is no longer in danger. I'm trying my best to convince myself, and I think I've finally done it."

Maeve said, "I have to admit that having her with us after we were captured did offer me comfort. I believed that she would protect him."

"I would say so. Thane confirmed that Odart's one palm was burned, the skin raw. I don't know how she did what she did, but I'm grateful."

"And I'm most grateful that Grant didn't seem bothered by it at all."

"Maeve, I have one more question for you. Sloan wondered if it was Grant who burned O's palm. It happened when he tried to touch you. That Grant glared at him and his hand burned immediately because the man touched his mother. He doesn't think that part was Lia at all. Is that true?"

"It could be. I'm not sure, Maitland. And we'll never know until he grows up."

Maitland said, "Do you think our son has something special in his future? I can't get that out of my mind. I think Connor said it. That Lia only protects those who have something they must accomplish in their future."

"Nay, husband. I just plan to love our only son with all my heart. The rest I'll not worry on. We are all here, all hale, and we have many to help us when the next trouble arises. According to Lia, he won't need her for many years."

"I'd like to ask her how many."

"Nay, you will not. I do not wish to know. Oh, and I just remembered something else I forgot to tell you. Something that should comfort you, because it surely did comfort me."

"What?"

"Sandor and Tora said Grandpapa Alex and Grandmama Maddie were sitting in the cellar, watching over all of them."

"And you believed them with all your heart?"

"Not at first, but when the smell of our apple orchard washed over me, I never doubted them again."

"Alex and Maddie were guarding the bairns *and* you, wife."

Maeve gasped. "They did! I remember something now. Tora said Grandmama Maddie told Alex we were too cold. And this blast of heat came in like someone lit a hearth behind us."

Maitland kissed his wife's hand. "You needed help, and you had it."

"Oh, Maitland. They were so close."

"Diamond, if it happens again, we're leaving Mull."

Alasdair chuckled from the staircase, and Dyna shook her head. "I am laird here, Derric. We're staying." Then she glanced at her parents entering the hall.

Alasdair said, "Well, I'm headed home to see if Emmalin wishes to return with our bairns."

Sela asked, "Will all the kidnappings keep her from coming?"

Alasdair snorted. "Emmalin thinks I'll save them from everything. She won't worry, but we'll see. Chief? What about you? You returning?"

Before Derric answered, Alaric flew down the stairs, running into the kitchens and back out again with something to drink and an empty bowl.

"Eli hale?"

Alaric shrugged. "Heaving her insides out again this morn. I promised something to drink, then I have to take my leave."

"I'll wager a laddie," Alasdair called out.

Dyna gave a wee whoop. "Nay, a lass."

Alaric took the steps two at a time, chuckling.

Tora, Sandor, and Sylvi were busy making toys for their new friends in anticipation of the upcoming holiday. It would take a while to make fabric animals plus a sword for Magni.

"Where's Logan?" Connor asked.

"He had a meeting with someone. Gwynie went with him. Took her bow too."

"Pheasant! I'm hoping for a nice plump pheasant," Dyna shouted.

Just then, Sandor got up from the floor and began to run in circles, Tora doing the same but in a different direction.

"Sandor, what are you doing?" Connor asked.

"Gwandda chaseen me," he said, giggling.

"Nay, I'm not chasing you. I need a day's rest from all the excitement. I'm an old man now."

Tora said, "Not you, Gwandpapa. Gwanda Alex chasing Sandor."

Connor looked up at Dyna, who whispered, "He saw them on Ulva too. Said they watched over them."

"They? Who?" Alasdair asked.

Tora said, "Gwanda Alex and Gwamma Maddie. Gwanda swim with Eva and Sandor. Gwamma swim with Eva and me."

"Eva had help swimming?" Alasdair looked from one adult face to the next, but no one said anything, the two bairns running and giggling.

Connor said, "I saw no one but Eva swimming as hard as she could, both bairns tied to her torso, and she struggled, but her strokes were powerful. There was no one visible in the water with them. But please ask Maeve. She believes that Mama and Da were in the dungeon with them. Said she could smell the apples and Mama's lavender. She found it comforting."

"Nay, Shakie, nay!"

Alasdair, wide-eyed, asked, "Who's chasing you now, Sandor?"

"Unca Shakie chaseen me."

Alasdair stood and froze, watching the boy run in circles and around the hall while he called out to some figment of the lad's imagination with his father's name. Jake, who died long ago. John Alexander Grant, nicknamed Jake by his twin brother Jamie.

"Papa?" Alasdair waited, but then Sandor stopped, looking over toward Alasdair.

Sandor pointed toward him and said, "Unca Shakie o'er dare."

The air around Alasdair filled with the powerful smell of mint leaves, exactly what his sire had chewed every day in the early morn, and the aroma filled him with all that Jake Alexander Grant had been in a matter of moments. "Da …"

Connor stood next to him and whispered, "Aye, he's here. Jake, you're missed!"

Sela had tears running down her cheeks. "Connor, we're staying. Alasdair, when you go back to get Emmalin, bring Hagen and Morgan back. Astra misses them. We're staying wherever your parents are. And Emmalin and your bairns need to be where Jake is."

Alasdair nodded. "We'll return, Aunt Sela. I cannot disagree with you." He peered up into his uncle's eyes. "Do you believe it?"

Connor nodded slowly. "I felt him too, Alasdair. That was my brother."

As fast as they'd gotten up, the two bairns returned to their animals in the middle of the hall, Sandor waving, "Bye, Unca Shakie." Then he stood up and ran back over. "What, Unca Shakie?"

Alasdair froze as if he were watching his dear father. Sandor ran again then stopped in front of him and said, "Unca Shakie say come back." Then he raced to his animals, waving goodbye to something.

Or someone. Shakie. Jake, his father.

The hall was silent as they all took in what they'd watched, but then Dyna asked, "Sandor, if Grandda Alex helped you and Grandma Maddie helped Tora, then who helped Grant?"

Sandor said, "Eva and Unca Shakie hep Gwant."

Tora nodded but added, "And Lia."

Connor mumbled, "We're staying. I promised Logan I'd help him with one more chore. We made a promise to a lad, and we have to do what we can."

Dyna asked, "To Magni?"

"Aye." Connor got up and went to the sideboard for a quick drink of Sloan's amber brew he'd given them.

"To do what exactly, Da?" Dyna asked.

"Help him find out what happened to his parents."

CHAPTER FORTY-THREE

Eva

———◆◆◆———

EVA CAME IN from the outdoors with Meg, laughing. They entered together and her mother called out to them, "Sit in front of the fire with me, you two."

She and Meg joined her mother as asked.

"And what were you two doing?"

"Axe throwing. It's fun," Meg said. "And Eva is so good at it."

"You are becoming fast friends, and it pleases me. I always wished for another daughter, Meg. You have filled that need and made my son happy besides."

"I do love Lennox."

"I'll have to attempt to find a wife for Taskill soon. But I don't know if he'll ever settle down."

"They all love Taskill, Mama."

Then Eva thought for a moment. "Except Alycia. She never liked him."

"She liked you well enough," her mother said. "So sad she turned greedy."

"Actually, she said she hated me. Because I was

so spoiled. I felt like she was my only friend for so long, and she was a phony."

"She betrayed you, Eva. That's the word."

Eva thought about how hurt she'd been over Alycia, but her mother was correct. And now she had other friends—Meg, Dyna, Eli, and Tamsin.

The door opened and Sloan stepped inside. Eva bolted out of her seat and ran to his side, giving him a quick kiss. "Sorry, Mama."

"Young love is always a joy to watch, Eva."

Meg said, "Excuse me, but I think I'll find Lennox. I believe he's in the lists." Then she disappeared.

Sloan moved toward the hearth. "Greetings to you, my lady. You look lovely."

"My thanks, Sloan. You have my daughter smiling wider than I've ever seen her."

"Mama, may we go up to the parapets? Do you mind? You know I love to look over the sound from there."

"Go, have fun. It's my favorite spot too."

Eva took Sloan's hand and tugged him up the staircase behind her. "What are you doing here? I just left you not long ago," she whispered.

Sloan nuzzled her neck from behind. "I missed you. And I wished to see how you were." He opened the heavy door for her and Sloan sat on one of the stools already there, tugging her onto his lap. After giving her a quick kiss, he whispered, "Are you sore?"

"Nay, not at all. Just happy that we handfasted."

"Did you tell your mother?"

"Nay, but I will. Did you tell Lennox?"

"Nay, but I might on the way out. I told him that I expected we would handfast soon. That you were not ready for a big wedding but that we wished to live together as husband and wife. He gave me his blessings."

"You did? You already asked him?"

"Lass, you are my betrothed, and I wished to do things right. We handfasted, so we are husband and wife. Now, when can I convince you to move to my castle?"

"How about on the morrow?"

"Truly? That soon? That would please me."

"Aye. Come back on the morrow and we'll chat with Mama. I'll talk with her first. But is your chamber ready for me? I think you might need another chest and a chair, Sloan. Your bed is big enough, but I do have some gowns."

"Och, nay. I have to go." He stood and kissed her. "Sorry, but I forgot to remove the bloody sheet. I don't want the maids to see it. I must hurry."

He opened the door but then stopped to lean down, giving her a big kiss. "I love you, Eva."

"I love you too. Did I please you, Sloan?"

"More than you could ever guess. Did I please you, Lady Rankin?"

She giggled. "More than I would have guessed."

Sloan said, "I'm going home to get our chamber arranged, love. I'll see you on the morrow."

He opened the door to head down the stairs, spoke to someone, then Eva asked, "Who is it, Sloan?"

He whirled around, conversing with someone

coming up the stairs. "I'm taking my leave. You have a visitor."

"Who?"

"Lia. She wishes to speak with you."

"Of course. Send the lass up." Eva had to admit that she was shocked to think the wee lass was here to visit with her. She'd had a powerful effect on so many, but not directly on Eva. "Greetings, Lia."

"It's so lovely to see you happy, Eva. But you are, are you not?" Lia asked, moving over to a stool to sit down. "It surely is a lovely place to center your thoughts."

"I am happy, Lia, and this place is beautiful."

"And it's in your own home. How fortunate you are to have such beauty from the parapets."

"It is." Eva peered out over the landscape, thinking on Lia's words and how true they were.

"You are in love. So do you finally accept that you are deserving of Sloan and his love, Lady Eva?"

"What? I'm not sure what you are asking." But in her heart, she did know, a sudden realization blossoming like the petals of the finest flower in her garden.

Lia said, "Sometimes, people are unkind to others in many ways, and people take that cruelty to heart and think they invited it or that they are deserving of the evil. But you never were, Eva. Of Alycia's or D's or any of it. I wish for you to know that."

Tears misted Eva's gaze, but she couldn't speak, memories flooding her mind.

"Dante thought he could quash your strength, but I'm telling you never to allow a stranger to ruin your self-worth. You let him control you for a short time, and he didn't have that right. I'm so glad you began to believe in yourself, that you deserve the good things in life."

"Lia, who are you?" Eva couldn't stop the tears this time and let them flood her cheeks. It was so odd speaking with a child who spoke like a wizened healer or priest. "Are you some kind of angel?"

"In a sense, aye. I come to help people for two reasons. One is to help right the evil in the world when it spins out of control. I help some people believe they have the strength to overpower evil. You did a fine job of it with Sloan's help."

"And the other reason?"

"To help people find their purpose. We need certain things to happen, and if they don't, we come to move things in the right direction. We send you inklings and feelings, but for some people, it's difficult to interpret through their pain."

"But why?"

"It's a simple premise, actually. Once you find your purpose, and you follow the path meant for you, all will be well in your world."

"What's my purpose?"

Lia giggled. "I think you know. It is to love Sloan and to be loved, because the two of you have many to bring into the world who will need your love and guidance. Many."

"My thanks to you, Lia. Will you stay?" The lass was so comforting that Eva wished she'd never leave.

"Nay, but you have another visitor."

"Who?"

Lia stood on the stool and held up her hand until a golden-winged bird flew down and perched on her fingers. "He's here for you, Eva." Lia brought her hand over and the bird jumped onto Eva's fingers, chirping.

"Da?"

EPILOGUE

Logan

———❧———

LOGAN STOOD IN the middle of the clearing, his informant a short distance away.

"This is the last time I'm coming, old man. I need to know how many score Grant has. Rankin has two, MacVey has four, MacQuarie two now. How many do Granthams hold at Duart?"

"Why? Who is asking because it surely is not you." Logan kept his eye on Gwynie in the tree not far away, her bow in her hand.

"You don't need to know."

"But I do. I know it's not Odart. He's dead. The arse named Dante will never walk again. Odart's two men each took a sword to the belly when they attempted to touch Alaric Grant's wife."

"You think you know so much, but you don't. All rumors."

"And how would you know?"

"Because you don't describe them exactly the way they happened." The man crossed his arms and chuckled. "You describe them wrong."

"Try this, wise arse. Odart had his neck sliced

after he had twelve of his teeth knocked out, one at a time. If he'd had more teeth, it would have been fifteen, but that's all he had. And one friend took a sword to his belly, the other an arrow straight to his heart."

The man's face went slack. "How did you know that?"

"Because my granddaughter put the arrow there. Oh, and the fool named Dante lived, but with an axe splitting his cock into two pieces, I doubt he'll ever plant his evil seed anywhere again. Think about that the next time you or any of your friends try to rape a woman. My female relations will pay you back."

The man paled and covered his private area briefly. "Dante died the next day. How did you know?"

"I know. Now, I know K, or Kelvan, whatever the hell you call him, is still in Kilchoan, but someone else is with him. And the two are making plans to do something. But I'm also going to tell you that if you don't want an axe in your bollocks, you better stay away from the bairns. I told you how I feel about that."

"No more bairns. Only the faery. And this woman with K says she owes someone."

"Who is she?"

"That's all I'll tell you until you tell me how many guards at Duart. Fair trade, old man, or I'm gone. And I'll never return."

"Fine. There are six score guards at Duart. And ten score more ready to come if ordered.

Now, the name of the woman, or I'll send my granddaughter aiming for your bollocks. What is it?"

"K's wife, Glenna."

Logan frowned because he didn't like this one bit. "Glenna?" And even Logan couldn't have prepared himself for the man's answer.

"Glenna of Buchan."

The End

http://www.keiramontclair.com

DEAR READER,

Thank you for reading book three of the Clans of Mull. I'm enjoying this new cast of characters so much that I'll keep going for two or three more.

I'm not sure whose story I will write yet. Here are my choices:

Taskill MacVey and Sheona Rankin
Broc MacNicol and an unknown lass
Dermot and Rut—likely to be a novella
Brian MacQuarie and Theebet MacKinnis
I'd love to write Mora's story, but she's a bit young yet.

I haven't quite decided, but I'm leaning toward #2. Let me know what you think!

And for those of you rushing to read about Glenn of Buchan again, the last book he appeared in was Kyla's book, but he began his reign of terror in Torrian's story, book 2 of The Highland Clan. Have fun!

Happy reading!

Keira Montclair

NOVELS BY
KEIRA MONTCLAIR

CLANS OF MULL
THE PLIGHT OF A SCOTTISH LASS
THE BURDEN OF A SCOTTISH
CHIEFTAIN
THE ANGUISH OF THE SCOTTISH
LAIRDS

HIGHLAND HUNTERS
THE SCOT'S CONFLICT
THE SCOT'S TRAITOR
THE SCOT'S PROTECTOR
THE SCOT'S VOW
THE SCOT'S DESTINY
THE SCOT'S WARNING
THE SCOT'S RECKONING
THE SCOT'S LEGACY

HIGHLAND SWORDS
THE SCOT'S BETRAYAL
THE SCOT'S SPY
THE SCOT'S PURSUIT
THE SCOT'S QUEST
THE SCOT'S DECEPTION
THE SCOT'S ANGEL

FALLING FOR THE CHIEFTAIN-3RD in a collaborative trilogy
HIGHLAND SECRETS –3rd in a collaborative trilogy

THE SUMMERHILL SERIES- CONTEMPORARY ROMANCE
#1-ONE SUMMERHILL DAY
#2-A FRESH START FOR TWO
#3-THREE REASONS TO LOVE

ABOUT THE AUTHOR

KEIRA MONTCLAIR IS the pen name of an author who lives in South Carolina with her husband. She loves to write fast-paced, emotional romance, especially with children as secondary characters.

When she's not writing, she loves to spend time with her grandchildren. She's worked as a high school math teacher, a registered nurse, and an office manager. She loves ballet, mathematics, puzzles, learning anything new, and creating new characters for her readers to fall in love with.

She writes historical romantic suspense. Her best-selling series is a family saga that follows two medieval Scottish clans through four generations and now numbers over thirty books.

Contact her through her website:
keiramontclair.com.